AN UNTHINKABLE INTERLUDE

"Do you plan to return here after you are wed to Lady Catherine?" Alethea asked Lord Worcester, searching for something to say alone with him in the garden.

Meanwhile, her mind was occupied with another question. Why did she find Worcester's closeness so sorely trying? Why did she feel such a maddening attraction to this man?

Before she could think of an answer, Worcester suddenly reached out to her. His lips were on hers, kissing her with a passion that caused a tremor to pass through her body. Then, losing all reason, Alethea returned his kiss with fervor.

It was Worcester who broke the kiss off. "Miss Brandon, I am sorry! I don't know what came over me."

Their eyes met then, and it was clear that they at last had found something upon which they could agree. This should not have happened, and must never happen again—if they possibly could help it . . . which at the moment seemed dismayingly doubtful indeed. . . .

Bewitching Lady

~~~~

Margaret Summerville

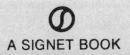

A SIGNET BOOK

SIGNET
Published by the Penguin Group
Penguin Books USA Inc., 375 Hudson Street,
New York, New York 10014, U.S.A.
Penguin Books Ltd, 27 Wrights Lane,
London W8 5TZ, England
Penguin Books Australia Ltd, Ringwood,
Victoria, Australia
Penguin Books Canada Ltd, 10 Alcorn Avenue,
Toronto, Ontario, Canada M4V 3B2
Penguin Books (N.Z.) Ltd, 182–190 Wairau Road,
Auckland 10, New Zealand

Penguin Books Ltd, Registered Offices:
Harmondsworth, Middlesex, England

First published by Signet, an imprint of Dutton Signet,
a division of Penguin Books USA Inc.

First Printing, September, 1997
10 9 8 7 6 5 4 3 2 1

Chapter 1

Geoffrey Charles Beauchamp, the Marquess of Worcester, sat at the desk in the library of his London townhouse, solemnly studying a large architectural drawing laid out before him. The room, with its dark oak wainscotting and austere furniture, was rather dim and dreary-looking on the sunniest of days. However, that afternoon in March, with a steady, cold rain falling outside, the library appeared positively gloomy.

Worcester's mood seemed to match his melancholy surroundings. After studying the drawings before him for some time, he looked up at the elderly gentleman who sat across from him. "The plans seem satisfactory, Crawford," he said. "You can instruct Hamilton to go ahead with the work."

The marquess's gray-haired solicitor nodded solemnly. "Very good, my lord." He paused. "The fire at Worcester Castle was very unfortunate, but I thank Providence that your lordship and Lady Prudence escaped from any harm."

"Yes," agreed Worcester, "it was lucky that no one was injured." The marquess thought of the wintry night scarcely three weeks ago when a fire had broken out at his country estate. It had been quite a disaster, with considerable damage to the house. But, as his solicitor had pointed out, it was a blessing that no one had been harmed in the blaze.

The fire had forced the marquess and his sister to return to town. Worcester, who preferred the country, wasn't pleased to find himself in London. He wished he could go back to Worcester Castle, but the extensive repairs there made that impossible.

Crawford could see that his employer was not in the best of humors. He shook his head sympathetically. "As I said, my lord, the fire at Worcester Castle was most unfortunate, but I think the renovation will please your lordship. There will be some significant improvements made to the house."

The marquess glanced back down at the plans and frowned. "I daresay you're right, Crawford, but it is a dashed nuisance. It is so dreary to be in London this time of year."

"Indeed, my lord," murmured the solicitor, regarding his employer sympathetically from behind his gold-rimmed spectacles. "Will your lordship remain in town?"

Worcester glanced up at the solicitor. "I suppose we might go to Oak Hill Lodge, but I have always found it an uncomfortable house."

Crawford seemed to ponder the matter for a moment. "What about the house in Derbyshire, my lord? Of course it isn't very large . . ."

The marquess cut him off. "Yes, it is too small for my plans." The elderly gentleman regarded Worcester expectantly, but his employer did not deign to tell him just what these plans were.

"Well, then," continued the solicitor, "there is your estate at Glencairn."

"Good God," muttered Worcester, "you can't think that I would go to Scotland now. And it is too far away, by half."

A slight smile appeared on Crawford's dour face. "Such a prospect is certainly not appealing, my lord."

Worcester impatiently got up from his chair and walked over to the window. Staring out at the gray sky, he frowned again. A creature of habit, the marquess did not like change. His life was ruled by routine and he did not relish any deviation in his ordered existence. In fact, Worcester was so set in his ways that he was considered by many in society as the stodgiest fellow in the kingdom.

One might have conjured up a picture of Worcester as a doddering old gentleman from this unflattering description. However, his lordship was very far from his dotage. Indeed, he had just turned thirty that very month. Worcester was an imposing-looking gentleman. While he was considered neither dashing nor particularly handsome, few could fault his appearance. He was tall and broad-shouldered, with dark hair and masculinely chiseled features. His countenance featured a prominent brow, cool gray eyes framed by thick dark, eyebrows, and a long aristocratic nose. It was a face of strong character, a serious face that seldom smiled. Indeed, Worcester's expression was usually one of disapproval or hauteur. This combined with his august rank made him an aloof, unapproachable figure.

However, despite the fact that many considered the young marquess a disagreeable sort of man there were many ladies who were perfectly willing to overlook his defects. After all, the marquess was one of the wealthiest men in England. Certainly a lady could tolerate such a husband if he was as rich as Croesus. As a result, the unmarried marquess was considered a great prize in the marriage mart.

Unfortunately for the ladies, Worcester had thus far shown no interest in matrimony. Many disappointed females decided that the cold-hearted marquess was destined to remain a bachelor for the rest of his life. These ladies would have been quite surprised to learn that Worcester had no such intention. As a matter of fact, the marquess had lately determined that it was time he found a wife.

As he stared out at the rain-drenched London street below him, Worcester once again reflected about choosing a bride. It was not that he wanted to marry. He was quite happy the way he was and he did not doubt that a wife would disturb his tranquil existence. However, since he had turned thirty Worcester knew that he could no longer delay the inevitable. It was his duty to marry and produce an heir and he was not one to shirk his obligations.

The marquess's reverie was broken when his solicitor coughed behind him. Turning around to face the man, Worcester waited for him to speak. "I do have a suggestion, my lord," said Crawford.

The marquess folded his arms in front of him. "Well?"

"Your lordship may remember that three months ago I had some business that took me to Towmouth. Since the village is in the vicinity of your estate Hartwood, I decided to take a look at the property."

Worcester looked slightly puzzled. "I don't remember you mentioning it, Crawford."

"Perhaps I did not, my lord," said the solicitor. "But that may be because I didn't see any problems there. The steward is an honest, capable fellow who has seen that the property has turned a fair profit. The housekeeper appeared a hardworking, efficient woman."

Worcester walked back over to the desk and sat down. He regarded the solicitor with considerable interest. "I have never even been to the place. I remember when I was a boy, my father talked of selling it."

Crawford nodded. "It is fortunate that he did not, my lord. It has proved a good investment."

"And what of the house? Is it liveable?"

"Oh, yes, my lord. Despite being unoccupied for so long, it is in good order. Indeed, it is a rather impressive structure and I think it could be made quite comfortable. Of course, it will need a score of servants to make it ready. The housekeeper and a very limited staff are there now."

"And what of the game thereabouts?" asked Worcester, quite interested.

"Oh, I talked to a local man who seemed to know about such things. He said there are plenty of birds for gentlemen's sport. And it is well situated, and not so far from London. The house is very near the coast and there are some excellent sea views nearby. The area is, if I may say so, my lord, quite picturesque."

"Is it?" said the marquess in a tone implying that scenery was of no importance to him. "Well, you have given me an excellent idea, Crawford. Lady Prudence and I will go there as soon as arrangements can be made. Indeed, I should like to be in the country again."

"Then I shall send word to have the house readied for you, my lord."

"Yes, do so immediately. I wish to leave town by week's end."

"Very good, my lord," said the solicitor, rising from his chair. After bowing politely, he exited the room.

A short time later, Worcester's butler Talbot appeared in the library. "Lord Edward is here, my lord," he said, ushering a young gentleman inside the room.

"Good morning," said the visitor, directing a broad grin at the marquess.

"Ned," said Worcester, smiling in return and displaying more animation in his expression than usual. "I thought you wouldn't arrive in town until next week."

"I had planned to stay longer at Newberry Hall, Geoffrey, but it was so deuced boring that I made excuses to leave early. Gad, it wouldn't stop raining. There was no sport to be had and I was sick to death of playing whist with Uncle Newberry and Cousin Jane. I was eager to come back to town for a change of scene."

Lord Edward Beauchamp sat down in an armchair. He was a

handsome young man of twenty-two with curly reddish blond hair. He was splendidly dressed in a well-cut coat of dove gray superfine and buff-colored pantaloons.

Although there was a slight family resemblance between the brothers, few observers would have guessed at their near kinship. The marquess was a good deal taller than his fair-haired brother and Worcester's face was leaner and more angular.

The greatest contrast between them, however, was in their demeanor and bearing. Edward was an affable, easygoing young man whose amiability showed in his smiling countenance. Worcester, on the other hand, was serious and aloof.

"And how were our aunt and uncle?"

"Oh, very well."

"And Cousin Jane?"

"Very well indeed. And her children are in excellent health, although Ralph is teething and making quite a fuss. And Marianne is walking. What a darling creature she is."

Worcester made no reply, but he was very glad that he hadn't been staying at Newberry Hall, where he would have been expected to admire his cousin's offspring. The marquess thought children nuisances who were best hidden away in the nursery.

"I am very happy to see you, Ned," said the marquess, "although if you found the rain so tedious in the country you're hardly escaping it in town. It has been raining endlessly here as well."

"But rain in town is much more tolerable, don't you think?" said Edward, smiling at his brother.

"What nonsense," said Worcester. "Nothing is worse than London this time of year. I can scarcely wait until I go to the country."

"What? You cannot mean you're not staying here?"

"No, I'm going to the country as soon as possible."

"Where will you go? Not Oak Hill?"

"No, I have never liked it. But Crawford has given me a splendid idea."

"Crawford?" said Edward. "That grim-faced curmudgeon? Good Lord, Geoffrey, the fellow makes me nervous. He always reminds me of Baxter, my old housemaster at Eton. I half expect Crawford to rap my knuckles with a ruler whenever I see him."

Worcester smiled slightly. "I assure you, Ned, he won't harm you."

"But what good idea has he given you? Don't tell me he suggested you return to Worcester Castle?"

Worcester shook his head. "Would that were possible. But the damage is too extensive. The repairs will take several months. Crawford suggested Hartwood in Devon. He happened to be in the area recently and seemed to think it suitable enough."

"Hartwood?" repeated Lord Edward in some surprise. "You can't intend to go there!"

"What do you mean?"

"Good God, Geoffrey, don't you remember Hartwood and the curse of the Beauchamps?"

Worcester raised his dark eyebrows and regarded his brother strangely. "The curse of the Beauchamps? What nonsense is this, Ned?"

Edward laughed. "I cannot believe that you don't remember! It is part of our family lore."

"I don't know what you are talking about," said the marquess.

"Surely you haven't forgotten. Nanny Hoskins used to speak of it until Mama told her to stop. Nanny was ordered never to mention it to Prudence for fear of scaring her."

The marquess looked thoughtful. "Oh, yes, I do remember her mentioning some ridiculous story. Even as a boy I knew it was nonsense. But that was so long ago that I don't recall the details."

"Well, I don't remember the details precisely myself," said Edward, regarding his brother with an amused look. "But I do know that there was a curse and evil befell any of our family that tried to live there. Perhaps Aunt Charlotte would know about it. I shall have to write her. You had best delay your plans of going to Hartwood until we hear from her."

"Don't be absurd," said Worcester. "Curse of the Beauchamps, indeed. May I remind you that we live in the modern era and have put medieval superstition behind us?"

"Perhaps you have done so, my dear brother, but I find it more sensible to stay away from such places as Hartwood. There are probably headless ghosts and howling demons running about."

"If there are, you certainly won't be bored," said Worcester.

Edward burst into laughter. "That may be, but I have no intention of going to Hartwood. I shall be perfectly happy staying in town. And since you will be in the country, I daresay you won't object if I reside here at Worcester House in your absence."

"I shall certainly object," said the marquess. "You are to come with me to Hartwood and, curse or no curse, you will do so."

"But I have just arrived in town. And several of my friends are here."

"Your family duties come first," said Worcester sternly. "It is important that you come to Hartwood as soon as arrangements can be made."

"Oh, very well," said Edward with some reluctance. "But I couldn't go immediately. I promised Charles Paget that I would attend his dinner party Tuesday next."

"Prudence and I shall leave for Hartwood before that, but I have no objections if you join us later. But you must come as soon as you can, for I am having a small house party and I shall need your assistance to keep the guests amused."

Lord Edward appeared quite astonished at this bit of news. "Egad, Geoffrey, as I recall, the last time you had such a party at Worcester Castle, you vowed that you would never again host a group of dunces and parasites."

Worcester nodded. "I admit that I don't enjoy such gatherings, but at times one must put up with it. I am inviting Feversham to Devon. I am anxious to settle the matter with Prudence and him."

"Settle the matter? Then she is to marry him?"

"It appears so," said Worcester.

Edward frowned. He had know that his brother was eager that Prudence marry Viscount Feversham. Since Edward heartily disliked Feversham, he did not approve of the match. "Does Prudence want to marry him?"

"Prudence knows that she must do her duty. And she has had two Seasons to choose a suitable husband. Although she was besieged with suitors, she found something lacking in all of them. She must marry someone, and Feversham is the best of the lot. At least he isn't a fortune hunter like so many of the others."

"But Prudence is still very young. If she has no affection for Feversham . . ."

Worcester cut him off impatiently. "Affection? What has that got to do with it? No, I won't hear any of your romantic nonsense, Ned. Prudence is nineteen and has had two Seasons in town. She is aware that her position in life allows her a very limited choice of husbands. She will be lucky to have Feversham. She will be a duchess one day, you know."

"I am well aware that Feversham will one day be a duke," said

Ned. "But what does that signify if Prudence would be miserable?"

"And why would she be miserable? In my view, he will be as good a husband as any other you might suggest. Tell me who you think would be a better choice."

"I really don't know," said Edward. "It seems that would be for Prudence to decide."

"Good God! You would have a girl of nineteen make such a decision? And, in any case, she has proposed no alternatives to Feversham. I suppose you would be far happier if Prudence married some penniless nobody with whom she fancied herself in love."

Edward frowned. He really didn't wish to argue with his brother. Notoriously stubborn and close-minded, Worcester had always been quite dictatorial where their sister was concerned. "Don't you think that you should be more concerned with your own matrimonial plans, Geoffrey? You are still a bachelor and you are now thirty. It is *you* who must do your duty."

Although Edward had thought Worcester would be annoyed at this remark, his lordship only nodded. "Yes, I realize that, Ned. And I plan to resolve that situation very soon as well."

His brother started. "What? Good God, Geoffrey. Don't tell me you have found a woman you wish to marry?"

Worcester shook his head. "Not exactly. I have no wish at all to marry. You are well aware that I am not eager to shackle myself to some female."

"Yes, I am well aware of that," said Edward.

"But I know that it is my duty to marry and provide an heir. And I have very seriously observed the young ladies in town during the Season. I have considered a good many prospects, I assure you. One must choose a future Marchioness of Worcester very carefully."

"By Jupiter, brother, you speak as if you were buying a new horse. One does not select a wife in such a dispassionate manner."

"And why not? I think it is the most sensible way to choose a wife. When one is the head of a great family, one must set aside romantic notions. Marriage is about property and providing heirs. It is essential to treat it with a cool head."

"It is clear that you are able to do that, Geoffrey," said Edward, regarding his brother with a bemused look. "But you said you are thinking of marriage. Does that mean you have decided upon the lady?"

Worcester nodded. "I have."

"Well, don't keep me in suspense. Who is she?"

"Lady Catherine Percy."

"Lady Catherine?" said Edward. "She is a very pretty girl."

"And her breeding is impeccable. She is well-mannered and dignified, just the sort of girl to be a marchioness."

Edward hesitated before replying. While he wasn't well acquainted with Lady Catherine, he was not disposed to like her. For one thing, he had little regard for her parents, the Earl and Countess of Huntingdon, who were both haughty and overbearing. And Lady Catherine was very much like her mother. Edward tried to be diplomatic. "But don't you think her a trifle . . . proud?"

"What is wrong with that?" said Worcester. "If one has reason to be proud, there is no fault in it. Lady Catherine comes from one of the most distinguished families in the kingdom. The future Lady Worcester should be aware of her rank and position in life."

"Then you are engaged to Lady Catherine?"

"Not yet," said Worcester, "but I have discussed the matter with Huntingdon. He is very much in favor of the match. I'm sure we will decide things when they are at Hartwood."

"So Huntingdon and his wife and daughter are coming?"

The marquess nodded. "Yes. And the Duke and Duchess of Cranworth and Feversham."

"I hope you haven't invited a future bride for me," said Edward.

"You know very well that I think you are too young to think of marriage. I have told you many times that I think it unwise for a man to marry before five-and-twenty."

"Yes, you've said that before," said Edward.

"In a few years if you are inclined to marry, I'm sure we will find you a suitable wife," said the marquess.

Edward refrained from making an indignant reply. His brother always thought he had the right to dictate to Edward what he should do. Ever since their father's death eight years ago, Worcester had assumed a paternalistic attitude toward his younger brother and sister.

Fortunately, Worcester had been persuaded in the last year to allow Edward more freedom. At twenty-one Edward had been given an income and he had gone off to live on his own. Yet, since the marquess controlled the purse strings, he still maintained his authority over his brother.

Edward hadn't chafed too much under Worcester's domination, although recently a complication had developed that might upset their relationship. Although he hadn't revealed it to the marquess, Edward had fallen in love with a lady whose family connections would certainly make her unacceptable to Worcester. Edward was very much in a quandary over this and he didn't appreciate hearing the marquess say that he would find him a suitable wife when the time was right.

Worcester glanced at the clock. "It is time for tea. You will stay, of course?"

There was something of a command in the request and Edward nodded. "Yes, I should like that very much."

"Good," said Worcester. "Come let us go to the drawing room and have some tea. And I will hear no more about this curse of the Beauchamps." Edward nodded and the two men left the gloomy library.

Chapter 2

Like most of the rooms in Crow's Nest Cottage, the library was small but comfortable. Filled with books and curious mementos, it was an interesting, pleasant room. The late-afternoon sun streamed in through the windows, making it bright and cheerful.

Alethea Brandon sat at an ornate oak desk, hard at work, busily applying ink to paper with a quill pen. Lying in front of the desk was a large tawny-colored dog, who slept soundly.

A servant, a stout young woman in a white cap and gray dress, entered the room, causing the dog to raise his head and regard her with a doleful expression. "Begging your pardon, miss," said the servant apologetically, knowing that her mistress disliked interruptions while she was working. "But Mrs. Truscott is here to see you. She's waiting in the drawing room."

Alethea didn't seem in the least perturbed at the announcement. Mrs. Truscott was her favorite aunt and she was always happy to see her. "Do have Sarah make tea, Molly. I'll join my aunt at once." The girl gave her a quick bob and left the room.

Putting down her pen, Alethea rose from the desk. "Come, Nelson," she said, addressing the dog, "we have a guest. It is Aunt Elizabeth."

The dog rose to his feet. An English mastiff, he was a huge animal whose appearance most people found rather daunting. Yet Nelson was a sweet, good-natured creature who wouldn't harm anyone except, of course, persons threatening his beloved mistress.

Followed by the mastiff, Alethea proceeded to the drawing room, where she found her aunt looking through the telescope that pointed toward the sea from the window.

"I do hope you see something interesting, Aunt Elizabeth," said

Alethea, smiling as she entered the room. "A pirate ship, perhaps?"

Elizabeth Truscott turned from the telescope to smile at her niece. "Nothing so exciting, my dear, but one does get a good look at seagulls this way. And I can't help but think of your father out at sea. I do wish my brother had stayed at home where he belongs."

Alethea laughed and then went over to her aunt to greet her with a kiss. "Now, Aunt Elizabeth, you know Papa would have been miserable if he hadn't gone on the expedition. One doesn't have many opportunities to explore the South Seas."

"I believe William has explored enough," said Elizabeth. "I cannot imagine how he could leave you alone here."

"I am perfectly fine," said Alethea. "And I am glad to be alone to work on my book. But I am happy to see you. Do sit down and we'll have tea."

"I should like that," said Elizabeth, taking a seat on the sofa. At forty, she was a handsome woman. She had dark brown hair, brown eyes, and fine classical features. "And, my dear Nelson, what a handsome fellow you are."

Going over to Elizabeth, Nelson wagged his tail delightedly. Alethea's aunt obligingly rubbed his thick neck.

Alethea took a chair near her aunt. She was a pretty young woman, who possessed an enviable complexion and excellent figure. While Alethea scoffed at those who would proclaim her a beauty, her remarkable hazel eyes fringed with long dark lashes were much admired. Her face was framed by curly black hair that had a tendency toward unruliness.

"My dear Alethea, I could scarcely wait to call. I have the most amazing news! You will never guess it. It involves a certain highborn personage who will be coming to our vicinity."

Alethea's eyes opened in a look of mock astonishment. "The Prince Regent is taking a house at Towmouth!"

Elizabeth laughed. "Do be serious, Alethea. But, actually the news is nearly as surprising as that."

"I pray you don't keep me in suspense any longer, Aunt."

"The Marquess of Worcester will take up residence at Hartwood." Elizabeth appeared well satisfied by her niece's look of astonishment.

"I can scarcely believe it," said Alethea. They were interrupted by the arrival of a servant bringing tea.

"Oh, look, Sarah's famous ginger cake," exclaimed Elizabeth, eyeing the tray. The dog Nelson, who was sitting near Alethea's aunt, also expressed considerable interest in the food being placed on the table. He sniffed the air excitedly.

"But do tell me more about this news of yours. Why would the Marquess of Worcester come to Hartwood?"

"I'm told there was a fire at the country home where he usually spends the winter and he needed another house."

"I shouldn't be surprised if Hartwood will go up in flames as well," said Alethea, a mischievous smile coming to her face as she poured the tea. "The curse of the Beauchamps, you know. This marquess must be very brave."

"Don't talk nonsense, Alethea," said her aunt. "Indeed, I hope you won't bring up that ridiculous curse business. There will be enough talk of that among the servants and local people. After all, we do want Lord Worcester and his family to stay here."

"Do we?" said Alethea, trying to maintain a serious expression. "My dear aunt, how could you wish that? Why, the Beauchamps are the sworn enemies of the Brandons."

Her aunt looked so alarmed at this remark that Alethea burst into laughter. "Oh, you were only gammoning me," said Elizabeth. "I should have known."

"Well, my father always reminded me that if it hadn't been for the nefarious first Marquess of Worcester, we Brandons would still reside at Hartwood."

"That may be," said Elizabeth, taking a bite of ginger cake, "but that was in the past and is best forgotten."

Alethea smiled. "It's not that I'd wish to live at Hartwood, of course. It is far too grand for me. But isn't it terrible to think of our poor ancestor Giles Brandon executed due to the evil Lord Worcester's treachery?"

"I don't think of it," said Elizabeth resolutely. "I never liked history overmuch, especially parts where persons lost their heads in the Tower."

Alethea laughed. "Well, when is this Lord Worcester to arrive at Hartwood?"

"Very soon," said Elizabeth. "Everyone is quite agog over the news. He is a very important man, and very rich."

"Well, I shall be eager to gape at him from afar," said Alethea. "I've never seen a marquess."

"That's because you've never come with us to London during the Season."

"Oh, no," groaned Alethea, "not this subject again!"

"I shall continue to badger you until you spend the Season in town with us. And now that your father is away, you can't think to remain here alone."

"I won't be alone. There are Sarah and Molly and John."

"But they are servants!" exclaimed her aunt. "It isn't the same at all. Before your father left, I told him that I would insist you come with us to London in the spring. Now, it is quite settled."

"Really, Aunt, I shall come and stay a fortnight or so, but you mustn't think I shall stay longer. I have my work to do here."

"Your work? You cannot mean to continue here, isolating yourself, never seeing anyone."

"Oh, I'm hardly a hermit," said Alethea with a smile. "I have all the society I desire."

"My dear Alethea, I have never approved of this work of yours. In truth, society here is too limited for a girl like you. There are so few eligible men about, after all. Indeed, you would do well to desert those musty books and concern yourself with more important matters."

"My dear aunt, I pray you won't start about my finding a husband."

"Alethea Brandon, you are nearly five-and-twenty. If you don't find a husband soon, you will die a spinster."

To her aunt's irritation, Alethea only laughed. "Is that such a dreadful fate? Why, I am perfectly happy as I am."

This remark exasperated her aunt. "You may say that, but I cannot believe it."

"If you prefer to think I'm miserable, you may do so," said Alethea with a broad smile. "And although I know that you have found an excellent husband in Uncle, I must remind you that most women aren't so fortunate. My acquaintance with the male sex has not made me so sanguine about the state of matrimony."

Elizabeth frowned but made no reply. She knew from experience that it was useless to argue with her strong-willed niece.

It was true that Alethea had been rather headstrong and independent. As a girl, she had loved nothing better than tramping about the woods or the seashore, her beloved terrier Wags at her side. Under the tutelage of her father, a renowed botanist, Alethea had developed a keen interest in plants. She would often return home from her rambles with a collection of leaves and wildflowers, her petticoats muddied and her dark hair wild and tangled.

Elizabeth sighed. Of course, it was her brother's fault that Alethea was so unconventional. William Brandon had been very pleased that his only child shared his botanical bent, and he had been eager to foster her interest. Her father had seen that she received a first-rate education and had taken her on some of his plant-finding expeditions. As a result, Alethea had become a serious scholar of botany herself. If she had been a man, she would no doubt be destined to one day be as highly regarded in academic circles as her father.

But Alethea was not a man and her aunt thought her brother quite wrongheaded in letting Alethea pursue such a life. It was not surprising to Elizabeth that Alethea was very nearly on the shelf, spending her time as she did. It seemed that she was always either out collecting her cherished plant specimens or thrusting her nose into some crusty old manuscript written in Latin.

Elizabeth thoughtfully took a sip of tea as she looked over at her niece. Surely it was not hopeless. After all, Alethea was very attractive. Of course, thought Elizabeth, it would help if Alethea gave a bit more attention to her clothes and tried to refrain from expressing herself so freely. She was very much like her father, who was something of a freethinker and the sort of man who always spoke his opinion. While this wasn't so objectionable in a man, Elizabeth considered it rather disconcerting in a girl. Certainly prospective suitors had been scared away by Alethea's outspokeness and her sometimes sardonic wit.

Taking a dainty bite of ginger cake, Elizabeth resolved that Alethea really must stay with them in town. Although Elizabeth and her husband were scarcely in the upper reaches of society, they had a respectable social position. She was certain that she could find some acceptable suitors for her niece in London, where gentlemen were quite plentiful. Elizabeth just wished that Alethea would become serious about finding a husband.

Although Elizabeth was determined to reopen the subject of her niece visiting them in town, she decided to change the topic for the time being. "I have had a letter from Frederick," she said. "I fear he is not happy at Oxford. Of course, Frederick was never the scholar in the family. You were always that, Alethea. I would not doubt that you would be getting on famously if you were in Frederick's position."

Alethea shrugged. While this was undoubtedly true, there was no point on dwelling on the impossible. It was her cousin Frederick who was able to go to university, even though he had no wish to be there. In his letters he was constantly complaining about his tutor and the boring lectures he was forced to endure.

Elizabeth was about to say something else about her son when Molly appeared in the room before them. Eyeing Elizabeth, the servant made a clumsy curtsy. She then turned to Alethea. "Beggin' your pardon, miss, but Mr. Brown is here and he says he must see you. 'Tis urgent, he said."

Alethea nodded. "Very well, Molly. Show him in."

Elizabeth, who knew that Brown was a poor farmer in the neighborhood, regarded her niece with a slightly disapproving look. "Good heavens, Alethea, you would have the fellow ushered in here?"

Before Elizabeth could reply, Molly returned, followed by a short, skinny man with carroty red hair. Clutching a well-worn hat in his hands, the man nodded at Elizabeth and then turned a worried expression on Alethea. "Good day, Miss Alethea. It's sorry I am to be disturbing you, but I fear my Jenny's poorly again."

Alethea's face took on a look of concern. "Oh dear."

"Aye, miss. I fear 'tis the same stomach complaint as last time."

Alethea stood up. "Well, I think I have something that will set her right again. Come with me, Dick, and I'll mix up something for her." She turned to her aunt. "I shan't be long, Aunt." Alethea left the room, with Brown and Nelson following behind her.

When she returned a short time later, Alethea sat back down and smiled at her aunt. "I'm sure old Jenny will be much better soon."

"Old Jenny," said Elizabeth with a frown. She was well aware that Jenny was a goat. "I don't know why you allow such persons as Brown to take advantage of you. You aren't an apothecary."

Alethea laughed. "But I enjoy helping when I can."

"I don't think it very seemly for you to physick animals. I am always hearing that you are going about the county treating sick cows and pigs. It is hardly the occupation for a lady."

"But I love animals and I can help them."

"And you're never paid for your labors, I'll be bound."

"Oh, I don't expect to be paid," said Alethea. "Why, I'm researching the medicinal powers of herbs. It is gratifying to see them working."

"You know that everyone talks about you."

"My dear aunt," cried Alethea, "everyone talks about everyone in Towmouth."

"But you know that there are superstitious persons claiming you have supernatural powers of healing."

"I suppose they think me some sort of witch," said Alethea with a laugh.

"That isn't so amusing," said Elizabeth. "George Phelps saw you talking to that pet crow of yours. He said you spoke to him as if he were human."

"I don't know how else one speaks to crows," said Alethea. She glanced over at Nelson. "Or to dogs. I imagine Mr. Phelps thought Hector my witch's familiar," said Alethea. "Well, some think he has a sinister appearance."

"I know you find it all very amusing, but one mustn't do things to cause the common people to gossip."

"And why not? Why shouldn't the common people gossip just as we do?"

Elizabeth smiled. "You are incorrigible, Alethea Brandon."

Alethea laughed in reply and offered her aunt another piece of cake.

build. Very pretty, with rounded soft hair, finely chiseled features,

Chapter 3

Three days after Alethea and her aunt had discussed the surprising news that the Marquess of Worcester was to reside at Hartwood, his lordship's large traveling coach was maneuvering the winding road that led to the estate. The two occupants of the vehicle, Worcester and his sister, Prudence, were silent as the carriage lumbered along toward its destination.

The marquess had found the journey extremely wearisome. In addition to the bone-chilling cold and bumpy roads, they had been forced to spend the night in a wretched, drafty inn. Worcester frowned and grimly stared out at the tree-laden hills surrounding them as he remembered the inn's unpalatable food and miserable accommodations.

Pulling his greatcoat closer around him, the marquess's frown grew deeper. As if these factors had not made traveling bad enough, Worcester was also beginning to feel unwell. The slight sore throat he had woken up with that morning was getting quite painful and he seemed to be experiencing alternating fever and chills. It was really quite irksome.

Prudence, who was unaware of her brother's illness, was rather enjoying the ride. A good-natured young woman of nineteen, Lady Prudence thought the journey an exciting adventure. She was especially eager to see Hartwood and stared out the carriage window with a look of anticipation on her face.

Those who were unfamiliar with the Beauchamp family might have been surprised to learn that the stern and unsmiling marquess was the brother of the sweet-looking young lady who sat across from him in the coach. Indeed, Prudence was much closer in looks and temperament to her brother Edward.

Kindhearted and shy, Prudence was of middle height and slight build. Very pretty with reddish gold hair, finely crafted features, and blue eyes, Prudence attracted considerable masculine admiration. And since she would undoubtedly receive one of the kingdom's largest marriage settlements, the lady had been very much sought after in town.

It was for this reason that Worcester was determined to find an acceptable husband for his young sister. Fearing that she might be foolish enough to fancy one of the unsuitable gentlemen that clamored about her, the marquess decided that he would see that Prudence made the right match.

Eleven years older than his sister, Worcester was used to managing Prudence's life. Since she had been an infant when her mother died and only eleven years old at the death of her father, Prudence had, for much of her life, been under the guardianship of her elder brother. In fact, Worcester had taken on the role of a strict, but fond, parent.

Prudence had always been a manageable girl and Worcester did not doubt that she would follow his wishes in regard to a husband. He was certain that his stay at Hartwood would end with satisfactory matches for both of them.

Unaware that her brother was planning to secure them both spouses during their excursion in the countryside, Prudence was looking forward to their residence in Devon. Bashful in large company, she preferred the smaller, informal gatherings the country offered. Also, as a nature lover, Prudence liked nothing better than finding herself out amidst bucolic scenery.

Prudence continued to look out the window, waiting to catch her first glimpse of Hartwood. The carriage turned a bend in the road and the house suddenly appeared before her. The young lady regarded it in some astonishment. A tall, imposing Gothic structure of gray stone, the ancient house very much appealed to Prudence's romantic nature.

"Look, Geoffrey!" she cried. "You can see the house!"

The marquess, showing none of his sister's enthusiasm, peered out the window. Although he was feeling too ill to fully appreciate the estate, he decided the house looked sufficiently grand for his purposes. Resting his head on one hand, he was just thankful that he would soon be out of the damnable coach.

Prudence continued staring at the house as the vehicle continued slowly up the lane toward it. As the driver pulled the equipage to a stop, she found herself filled with a strange excitement. When the groom opened the door and assisted her down, Prudence eagerly approached the house. Worcester, who was feeling increasingly ill, followed slowly after her.

Talbot, who had come up a few days previously from town, hurried out to greet them. "My lord, my lady," said the butler, bowing gravely. "I do hope your journey was pleasant."

The marquess made a grimace. "It was dashed unpleasant, Talbot. I was jolted unmercifully in that damnable carriage and I thought that we'd never get here."

After murmuring his regret at his master's words, the butler led Worcester and Lady Prudence up the ancient stone steps to the massive front door of the house. As Worcester and Prudence stepped inside, they found themselves in a cavernous entryway decorated with suits of armor. The walls were hung with numerous pieces of medieval weaponry that gave the place a grim, forbidding aspect.

Standing before them was a stout, middle-aged woman in a prim blue dress. Talbot quickly introduced her as Mrs. Graham, the housekeeper.

Mrs. Graham, eager to finally meet her employer, made a curtsy and smiled. "Welcome to Hartwood, my lord and my lady. I do hope everything will be to your liking."

Worcester gave her a cursory nod, but Prudence smiled at her. "Thank you, Mrs. Graham. I am sure it will be," she said. The housekeeper was quite pleased by the young lady's pleasant tone. Although she was not altogether sure about the grim lord standing before her, Mrs. Graham decided that Lady Prudence seemed amiable enough.

Talbot, who was used to his employer's unsmiling countenance, took his lordship's hat and coat and handed them to an awaiting maid. The butler did not fail to take note of his employer's pallor and his pained expression. "Are you feeling unwell, my lord?" he said.

Worcester, who was feeling quite wretched, tried to make light of it. "It's nothing, although I am rather tired."

Talbot nodded, regarding Worcester with some concern. "Perhaps your lordship would wish to retire to your room to rest."

"I believe that would be a good idea, Talbot," replied the marquess.

Prudence viewed her brother with some alarm, thinking that he must be feeling miserable. He was scarcely ever sick and she couldn't remember him ever retiring to his room in the middle of the afternoon.

"Geoffrey, I didn't know you were ill," she said, her blue eyes suddenly fixed upon him with a worried look. "You should have said something."

"There is no reason to make a fuss, Pru. I shall be fine after resting a bit."

"I shall show you to your room, my lord," said Talbot. "Please follow me." He led Worcester and Prudence up the imposing staircase and stopped in front of a door. Opening it, he turned to the marquess. "This is your room, my lord. I shall have Weeks sent to you."

Worcester nodded. "Thank you, Talbot."

Prudence placed a gentle hand on her brother's arm. "Are you certain you shall be all right, Geoffrey?" she asked. "Perhaps we should fetch a physician . . ."

Worcester abruptly cut her off. "Don't be ridiculous, Pru. No need to send for a leech. It is a trifling thing." He managed to smile at her and then he went into the room. His valet Weeks appeared shortly to assist him, and the marquess was soon changed out of his traveling clothes and into a nightshirt.

Climbing into the large canopied bed and shivering, Worcester pulled up the covers thankfully around him. Closing his eyes, he decided he had made a rather inauspicious start to his stay at Hartwood.

Chapter 4

While Worcester stayed in his room, Prudence spent the afternoon receiving a tour of Hartwood from Mrs. Graham. She was very pleased with the house despite its old-fashioned furniture and often gloomy rooms. While she was well aware that the house needed a significant amount of interior decoration to make it more comfortable, Prudence liked it very much. It had a brooding aspect that struck her as romantic and she loved the splendid views afforded by many of the windows.

In the evening Prudence received word that Worcester would not join her for dinner. Concerned, she hurried to his room, where she found him feverish and miserable. Still, the marquess insisted that there was no call for worry and that she must have dinner without him.

Prudence, left to dine alone in the vast dining hall, could not help but worry about her brother. Her concern prevented her from enjoying the elaborate dinner that had been prepared in honor of their arrival.

After the meal, she returned to Worcester's room, but finding him sleeping soundly, she retired to her own bedchamber. As she got into bed that night and blew out her candle, Prudence devoutly hoped that her brother would be feeling better the next day.

However, the following morning Worcester's condition had worsened. He seemed even more feverish and his throat was painfully sore. The marquess was also in an exceedingly bad temper, barking hoarsely at his valet and snapping at the maid.

When Prudence urged her brother to let a servant fetch a doctor, the marquess stoutly refused. Worcester had never had much faith in the medical profession, dismissing most doctors as ignorant quacks.

Worcester insisted that all he needed to recover his health was more rest and to be left alone. Prudence wasn't to stand about fussing over him like a mother hen. Frustrated by her brother's stubborn resistance to seeking medical advice, Prudence left him.

Although she tried to busy herself talking about household matters with Mrs. Graham and taking walks about the grounds, Prudence continued to worry about the marquess. When evening came and he still seemed to be getting much worse, she again urged him to allow her to send for a physician. Yet Worcester wouldn't hear of it and once again Prudence went to bed full of concern about him.

Early the next morning, Prudence's maid entered the room to inform her that the marquess was no better. Dressing quickly, Prudence hurried out to see him. She found Talbot and Mrs. Graham in serious consultation just outside her brother's door. "Talbot," she said, alarmed at their solemn expressions, "what is the matter?"

After exchanging a glance with the housekeeper, the butler fixed a grave look upon his young mistress. "I fear, my lady, that his lordship appears to have a high fever this morning." He paused. "He is quite restless and somewhat disoriented."

"Oh dear," said Prudence. "The doctor must be sent for at once."

"We have already done so, my lady. I was certain that you wouldn't object."

"Oh, yes, of course," said Prudence. "Oh, why didn't I insist that he see a doctor yesterday? He is so frightfully stubborn and he hates physicians."

Talbot, who was well aware of this, nodded. "I'm sure there is no call for alarm, my lady," he said. "The physician will be here shortly and Mrs. Graham tells me he is quite competent."

"Oh yes, my lady," said Mrs. Graham. "Dr. Chandler is a very capable young man."

Prudence nodded and managed a faint smile at the older woman. "Then I shall go in and see my brother now," she said. Opening the door, Prudence tiptoed over toward the large canopied bed where the marquess lay. A frazzled-looking maid sat in a chair at the head of the bed, attempting to put a compress on Worcester's forehead. The servant looked up as Prudence entered.

"How is he, Mary?" asked Prudence.

The maid shook her head. "I fear he is rather poorly, my lady." Prudence looked down at her brother. He seemed quite agitated, tossing and turning on the rumpled bed and muttering in a low, incoherent voice.

Prudence, seeing how ill he was, felt suddenly weak herself. What would she do if Geoffrey . . . Prudence could not even force herself to finish her thought. She turned to the maid. "The physician will be here soon, Mary," she said, trying to remain calm. "I will look after his lordship now."

The servant nodded and left the sickroom. When she was gone, Prudence took up the compress and managed to press it against her brother's fevered brow. She could only pray that the physician would come soon.

After what seemed to Prudence a very long time, the door opened. Looking up eagerly, Prudence was disappointed to find that it was only Talbot, who appeared very solemn. When Talbot motioned to her, Prudence quickly got up and followed him out into the hallway. There stood Mrs. Graham with a short young man with a thatch of blond hair. Prudence turned to the butler. "What is wrong, Talbot?"

"I am afraid, Lady Prudence, that the local physician isn't available. Jeremy here went to Dr. Chandler's house in the village and his housekeeper said that he was called away to his aunt and won't be back until tomorrow morning."

"Tomorrow morning!" cried Prudence in dismay. "But there must be someone else . . ."

"I fear the next closest physician would be in Hadley Dale, my lady," said Mrs. Graham apologetically, "and that is some twenty miles distant."

"Oh dear," said Prudence, "what shall we do? My brother is burning up with fever! And he has become delirious!" Prudence looked as if she might burst into tears.

The housekeeper hesitated for just a moment. "If I might suggest something, my lady."

Prudence fixed her blue eyes on the woman with a desperate expression. "Yes, Mrs. Graham?"

"There is a lady who lives not far from here. Miss Alethea Brandon is her name. She is very knowledgeable in plant cures. I'm sure she could help his lordship. I believe she should be sent for at once."

"Then do so, Mrs. Graham," said Prudence, eager to try anything.

"Jeremy, run as fast as you can and fetch Miss Alethea."

"But, Mrs. Graham," said the boy, "I don't think Miss Alethea would come to Hartwood."

"Don't speak nonsense," said Mrs. Graham. "Now be off with you."

"Wait," said Prudence, looking closely at Jeremy. "Whatever do you mean? Why wouldn't this woman come to Hartwood?"

The boy stared sheepishly at her.

"Pay him no mind, my lady," said Mrs. Graham, frowning at him. "Hurry on then. And make sharp, lad, or I'll box your ears." This threat caused the young man to scurry off.

"But why did he say that, Mrs. Graham?"

The housekeeper shook her head. "Oh, 'tis only silly nonsense. I know Miss Alethea very well and she'll be here in a trice."

"But I must know what he meant, Mrs. Graham."

"Oh, very well, my lady. It is that Miss Alethea is a Brandon." When Prudence only looked perplexed, she continued. "Then you have never heard of the feud between the Brandons and your family?"

"Feud?" said Prudence. "Indeed, I have never heard of these Brandons."

"It was all very long ago and best forgotten. I have known Miss Alethea since she was an infant, and she is a good and kind lady. And as I said, she has considerable knowledge about plant remedies for ailments. Why, 'tis she who helped my little nephew Ben when he had the croup last winter. Some local folk think Miss Alethea has the powers of sorcery in her healing. And she lives very close by. She'll be here very soon."

At that moment Prudence thought she heard Worcester say something, so she hurried in to him. Finding him muttering to himself, she took the seat beside his bed. "What is it, Geoffrey? Would you like anything? Perhaps some water?"

The marquess, who seemed barely to comprehend her, only shook his head. As she stared down helplessly at his prostrate form, she hoped that Mrs. Graham was right about this Miss Brandon's healing powers.

Alethea had been quite surprised when Jeremy had arrived at Crow's Nest Cottage with the summons for her to go to Hart-

wood. Hearing about the ailing marquess, she couldn't help but
think of the ancient curse that had been placed on the Beauchamp
family. Even though Alethea was far too sensible a woman to believe in such superstitions, she did think it an odd coincidence
that the Marquess of Worcester had been struck ill on his arrival
at the house.

Hurrying to put together a basket of medicinal herbs, Alethea
was soon ready to go. Flinging her old blue cloak around her
shoulders, she followed Jeremy to the waiting trap that was to
take her to Hartwood

A short time later, the vehicle pulled up in front of the imposing gray stone house. Alethea glanced up at the towering building. She was struck again by the strange feeling she had whenever
she saw Hartwood. Alethea felt as if she belonged there.

Of course, she knew that her unusual attachment to the house
was probably due to her ancestral connection to it. After climbing
down from the trap, she made her way to the front entrance.

Talbot met her at the door. "Miss Brandon?"

Alethea nodded.

Although the butler was rather taken aback to find that Miss
Brandon was such a young and comely lady, he tried to mask his
surprise. "Do come in."

Mrs. Graham hurried across the entry hall. "My dear Miss
Alethea. Thank heaven you are come so quickly. We are so worried about his lordship. He is very ill indeed."

"Then do take me to him at once," said Alethea, taking off her
cloak and bonnet and handing them to Talbot. The housekeeper
nodded and led the way upstairs.

Arriving at Worcester's door, Mrs. Graham ushered Alethea inside. "Lady Prudence, Miss Brandon is here."

Alethea looked into the room and saw a pretty young woman
with reddish gold hair sitting next to a canopied bed. Rising from
her chair, she came forward, a worried expression on her face.
"Oh, Miss Brandon, thank you for coming! I am Lady Prudence
Beauchamp."

Alethea took the lady's outstretched hand and smiled warmly at
her. She looked over toward the bed.

"I fear my brother is very ill, Miss Brandon. I do hope that you
might help."

"I shall certainly try," said Alethea. Putting her basket down on
the table, Alethea walked quietly toward the bed and stared down

at the recumbent figure stretched out on it. So this was Lord Worcester, she thought.

The marquess lay with his eyes closed, his black hair tousled and damp with sweat, and dark stubble upon his chin. He suddenly began to move about and mutter something incomprehensible.

As she stared down at him, he opened his eyes and fixed a wild-eyed gaze upon her. "I have come to help you, Lord Worcester," said Alethea, placing a hand upon his brow. The marquess continued to gaze up at her, a strange expression in his gray eyes. "Who are you?" he murmured in an odd voice.

"I am Miss Brandon," said Alethea, smiling at him. "Do try to rest, my lord." The marquess closed his eyes but remained agitated, tossing from side to side and murmuring unintelligibly.

Prudence regarded Alethea with a piteous look. "He is very ill, is he not, Miss Brandon?"

"His fever is dangerously high. We must do something to lower it." Alethea gestured toward her basket. "I have brought some herbs that should help. I shall need to use your kitchen to prepare them."

"Oh, certainly. I shall have one of the servants take you there right away, Miss Brandon." Alethea nodded and went to retrieve her basket. Responding quickly to Prudence's summons, a maid soon appeared and escorted Alethea to the kitchen.

Some time later, Alethea reappeared in the sick room, carrying a glass which contained a greenish liquid. She walked over to the bed, where Prudence sat in a chair next to her brother. "This should help bring down the fever and let him get some rest." She put a gentle hand on Worcester's burning forehead. The marquess, who was mumbling something, suddenly opened his eyes again.

"Nanny Hoskins!" he cried in an eager voice. His gray eyes rested on Alethea with a perplexed expression. "You are not Nanny," he said.

Alethea smiled and leaned over toward him. "No, my lord. But Nanny wants you to drink something to make you feel better." She lifted the glass to his lips and after a moment's hesitation, he drank it down. "There," said Alethea, pleased by his obedience, "now you must rest."

Worcester continued to gaze up at her for a while, but then he closed his eyes. Alethea sat down in a chair that had been placed next to Prudence and the two women sat silently watching the marquess. Worcester remained restless for a time, but then he slowly seemed to settle down. After about an hour had gone by, he finally fell asleep.

Alethea was very encouraged that her patient was finally resting peacefully. Knowing that Prudence was very worried, she tried to speak in an encouraging tone. "This medicine is very useful in reducing fevers," she said in a low voice.

"Oh, Miss Brandon, will he be all right?"

"I'm sure he will be fine," said Alethea.

Prudence was so relieved she almost burst into tears. "I'm so glad you are here. When I heard that there was no physician, I didn't know what to do."

"Well, you mustn't worry. He is doing much better," said Alethea, hoping that the promising turn in the marquess's health continued. She knew that fevers could be quite unpredictable and so she could not be too sanguine on the matter. She looked closely at Prudence. The young woman appeared rather pale and drawn and Alethea was afraid she could also be subject to the illness. "I can sit with him, Lady Prudence," said Alethea. "You should get some rest yourself. It wouldn't do for you to get sick as well. Why don't you lie down for a while in your room?"

Prudence hesitated, but then agreed. The worry over her brother had made her feel quite exhausted. After profusely thanking Alethea again, Prudence left the room.

Sitting alone with the sleeping marquess, Alethea looked down on him. A slight smile crossed her lips as she thought that she, Alethea Brandon, was ministering to her family's sworn enemy at his sickbed.

Chapter 5

The marquess slept for several hours. For the most part, he rested quite soundly, although occasionally he would toss and turn and start mumbling incoherently. Alethea sat in her chair by his bedside, watching him. Throughout her long vigil she found herself wondering what sort of man he was.

She was disinclined to think well of him. After all, from what she knew about wealthy lords such as Worcester, he was probably arrogant, dissolute, and extravagant.

Since her station in life was relatively modest, Alethea had not made the acquaintance of a marquess before. Noblemen of such rank were not in the habit of associating with the local gentry of the area.

Rising from her chair, Alethea leaned over the sleeping marquess and placed a hand on his brow. She was relieved to find him cooler. The fever had broken. Picking up his wrist, Alethea felt his pulse. It was strong and regular.

Worcester's eyes opened. "What?" he said, looking about the room as if trying to remember where he was.

"Lord Worcester," said Alethea, placing his arm back down on the bed. "You are awake. You appear to be much better. I must fetch Lady Prudence. She has been so terribly worried about you. You've been very ill with fever."

"Who are you?" said Worcester, regarding her in some confusion.

"I am Miss Brandon," said Alethea.

"Miss Brandon?" Worcester stared at her. He had a vague realization that he had seen her before. A vision of a dark-haired woman hovering over him suddenly rose before him. He found himself thinking that she had lovely hazel eyes.

Suspecting that he was wondering about her position in the scheme of things, Alethea smiled. "I live nearby, Lord Worcester. I was summoned here because Dr. Chandler had been called away. I hasten to say that I am a very poor substitute for Dr. Chandler, but I do have some knowledge of herbal medicines."

Worcester continued to regard her with a rather dazed look. "I seem to remember drinking some foul liquid."

Alethea nodded. "Yes, it tastes quite wretched, but it can be very effective. You appear to be proof of that, my lord. But I must send word to Lady Prudence." Alethea rang for a servant. When the maid appeared, she sent her to inform Prudence of the good news of his lordship's apparent recovery.

"How long have I been sleeping?" asked the marquess.

"A few hours. We were really concerned. I'm afraid you were quite delirious."

"Good God," muttered Worcester.

"But how do you feel?"

"I feel dashed rotten," said the marquess.

Alethea smiled. "I daresay it will be some time before you are completely well. Can you sit up, my lord? Would you like a drink of water?" When she leaned down and assisted him into a sitting position, he was aware of the faint floral scent of her perfume.

Turning away from him, Alethea poured a glass of water from a pitcher by the bedside. "Drink this, Lord Worcester." When he took the glass with seeming reluctance, she smiled again. "Don't worry, it's only water."

Realizing that he was very thirsty, Worcester drained the glass. At that moment Prudence entered the room, followed by Talbot. She rushed to his bedside. "Oh, Geoffrey, Mary said you were better! You cannot know how glad I am. I was so frightfully worried."

"Good Lord, you act as though I was nearly in my tomb," said the marquess.

"But you were very ill," said Prudence.

"Nonsense," returned the marquess, "it wasn't in the least serious."

"It was serious enough for you to take Miss Brandon for Nanny Hoskins," said Prudence.

This remark silenced Worcester, who frowned and hoped that he wasn't reddening with embarrassment. It seemed he had made an ass of himself.

Prudence turned to Alethea. "Is he out of danger, Miss Brandon?"

"I believe so," replied Alethea. "But I must urge his lordship to get more rest. Indeed, perhaps we should leave him, Lady Prudence."

"Shouldn't I stay with him?" said Prudence.

"That isn't necessary," said the marquess. "I should sleep better without females hovering about me."

"Yes, I'm sure Lord Worcester is right," said Alethea. "We can look in on him later. Come along, Lady Prudence." The two ladies left the sickroom and went to the drawing room.

"Oh, Miss Brandon, I cannot express my gratitude to you. What a relief to see Geoffrey so much better. Your medicine must be quite wonderful."

"I do think it helped bring his fever down," said Alethea.

"It was very bad of me to leave you alone for such a long time. I didn't think that I would fall asleep, but I did."

"You mustn't concern yourself with that. I didn't mind at all."

Prudence smiled. "Well, I can never repay your kindness to us. But at least, I hope you'll stay for dinner."

When Alethea readily accepted this invitation, Prudence looked quite pleased. The two ladies sat down. "I fear your stay at Hartwood hasn't started off well, Lady Prudence. But now that Lord Worcester is better, I'm certain you will enjoy it."

"I do hope so," said Prudence. "I like Hartwood very much."

"I must say your arrival has generated a good deal of interest, Lady Prudence. Hartwood has been empty for so many years."

"Indeed, I never knew a thing about Hartwood until my brother announced we were coming here," said Prudence. "We normally spend the winter at Worcester Castle. But there was a fire. Fortunately, no one was hurt and all of the paintings and most of the furniture were saved. I nearly cry thinking of all the damage.

"We had to go to London, but my brother doesn't like town even during the Season. He was most eager to go to the country. Hartwood was suggested and so here we are. I know I'll love Hartwood as soon as Geoffrey is well again."

After smiling in reply, Alethea glanced about the drawing room. Her eye fell upon a portrait hanging above the fireplace. "That is an interesting picture," she said, rising to stand before the painting. Staring down at her was an arrogant-looking, dark-haired gentleman attired in Elizabethan garments.

"That was Geoffrey Beauchamp, the first Marquess of Worcester," said Prudence. "There is a portrait of him at Worcester Castle. I have always thought my brother resembles him. And they are both named Geoffrey."

Alethea raised her eyebrows and gazed at the portrait. "I must confess I can't discern any likeness between them."

"Perhaps it is merely something in the expression," said Prudence. "That is how Geoffrey looks when he gets on his high horse about something."

Smiling, Alethea continued to gaze up at the first marquess. She decided that he didn't appear at all pleased to have a Brandon standing there before him. She regarded the portrait with interest, thinking that if it hadn't been for this man, her family would still reside at Hartwood.

At that moment Talbot appeared. "Dinner is ready, my lady," he said.

Prudence nodded and she and Alethea followed the servant to the dining room. Alethea could not help but be impressed by the size of the room, with its large cherry table adorned with silver candelabra. Taking the chair that Talbot pulled out for her. Alethea thought that many years ago her ancestors had sat down for dinner in that very spot.

As a footman ladled out the soup from a large silver tureen, Prudence regarded Alethea with a curious look. "There is something I must ask you, Miss Brandon. The boy who was sent to fetch you said something about a feud between our families."

Alethea smiled. "Well, I fear that there was a feud, but it happened a very long time ago."

"I never heard about it. Do tell me!"

"Very well," replied Alethea, nodding at her young hostess. "You see, it was the Brandon family who first owned Hartwood."

"Owned Hartwood?"

"Yes, Hartwood was built by one of my ancestors. That was during the reign of Henry VII. And then during Queen Bess's time, a certain ambitious young gentleman named Geoffrey Beauchamp took a fancy to Hartwood and wanted it for himself. He convinced the Queen that my ancestor, Sir Giles Brandon, was a traitor. Poor Giles was brought to trial. Apparently a number of witnesses had been paid to testify against him and he was convicted of treason. My ancestor was beheaded and his estate forfeited. Hartwood was given to the first Lord Worcester."

"Oh, Miss Brandon, that is terrible!" cried Prudence. "But are you sure the story is true? I can scarcely believe that my ancestor would act in such a fashion."

"Well, my family has always accepted the story as truth."

"Then you must think that my brother and I are terrible!"

Alethea laughed. "I can hardly blame you or Lord Worcester for something that happened more than two hundred years ago. One can hardly be held accountable for one's ancestors. I assure you that my family holds no grudges. And the Brandons have done very well. We have had a good many distinguished scholars and military men in the family. My father, for example, is a well-known botanist."

"How wonderful," said Prudence, although she wasn't quite sure what a botanist was. "I must say, Miss Brandon, it is very good of you to take it so well."

Alethea laughed. "Well, it has been a very long time, after all."

Prudence smiled. She liked Miss Brandon very much. For some reason it seemed easy to talk to her and the usually shy Prudence was soon telling her all about London. By the time the meal was finished, both ladies were talking and laughing as if they were old friends.

After dinner they went to the drawing room for a time. Then Alethea glanced at the mantel clock. "Oh dear, it is growing late already. I shall look in on Lord Worcester and then I must return home."

Prudence's face fell. "Oh, I wish you didn't have to go." But why must you? Couldn't you stay? I should feel much better if you did. Oh, please stay, Miss Brandon. I shall be worried if you're not here."

"Very well, I suppose I could stay the night."

"Oh, I am so glad!" cried Prudence. "If you stay for a few days it would be such a help."

"A few days?" said Alethea. "Oh, I don't see that I could manage that. I have a good deal of work to do. You see, I am writing a book."

"A book! So you are a writer, Alethea! How wonderful! I do so love to read novels."

"I fear it isn't a novel. It is a book about herbs."

"Oh, of course," said Prudence, rather disappointed. "How wonderful to be able to write a book about such things." She looked thoughtfully at Alethea for a moment. "But couldn't you work on your book here? There is a library with a good many books. And I promise I shan't plague you. But if you are here while Geoffrey is ill, I shall be so much happier. Do say you will stay, Miss Brandon."

Alethea hesitated again, but then she nodded. "Very well. I will stay until Lord Worcester is well."

Very pleased at the prospect of having Alethea as a guest, Prudence smiled happily. Then the two young women rose and made their way to Worcester's room.

Chapter 6

The next morning Worcester awoke to find the maid Mary and his valet Weeks staring down at him with serious expressions. Regarding them with an irritated look, he muttered, "Why the deuce are you two standing about?"

"We just wondered how you were, my lord," said Weeks, trying hard not to smile. "How does your lordship feel?"

Worcester sat up in bed. "A damned sight better than I was." A thoughtful expression on his face, he ran a hand along the stubble on his chin. He knew he had been miserably ill, but his memories of the last couple of days were hazy.

"My lord?" asked the valet.

"Yes, Weeks?"

"Would your lordship be wanting anything?" said the valet.

"I daresay a shave would seem to be in order," said the marquess, still fingering his chin. "And a bath."

The maid interrupted, shaking her head. "Oh, my lord, I don't think a bath a good idea, what with you having had a fever and all. You might catch another chill . . ."

"Mary is right, my lord," said Weeks. "We must see what Miss Brandon says first."

"Miss Brandon?" said the marquess. "Why the devil should she be consulted about my taking a bath?"

"Oh, here is Lady Prudence, my lord," said Weeks, pleased to see that his master's sister had entered the room.

Hurrying over toward him, she greeted him happily. "Geoffrey! You're better! Oh, I am so glad!" She leaned down and gave him an impulsive hug.

"Really, Pru," said the marquess, extricating himself from her embrace, "it wouldn't do to strangle me now that I am better."

Prudence laughed and stepped back from him. "I was so worried about you, Geoffrey," she said, taking the seat beside the bed. "I thank Providence that Miss Brandon was here to help you."

"I'm sure Miss Brandon's quack cures had nothing to do with my getting better."

Prudence shook her reddish gold curls. "Oh, it was not quackery. And it was Miss Brandon's medicine that brought your fever down. I'm sure of it. And she agreed to stay on here at Hartwood until you are well again."

"You invited her to stay here?"

"Yes, of course. I like her so very much, Geoffrey. She is such good company."

Worcester frowned. "I'm sure Miss Brandon is pleasant enough, but I don't know if she's the sort of person one invites to stay here."

"Indeed, some might say she has as much right to stay at Hartwood as we do," said Prudence.

Before the marquess could demand an explanation for this remark, Alethea appeared at the door. "Good morning, Lord Worcester," she said, entering the room.

The marquess watched her. She wore a plain muslin frock of pale green with long sleeves and a high collar. While Worcester expressed little interest in such fripperies as female fashion, he had to admit that there was something pleasing about Alethea's appearance.

Worcester, who had always been quite proud of being extremely sensible in regard to the opposite sex, experienced a strange, rather unsettling sensation as he looked at Alethea. He found himself noting that she had an excellent figure and a stateliness in her bearing that would be admired at court.

"How do you feel, my lord?" said Alethea, coming up beside him.

Worcester found himself acutely aware that he was unshaven and disheveled. "I feel much better."

Prudence, unaware of her brother's reaction to Alethea, got up from her chair. "My brother appears much improved."

"I am very glad of it," said Alethea, reaching out her hand and placing it on his forehead. "Yes, your fever does appear to be gone," she said, removing her hand after a moment.

Although Worcester had been strangely discomfited by her touch, he had sufficient self-control not to reveal it.

"I have made up some more medicine for you, Lord Worcester. It will help clear congestion in your lungs." Alethea extended a glass to Worcester.

"That is good of you, Miss Brandon," he said, frowning at the medicine, "but I don't believe I need anything further."

"But I have made the medicine, Lord Worcester, and since I have gone to the trouble, I must insist you drink it. I assure you it will do you good." She continued to hold the glass out to him. "You may as well take it, my lord. I shan't leave until you do."

Worcester regarded Alethea in some surprise. He was not accustomed to anyone insisting he do anything. Ordinarily he was treated with such deference by everyone. Of course he had noted that on both his meetings with Miss Brandon, she had not been in the least intimidated by him.

His gray eyes met her hazel ones for a moment. "Very well, Miss Brandon," he said, taking the glass and drinking the potion. It had a sharp, bitter taste. "Good God, what was that?" said Worcester.

Alethea smiled as she took the glass from his hand. "Oh, I can't reveal my secrets, my lord. Now I do think it best if you rested. You may feel much better, but you are still unwell."

He frowned again and Alethea only smiled. Prudence directed an admiring gaze at Alethea, pleased with the lady's easy manner of speaking with him. Most of the time people seemed so in awe of Worcester.

At that moment Talbot entered the room. "Dr. Chandler is here, Lady Prudence."

Prudence appeared surprised. "Dr. Chandler? Oh, good."

"I certainly don't need a doctor," said the marquess. "I've already suffered Miss Brandon's cures. And apparently I am recovering well enough. I won't have anyone else fussing about me."

"Now, Lord Worcester," said Alethea in the tone a mother adopts when dealing with a stubborn child, "you must see him."

"Indeed, I won't," said his lordship. "Talbot, send him away."

"Do send him in, Talbot," said Alethea in a commanding tone. The butler hesitated. "Don't worry about what his lordship says. He is not thinking clearly."

"I assure you I am thinking quite clearly," protested the marquess, but Talbot had already retreated from the room.

Dr. Chandler appeared a few moments later. A tall, fair-haired man in his midtwenties, the doctor smiled at the occupants of the room.

"Lady Prudence," said Alethea, "may I present Dr. Chandler?"

"Your servant, Lady Prudence," he said, bowing to her. "I must apologize that I wasn't able to call yesterday. My housekeeper told me when I returned this morning that Lord Worcester was gravely ill." He looked over at that gentleman. "I am gratified to find that you are so much improved, my lord." He looked over at Alethea. "It appears Miss Brandon has taken good care of you." He smiled at her. "I fear this lady will steal all my patients away from me. I may have to move elsewhere."

Alethea laughed. "Don't be ridiculous, Robert."

The marquess noted the use of the physician's Christian name with disapproval. It appeared Miss Brandon and the doctor were well acquainted.

Chandler looked back at Worcester. "Ever since Alethea cured Tom Robertson's sow, the local farmers think her a marvel. And as she is also much prettier than I, I can't blame the fellows for wanting her opinion."

Worcester found himself irritated by the doctor's familiar tone. Alethea? So that was her name. He regarded her closely, noting her radiant smile and bright hazel eyes. She was a dashed pretty girl, he thought and there was something about her he found very much to his liking. Yet he only frowned and regarded Chandler with a grim expression.

"Lord Worcester made an amazing recovery, Robert," said Alethea.

"Doubtlessly due to your potions," said the doctor. "I will have you know, Lord Worcester, that some regard Miss Brandon's abilities as akin to sorcery. She is always making some sort of witch's brew."

"Yes, I had the misfortune to drink some of it," said the marquess.

Chandler smiled. "Whatever it was, it appears to have worked very well. You are breathing without difficulty. If you would open your mouth wide, my lord," he said.

"What the deuce for?" said the marquess.

"So that I might have a look at your throat, sir."

"Oh, very well," muttered Worcester, reluctantly complying with the request.

"There is still some inflammation," said the doctor. He turned to Alethea. "I expect you have given his lordship some of your famous remedy." Alethea nodded and Chandler smiled. "Keep taking that and you will be completely well in a few days."

Worcester eyed him with a curious look. "You do not dispute Miss Brandon's cures?"

"Indeed not. Why, I prescribe them myself. I am always in consultation with Alethea. Yes, Miss Brandon is a remarkable lady. Were she a man, I don't doubt that she would be an eminent physician." He directed an admiring look at Alethea, who smiled in return.

From some inexplicable reason, this display of regard irritated the marquess. It was clear that the doctor was fond of Miss Brandon.

"Well, then," continued Chandler, "I believe we should leave his lordship so that he might rest. You must be careful not to overexert yourself, Lord Worcester. Allow yourself several days to completely recover. I should think you should stay in bed for at least a week."

"A week?" said the marquess. "That is ridiculous."

"Dr. Chandler is the physician, sir," said Alethea severely. "Indeed, you must heed his advice." She looked over at Chandler. "Lady Prudence and I will make certain that he does, Robert."

"You are a very fortunate man to have two such diligent and lovely nurses, Lord Worcester," said the doctor. "Now I shall leave you to their care. I'll return tomorrow."

Worcester muttered some response and Chandler made a formal bow to his patient.

"I'll show you out, Robert," said Alethea, escorting Chandler from the room.

When they had gone, Prudence sat down beside her brother. "Dr. Chandler seems to be a very pleasant gentleman."

"Pleasant?" said the marquess. "I found nothing so very pleasant about him. Imagine him telling me to spend a week in bed. That is only so that he can justify what will be his doubtlessly exorbitant bills."

"I'm sure he has only your best interests at heart," said Prudence gently.

"Yes, to be sure," said the marquess sarcastically.

"But you must take care not to attempt too much, Geoffrey."

"Oh, very well. Now do leave me, Pru. And have Weeks come to me. I'm in need of a shave. And don't tell me I must have Miss Brandon's permission to shave."

Prudence laughed and went to fetch the marquess's valet.

Chapter 7

After leaving Worcester, Alethea volunteered to escort Chandler to the door.

"So you're staying here at Hartwood, Alethea?" said Chandler.

She nodded. "Yes, I shall stay another day or so. Lady Prudence needs someone to be with her."

"She appears to be a very nice girl. And very pretty, too. But her brother." The doctor rolled his eyes. "He is very much the great lord, isn't he?"

"In truth, we are scarcely acquainted. When I first met him, he was delirious. He thought me his nanny."

"Good Lord," said Chandler, bursting into laughter.

"It is clear he isn't accustomed to receiving orders. But I shan't be cowed by him. I shall see that he takes his medicine."

"What a formidable lady you are, Alethea," said the doctor. "But I must tell you that my housekeeper was amazed when she heard you were at Hartwood. She babbled on about this ancient feud of your family's and the curse of the Beauchamps. I daresay she feared you would poison Worcester."

Alethea laughed. "Everyone in Towmouth knows the tale of poor Sir Giles and the curse. If the marquess doesn't recover, I shall doubtless be accused of foul play."

"Well, fortunately he appears improved," said the doctor with a grin. "As a Brandon you certainly have a motive to do him in."

"Don't be absurd," said Alethea, laughing again.

"Now confess, my dear Alethea, now that you are at Hartwood, you feel some resentment toward the dastardly Beauchamps. After all, this was your family's home."

"I assure you I have no intention of slipping some deadly nightshade into his lordship's tea, Robert," said Alethea. "And I don't find much point in holding grudges for more than two hundred years. I am quite happy at Crow's Nest Cottage. It is far more comfortable than Hartwood."

Chandler smiled. He was sure that she meant it. Alethea Brandon had never been concerned with the trappings of wealth. He, on the other hand, would have been very happy to be the owner of a fine manor house like Hartwood.

When they reached the door, Chandler took his leave, saying he would return the following day to see how the marquess was doing. Alethea went to the drawing room, where she took up a newspaper she found lying on a table and sat down. After a time, she was joined by Prudence.

"I finally persuaded my brother to rest," said Prudence, taking a seat on the sofa across from Alethea. "Dr. Chandler appears to be a very knowledgeable gentleman."

"Oh, yes," said Alethea, putting down the newspaper. "He is an excellent doctor."

"Do you know him very well?"

"Oh, I have known him since we were very small children. He is like a brother to me."

"Like a brother?" said Prudence.

"Oh, yes. Robert is a wonderful man, kind and thoughtful. Indeed, I don't think I know a more admirable gentleman. He would make some fortunate lady an excellent husband, but he says he has no time to think of matrimony."

"He did seem very nice," said Prudence, a thoughtful expression on her face. She had found the physician a very handsome and charming man. "I imagine a good many ladies of the vicinity have set their caps for him."

"Oh, yes, I daresay they have." Alethea smiled. "For a time my Aunt Elizabeth had fastened upon the idea that Robert and I should marry. It was some time before she would let loose of it. My poor aunt. She despairs that I am an old maid."

"Why, you aren't old at all," said Prudence.

Alethea laughed. "I am nearly five-and-twenty and, I assure you, I am firmly on the shelf. But, in truth, I am glad of it."

"Are you?" said Prudence, regarding her in some surprise. "Then you don't wish to marry?"

"No, I have no wish to do so. It isn't that I'm opposed to marriage. A good marriage is something quite wonderful, but if a woman chooses the wrong husband, it is the worst sort of misery. I shouldn't like to be at the beck and call of some male tyrant.

"No, I am quite happy as I am. I have my work and a comfortable home. I don't lack for family and friends. And I am my own mistress and do as I please. Yes, I consider myself very fortunate."

Prudence regarded her with a solemn expression. "Yes, I do think you are very fortunate, Miss Brandon. It must be marvelous to be so clever and useful." She sighed. "My brother says that I must marry, and I fear that I shall have little choice in the matter."

"But surely Lord Worcester will take your wishes into account on such an important thing as this."

She shrugged. "I really don't have any wishes. You see, I haven't met any gentlemen that I would like to marry even though I have been introduced to all manner of eligible men. I have had two Seasons in town and a score of suitors."

"And you haven't found any to your liking?"

She shook her head. "I never seem to like anyone my brother finds acceptable."

"I imagine that when one is the sister of a marquess, the number of acceptable young men from which to choose is rather limited."

"Yes," replied Prudence, "Geoffrey insists that I marry someone of sufficiently high rank and ample fortune."

"And does Lord Worcester have anyone in mind?"

"I believe he would be most happy if I married Lord Feversham. But I don't like him in the least. I know I should be very unhappy if I married him."

"You mean that Lord Worcester would force you to marry against your will?"

"No, I don't think that, but my brother believes I am being silly and far too particular."

"Well, one should be particular in selecting a husband," said Alethea. "I shall advise you to stand your ground. Don't marry someone you dislike. You will only regret it for the rest of your life. And you are still very young, Lady Prudence. There is no need to rush into marriage."

"But I am nineteen and Geoffrey feels that is quite old enough to marry."

Alethea frowned. She was beginning to dislike Worcester. If he

was the sort of man to pressure his sister into marriage without regard to her happiness, it was a serious fault indeed.

The two ladies continued their conversation in the drawing
room for a long time. Prudence found herself talking about her
life in London during the Season. Alethea listened sympathetically.

It seemed that Lady Prudence Beauchamp was a rather unhappy young lady. Alethea had never given much thought to the
fact that young ladies of rank and fortune might be miserable. It
was rather enlightening to find that life could be difficult for
someone who seemed to be so blessed.

Finally they were interrupted by the appearance of the butler,
who announced that luncheon was being served. When they sat
down in the dining hall, Prudence looked over at her guest with a
rather sheepish look. "I am sorry to go on and on. You're scarcely
getting a word in, Miss Brandon. You are kind to listen to me."

"It does one good to speak of things that are troubling. I don't
mind listening in the least."

"You are very good," said Prudence, realizing that she had
opened up to Alethea more than she ever had to anyone else. She
had never been one to make friends easily, but now, after such a
brief acquaintance, she was speaking to Alethea as if she had
known her for ages. "Really, we must cease talking about me,
Miss Brandon. I should allow you to speak of your self and your
family."

"I caution you, Lady Prudence, that such an invitation may
cause me to talk for hours. I find my family so frightfully interesting. I'm not so sure that everyone else shares my fascination with
them."

Prudence laughed. "Oh, I should like to hear about them."

Alethea needed no further encouragement. She began to talk
about her father and his scientific expedition. Prudence found the
subject fascinating and soon she forgot the unhappy business of
the marriage mart.

Chapter 8

That evening Worcester lay in his bed, propped up with pillows, reading by the light of an oil lamp. While not overly bookish, the marquess enjoyed a novel now and again. Earlier that afternoon, he had thought to relieve the boredom of his confinement in bed by finding some diversion in reading. He had sent one of the footmen on the mission of bringing him some books from Hartwood's library.

Finding himself not up to the formidable task of selecting his master's reading material, the servant had enlisted Talbot's aid. Talbot in turn had sought out Mrs. Graham's advice. Since no books had been added to Hartwood's library for many years, the housekeeper was forced to provide some volumes from her own collection, which she sent up with the footman.

The marquess had cast his critical eye on each of the books, his expression making it clear that he had found the suggested reading matter less than desirable. Worcester had finally settled upon a dry-looking tome entitled *The History of the Crusades*. To his surprise, the marquess found the book very interesting. So engrossed was he in his reading that he barely noted the knock on his door. It opened and Prudence entered, followed by Alethea.

"Good evening, Geoffrey," said Prudence. "We were just going to dinner and we thought we'd come to see how you were doing."

Putting down his book, the marquess frowned to see Alethea. He wasn't sure that he liked this young woman visiting him in his bedchamber. It seemed deuced awkward receiving company in bed. At least he had been shaved and made more presentable.

"There is no need to delay your dinner on my account," said the marquess. "I am feeling remarkably better."

"I am glad," said Alethea, coming forward.

Worcester noted that Miss Brandon was now attired in an ivory silk evening dress. Someone more versed with ladies' styles would have noted the dress was several years old and hardly fashionable. Yet the marquess only found himself thinking that Miss Brandon looked exceedingly well in the high-waisted creation, with its low neckline and short sleeves. She was a very handsome woman, he acknowledged to himself.

Alethea regarded the marquess with interest. His expression was cool and aloof and hardly welcoming. "Miss Brandon," he said, nodding politely.

"I see you are reading, my lord," said Alethea.

"It passes the time," said Worcester.

"But what is that book?" asked Prudence.

"The History of the Crusades," replied the marquess, holding it up.

"Oh, yes, by Mr. William Melton," said Alethea, recognizing the hefty volume. She was rather surprised and favorably impressed to find Worcester reading such a serious work. "That is excellent. His history of Richard the Lion Heart is even better. I shall be happy to loan it to you if you wish."

Worcester frowned. It appeared Miss Brandon was something of a scholar. Being firmly of the opinion that there was a danger in overeducating females, he didn't approve of learned women. "That is good of you, Miss Brandon," he said, "but I am having quite enough of Richard the Lion Heart in this book. And I must confess that I chose this only because it seemed the least distasteful of several choices brought to me by a footman." He gestured toward a number of volumes stacked on the table by the bed. "Why the man thought I might have been interested in the sermons of John Knox is altogether perplexing."

Alethea smiled. "I have many books at Crow's Nest Cottage. I shall send a note requesting some be brought over."

"That is kind of you, but I shouldn't like to have you take the trouble."

"Oh, it isn't any trouble, I assure you." Alethea smiled again.

"Well, we must be going, Geoffrey," said Prudence. "I have had Cook prepare some chicken broth. Miss Brandon says it is the very thing for you. Mary will bring it shortly. And I shall come to see you directly after dinner."

The marquess nodded and the ladies left him. He was a trifle annoyed with the brevity of the visit. Prudence had seemed quite eager to be off to dinner while he was stuck sitting in a dreary room with the prospect of chicken broth to eat. He detested chicken broth, after all.

Worcester glumly turned his attention once again to his book. It wasn't until nearly three hours later that Prudence returned to his room.

"Geoffrey, how are you?"

"Well enough," said the marquess. He was irked with his sister. She had said she would be up directly after dinner and he had expected her a long time ago.

"Did you enjoy your broth?" said Prudence, sitting down in the chair beside the bed.

"As much as one might be expected to enjoy it," said the marquess.

"We had a lovely dinner," said Prudence. "I am sorry that I didn't come sooner. Miss Brandon and I were talking and the time just flew by."

"So your silly prattle took precedence over me, did it?" said Worcester.

"Oh, of course not," said Prudence. "It's only that Miss Brandon is so very interesting. I was quite amazed to see the clock and realize so much time had gone."

"It seems you are becoming very friendly with this woman. We don't know a thing about her. Who is she? Who is her family?"

"The Brandons are an old family. She told me all about them. Her father is a botanist. Yes, I'm sure that is what she called him. He is a very great man who has written books on plants and things. And now he is on a ship exploring the South Seas. Isn't that wonderful?"

"I don't see anything wonderful about it. Roaming about the world among heathen savages is hardly commendable in my view. But I suppose it's better than him being in trade." He paused. "What was it you said to me? Miss Brandon had as much right to be here at Hartwood as we did. What did you mean by that?"

"It's true, Geoffrey. Miss Brandon told me that her family first owned Hartwood. Our ancestor, the first marquess, conspired against Miss Brandon's ancestor. He was falsely accused of being a traitor and executed. Our family was awarded his estate."

"I'm sure that's utter poppycock," said Worcester. "I wonder if that has something to do with this curse business Edward was telling me about before we came here."

"Curse?" said Prudence, regarding him in some alarm.

"Yes, he said something about a curse. Of course, I have a vague recollection of hearing some such ridiculous tale when I was a boy, but Edward said our aunt might know more about it."

"Oh dear, perhaps that's why you became sick," said Prudence.

"Don't be absurd," said the marquess.

"But you're never ill," said Prudence. "You have the strongest constitution. I shall have to ask Miss Brandon about this curse."

"She will think you a gudgeon to be sure," said Worcester. "Curse, indeed. Of all the preposterous notions."

Prudence knew better than to say anything further on the subject, but she was quite bothered at the idea that some old family curse was hanging over them at Hartwood. Her brother's sudden and very serious illness was disturbing.

"I am so glad you are looking so much better, Geoffrey," she said. "I was very worried."

"I assure you, Pru, there was never any reason to worry. And I shouldn't be surprised if I am up and about tomorrow."

"But the doctor said you must stay in bed."

"I'll not be ordered about by him," said Worcester.

"Then you'll be ordered about by me and Miss Brandon," said Prudence with surprising spirit. "We'll see that you do as you're told."

Finding Prudence's tone uncharacteristically assertive, the marquess raised an eyebrow slightly. He suspected it was the influence of Miss Brandon, who seemed to be a bold and strong-willed female. "Neither you nor your newfound friend will keep me in bed longer than necessary. God in heaven, it is such a dreadful bore being stuck in this room. And there is far too much to be done for me to lie about here like an invalid."

"What do you mean, Geoffrey?"

"In but a fortnight, our guests will arrive. I must see that the house is put in order."

"Guests?" said Prudence, regarding him in surprise.

"Yes, of course."

"But you didn't mention to me that you had invited guests to Hartwood."

Worcester nodded. "You can't think that I'd wish for us to be marooned out here without any suitable society."

Prudence appeared surprised. Worcester was not a man who loved society. Indeed, he valued his privacy and seldom invited houseguests. "Who will be coming?"

"Lord and Lady Huntingdon and their daughter Catherine." He paused. "And the Duke and Duchess of Cranworth and their son Feversham."

"Lord Feversham?" she said in dismay." Oh, Geoffrey, you know I dislike him."

"Why, you scarcely know the man. I can't understand your taking such an aversion to him. He seems pleasant enough to me and he is well regarded in society."

Prudence fixed a long-suffering look on her brother. She knew that he had decided that the Viscount Feversham was an excellent marriage prospect. The fact that she found him overbearing and obnoxious didn't seem to matter in the least.

Rather than provoke a lecture, Prudence rose from her chair. "I shouldn't tire you," she said. "You must have your rest. I am tired as well. Good night, Geoffrey."

"Good night, Prudence." Worcester watched his sister leave the room. He wished she were more open-minded where Feversham was concerned. A man of impeccable lineage with powerful connections, the viscount was a man of considerable property.

His thoughts turned to his prospective bride. He wasn't very well acquainted with Lady Catherine Percy. She was considered a great beauty and was much sought after. Yet he could hardly be less enthusiastic about the idea of marrying her.

The marquess looked thoughtful for a while. Then he put down his book, turned off his oil lamp, and went to sleep.

Chapter 9

The next morning Prudence lost no time in asking Alethea about the curse. They had scarcely sat down to breakfast when Prudence brought up the subject. "Miss Brandon?"

"Oh, do call me Alethea."

"I should like that very much," returned Prudence. "And you must call me Pru."

"Very well, Pru," said Alethea with a smile.

"I wanted to ask you something. My brother spoke of a curse."

Alethea's fork paused midway to her mouth. "Oh dear. I had hoped you didn't know about that. Well, I suppose I must explain. You remember the story of my unfortunate ancestor, Sir Giles?"

"Yes, of course."

"I fear his widow placed a curse on your family. It was something to the effect that any members of the Beauchamp family who would dare cross the threshold of Hartwood would have something horrible happen to them."

Prudence's eyes grew wide. "Like my brother becoming ill?"

"Oh, I'm sure that was only coincidence. I must confess I have little faith in curses. I assure you, Pru, it is only an old story."

"But that is why none of my family has lived at Hartwood for so many years."

"But it's just superstitious nonsense. And don't forget, nothing really horrible happened to Lord Worcester. He recovered in a very short time. Why, many of these sorts of fevers are far worse."

Not wanting Alethea to think her a silly goose, she nodded in agreement. Yet Prudence was uneasy. She was the sort of girl who knocked wood and threw salt over her shoulder if she spilled it. Credulous by nature, she believed in ghosts and supernatural happenings. Having read several novels in which curses figured prominently, she wasn't at all glad to hear that a curse had been placed on her family.

Alethea changed the subject and the two spoke of other things. They had scarcely finished breakfast when Talbot appeared. "Your pardon, my lady, but Dr. Chandler is here. He is waiting in the morning room."

"Oh, good," said Prudence, rising from her chair. When they arrived in the morning room, they found Chandler looking cheerful and dapper.

While he wasn't at all a wealthy man, Chandler took care to dress as well as possible. His dove gray coat looked very well on his broad-shouldered form. He smiled brightly at the ladies before bowing politely. "Good morning, Lady Prudence, Alethea."

"Good morning, Robert," said Alethea. "You are here very early."

"I have a good many calls to make. And I was eager to see how his lordship was faring. I hope he is much improved."

"Yes, he is, sir," said Prudence. "Shall we go to him now?"

There were no objections from Alethea or the doctor, so the three of them proceeded upstairs. After knocking on the door, Prudence pushed it open to find the marquess propped up in bed. "Good morning, Geoffrey. Dr. Chandler has come to see you."

The marquess frowned at the physician. "I assure you, sir, I am completely recovered."

"I'm gratified to hear that, my lord," said Chandler, approaching Worcester's bedside. "It appears that you are greatly improved. If you would open your mouth."

Worcester reluctantly submitted to this request and the doctor examined his throat. "Yes, much improved," Chandler repeated. "You will be completely well in a short time."

"I feel completely well now," said the marquess.

"One mustn't be hasty in such matters," said the doctor. "But in a few days you will be able to leave your bed."

"What!" exclaimed Worcester. "See here, if you think I shall spend more days in this bed, you are very much mistaken."

"I must insist, my lord, that you don't overexert yourself."

"I won't overexert myself,'" said Worcester. "And surely there is nothing wrong with my getting out of this accurst bed and sitting in a chair."

Chandler turned from his patient to direct a look at the ladies. He then turned back to the marquess. "Perhaps you are right, Lord

Worcester. If you stay indoors and rest quietly, you may sit in a chair."

"I am very grateful for your permission, sir," returned his lordship testily.

Alethea suppressed a smile. The marquess could be a very disagreeable man, she thought.

"And I should like it if you would all leave me," continued the marquess. "I don't enjoy having people stand about my bedchamber gaping at me."

"Then I shall take my leave," said Chandler. "I shall call tomorrow."

"That isn't necessary," said Worcester. "I daresay you are a busy man."

"Oh, I'm sure Lady Prudence would feel much better if you did call, Robert," said Alethea.

"Yes, I would," said Prudence.

Before the marquess could make further protests, his visitors retreated from the room. The ladies accompanied Chandler down the stairs. "It appears he has made remarkable progress," said the doctor. "It wouldn't hurt to have him take a bit more of your elixir, Alethea."

"If he will do so," replied Alethea. "It seems he is quite convinced he's completely well. But we'll keep a tight hand on his reins, won't we, Lady Prudence?"

"We will try," said Prudence.

Chandler took his leave of them and left Hartwood. When he had gone, Prudence turned to Alethea. "Thank you for staying, Alethea. I should have been lost without you."

"Well, his lordship appears much improved. Perhaps it's time I returned home."

"Oh, please stay a bit longer," said Prudence. "It would be quite dreadful here all by myself."

"I shall be happy to stay another day or so. I have an idea, Pru. Why don't we walk to Crow's Nest Cottage? It isn't far. I could get some books for Lord Worcester to read. And there are such lovely views of the sea from there. I know you would like it."

"Oh, I'm sure I would," said Prudence eagerly. "But I must ask Geoffrey."

"Then do ask him," said Alethea. Prudence hurried back up the stairs to her brother's room. When she returned a few minutes later, she appeared very happy.

"He said that I might go. But we are to take the carriage."

They were ready in a short time. Since Crow's Nest Cottage was scarcely two miles distant from Hartwood, it didn't take long to get there.

As Alethea had expected, Prudence was thrilled at the expansive views of the sea that became visible as the vehicle neared Alethea's home. When they arrived at Crow's Nest Cottage, Prudence pronounced it the most charming house she had ever seen.

It was an attractive, unpretentious residence with ivy covering its redbrick walls. The views from several aspects of the house were quite striking. That morning the sky was gray and overcast.

They paused before entering the house to stare out at the sea. "What a marvelous place, Alethea," said Prudence, watching the waves rolling toward shore.

"Yes, isn't it?" said Alethea. "I think it's the most wonderful place in the world. Now do come in. I have so many things to show you."

The young ladies were greeted by an ecstatic Nelson. Prudence seemed a bit surprised to see such a large dog approaching them, but she was soon convinced that the mastiff was a friendly fellow.

Alethea led Prudence through the house, with Nelson following behind them. "It isn't a very large house," she said.

"But it is delightful," said Prudence.

"Oh, here is the library. We'll find some books for his lordship." They entered the room and Alethea began to peruse the shelves. While she was selecting volumes, Prudence was diverted by a large bronze statue sitting upon a table. It was an exotic figure with several arms.

"But what is that, Alethea?" she cried.

Alethea glanced over. "Oh, that is Shiva, the Hindu god. My grandfather brought him from India many years ago. There are many interesting things lying about the house. My grandfather lived in India for several years. He was something of an adventurer. He sailed with Captain Cook on his first voyage."

"Really?" said Prudence, very much interested.

"Oh, yes. He left a fascinating journal of his experiences. Papa has also traveled the world. He's been to the West Indies and South America. My father brought back many specimens of plants." A sigh escaped Alethea. "If only I had been a man so that I might have gone with him."

Although Prudence had no desire to visit the four corners of the world in a sailing ship, she could understand how someone with a more adventurous spirit would want to do so. "But then you wouldn't have been here to help us, Alethea."

Alethea smiled. "I suppose not. And I must confess I would miss Crow's Nest Cottage terribly if I went away."

"Do you think of your father often?"

"Oh, constantly. I wonder where he is and if he's safe. He told me I mustn't worry, but one can't help it. But I know he is doing what he loves." She pulled another book from the shelf and set it on the desk. "Oh, I must show you my herbs."

Alethea led Prudence from the library to the small room at the back of the house where bunches of herbs hung from the ceiling. Prudence sniffed at the pleasant, pungent odor of the place. "And you know what all of these are?"

"Yes, of course," said Alethea, "but then I have been studying herbs since I was a young girl." She gestured toward the desk in the corner of the room on which was piled a great stack of books. "I am particularly fascinated by medieval herbals." Taking a large volume from the top of the pile, she opened it to show her visitor. "This book is very old. It was written more than three hundred years ago."

"Oh, my," said Prudence, looking down at the text. "But it is in Latin. You cannot mean that you are able to read that."

Alethea laughed. "Why, yes."

"How clever you are," said Prudence, gazing down at the incomprehensible words. She picked up another old volume. "But what is this, Alethea?"

"Oh, that is a great favorite of mine. It is a book of potions and charms."

"You mean witchcraft?"

Alethea shrugged. "I suppose it is, but it is only an academic curiosity to me."

"Then you haven't tried any of these?"

Alethea laughed. "Oh, I haven't got round to that. Perhaps one day I'll brew up a love potion when I find a suitable gentleman." Prudence regarded her with wide eyes. "Oh, Pru, I'm only joking." Prudence laughed and Alethea took the book from her hand. "I shall take this back with me to Hartwood. There are several passages I must consult for my book. And I shall bring my watercolors."

"Are you an artist?"

"I shouldn't be so bold as to call myself that. I do drawings and paintings of plants. I've illustrated some of my father's works. Come, I'll show you." She led Prudence back to the library, where she fetched a portfolio from the shelf.

Opening it on the desk, she displayed a number of large sheets for her guest's examination. "Oh, Alethea," exclaimed Prudence, looking down at the delicate drawings of flowers and plants, "you are an artist! These are beautiful!"

"Thank you, Pru," said Alethea with a smile. "I must confess I'm rather proud of these."

Prudence continued to survey the drawings. "Good heavens, Alethea. You're so very accomplished. You know so much about herbs and you read Latin and draw so well."

"I have been at it a long time," said Alethea.

"And I can't do anything."

"Oh, I'm sure that's not at all true."

"It is, Alethea. Why, I am hopeless at drawing. And I am so untalented at the pianoforte. I expect that you are an accomplished musician."

"Why, I wouldn't say that. I do play a little."

"And I shouldn't be surprised that you write poetry."

Alethea laughed. "Now, I can truly say that I have never written a word of poetry in my life."

"Thank heaven, that is something," said Prudence, bursting into laughter. Nelson came over to Prudence, who stroked his enormous head.

Suddenly there was a noise at the window. Prudence and Alethea turned to see a large crow land on the windowsill. "Oh!" cried Prudence, viewing the bird with alarm.

Alethea hastened to reassure her. "Oh, that's only Hector. He comes by for a biscuit. Good morning, Hector." The crow cocked his head at Alethea and responded by cawing loudly. Alethea laughed. "He is vexed with me for being gone. Now, mind your manners, sir, or you won't get your biscuit." Alethea took up a tin that was sitting on a table and opened it. "Would you like to give him one, Pru?"

"Yes, I would," said Prudence, eagerly coming forward to take a biscuit from the tin.

"Go ahead. He won't hurt you."

Prudence extended the biscuit to the bird, who snatched it from her hand and flew away. She smiled delightedly. "What a clever fellow."

"He is too clever by half," said Alethea. Nelson, who had watched the avian visitor with keen interest, now turned to his mistress, who was holding the tin of biscuits. "I suppose you'd like one as well, Nelson." She took one from the tin and tossed it to the dog, who gobbled it down.

Prudence laughed again and thought that Crow's Nest Cottage was a most diverting place.

Chapter 10

While his sister and Alethea were gone, Worcester called for his valet. He informed Weeks that he was getting dressed, causing the worthy servant to remind his master about his weakened condition. The marquess, who was thoroughly tired of being thought an invalid, suggested that Weeks concern himself with his duties.

When Worcester was dressed, he viewed his reflection in the mirror. It was a great satisfaction to him that he would be able to face his sister and her new friend in his well-tailored suit. Indeed, he hadn't been very glad to have Miss Brandon see him in his nightshirt.

Now he was decently attired. The marquess continued to stare at himself in the glass, more concerned than usual with his appearance. Worcester had always said that he never gave two figs for fashion, and the preoccupation with dress expressed by the dandy set invariably disgusted him. But now, for some unaccountable reason, he found himself wanting to look his best.

The marquess refused to admit to himself that he hoped to impress Alethea. No, it was only that a gentleman should appear presentable before company.

After a few moments, Worcester left the room and proceeded downstairs. While he liked to believe that he was completely well, in reality the marquess was still weak and a bit light-headed. When he arrived in the drawing room, he sat down in an armchair near the fire.

Talbot, who thought his master's emergence from the sickroom somewhat premature, hastened to his side. "Will you be wanting anything, my lord?"

"A newspaper if one can be found."

"Of course, my lord," said the butler, bowing and exiting the room. When he returned, he brought not only a newspaper but a blanket, which he insisted on draping over Worcester's knees.

The marquess then sat quite comfortably reading. After perusing the newspaper for a long time, he tossed it aside and stared into the fire.

"Excuse me, my lord." Worcester turned to see the housekeeper approaching him, a glass in her outstretched hand. "Yes, Mrs. Graham?"

"Miss Brandon said I was to have you drink this."

"More of her foul-tasting concoction, I'll be bound," said Worcester. "Oh, very well, I'll have it."

The housekeeper gave the marquess the glass and stood watching him as he drank it. "There," he said, returning the glass to her. "I've taken every drop."

"Good, my lord, I'm sure it will do you good. But are you certain you should be up? Perhaps your lordship should return to bed."

"I'm perfectly fine here, Mrs. Graham."

"But do take care, my lord," said Mrs. Graham, giving him a look of grandmotherly concern. "We were all so very worried about you."

"Yes, yes," said his lordship rather impatiently.

Mrs. Graham left him alone and he sat looking at the clock, wondering when Prudence and Alethea would return. It was nearly noon. Rising from his chair, he wrapped the blanket about his shoulders and moved to a seat near the window where he could view the front lawn. After half an hour had passed, Worcester saw the carriage appear in the lane that led to the house.

It wasn't long before the door to the drawing room opened and Prudence and Alethea came in. "Geoffrey," cried Prudence, hurrying up to him. "Talbot said you were in the drawing room. I was quite surprised. I do think that you should return to your room."

"I have no intention of doing so," said Worcester.

"Don't you think he should go to bed, Alethea?" said Prudence, turning to her new friend.

The marquess did not fail to note that his sister had addressed Miss Brandon by her Christian name. Worcester considered such familiarity premature and uncharacteristic of his usually very reserved sister.

"I suppose there is no harm in his lordship being up as long as he feels well enough," said Alethea. She smiled slightly at the marquess, who responded by regarding her somberly.

Alethea found herself thinking that Worcester would be handsome if he would adopt a more pleasant expression. She found herself thinking he had very striking gray eyes.

"We had such a splendid time, Geoffrey," said Prudence, taking a seat on the sofa near her brother's chair. Alethea sat down beside her. "Crow's Nest Cottage is quite wonderful."

"Is it, indeed?" said the marquess.

"Oh, yes. There is such a splendid view of the sea. And Al . . . that is, Miss Brandon has a wonderful dog named Nelson and a pet crow named Hector."

"A pet crow?" said the marquess, raising an eyebrow at this.

"I don't really think of him as a pet," said Alethea. "But he does visit me from time to time."

"He sat on the windowsill," said Prudence, "and he was very tame. I fed him a biscuit. He's a very clever bird, Geoffrey. Don't you think it wonderful that Crow's Nest Cottage should have a crow?"

Not allowing her brother the opportunity to respond to this question, Prudence continued. "And there are so many other interesting things there. I saw all of Miss Brandon's herbs and some very old books. There were statues and masks and things from foreign places. And you will find this quite fascinating, Geoffrey. Miss Brandon's grandfather sailed with Captain Cook."

Even Worcester couldn't feign indifference at this remark. He knew all about Captain Cook and his voyages, having read all about them as a boy. "Did he?"

"Oh, yes," said Alethea, "as I was telling Lady Prudence, he was something of an adventurer." Noting the marquess appeared interested, Alethea was more than happy to launch into the tale of her grandfather's journey to the South Seas.

When luncheon was announced, they went to the dining hall, where Worcester pronounced himself famished. "And don't even attempt to suggest I restrict myself to chicken broth," he said as the footman pulled out the chair so that he might be seated.

Alethea laughed. "No, I shouldn't dare, my lord. But I shall enlist Lady Prudence's aid in seeing that you take your rest in the afternoon." Worcester made no protest and lunch proceeded in a most enjoyable fashion.

Although he would have never admitted it to his sister, his

lordship considered Alethea an interesting young woman. As he sat there eating his meal, he reflected that her conversation was far more diverting than the usual gossip discussed by most ladies of his acquaintance.

And Alethea was a dashed good-looking girl, he thought, taking in her dark curls, pale creamy complexion, and lovely hazel eyes. Worcester also noted the admirable feminine curves confined within the bodice of her dress.

Alethea was completely unaware that the marquess was regarding her with more than a passing interest. He was acting with cool civility toward her in the way a man of exalted rank might be expected to act with someone he considered his social inferior.

After luncheon, Worcester was persuaded to retire to his room to rest. The afternoon passed quickly and before long it was time for the ladies to dress for dinner. When Alethea came downstairs attired in a peach-colored silk dress, she found Prudence waiting for her in the dining room. "Oh, how pretty you look, Alethea," said Prudence.

Noting that her hostess was wearing a stunning gown of blue satin and a fashionable matching turban atop her red-gold curls, Alethea smiled. "I confess I feel quite dowdy beside you," she said. "What a lovely dress."

Prudence glowed with pleasure and thanked Alethea for the compliment. They were soon joined by Worcester, who looked very distinguished in his close-fitting evening coat and knee britches.

"You are looking well, my lord," said Alethea.

"I feel very well indeed," returned his lordship, who, upon waking from his nap, was glad to find that he seemed quite back to normal. They went in to dinner and enjoyed a delicious repast.

After lingering over the meal for some time, they retired to the drawing room, where the ladies once again sat down upon the sofa. "That was a lovely dinner," said Alethea. "I must say I shall miss the wonderful food I have enjoyed here when I return home."

"I pray you don't even mention returning home, Alethea," said Prudence. She looked at her brother. "I should be lost without Miss Brandon. Don't you think she should stay longer, Geoffrey?"

"Miss Brandon is welcome to stay as long as she likes," said the marquess.

"Well, I can only stay another day or two at most," said Alethea.

Prudence's face fell. "You must stay at least another week."

"Oh, I fear I couldn't possibly. And I heard from Mrs. Graham that you will be having houseguests soon. I'm sure you'll be very busy with preparations for them."

Prudence made no reply, but only looked gloomy at the prospect.

"Yes, there are many arrangements to be made for our guests, Prudence," said the marquess. "It will be necessary to find them diversion. I thought that I would have some parties and entertainments here. And then I had thought of giving a ball here at Hartwood."

"A ball?" said Prudence, regarding her brother in some astonishment. Worcester detested balls and Prudence was well aware that he hated to toss his money away on such frivolous expenditures.

"A ball at Hartwood?" said Alethea. "It will certainly cause a sensation."

Although causing a sensation had never been his lordship's intention, he could only shrug. "Since we aren't acquainted with anyone here, Miss Brandon, perhaps you will be able to assist Prudence with the invitations. You would know whom to invite."

"And what is even more important, whom *not* to invite," said Alethea with a bright smile.

Prudence laughed, but since he wasn't sure how to take the remark, the marquess only raised an eyebrow.

"A ball will be quite a lot of work," said Prudence. "Are you sure it's a good idea, Geoffrey?"

"Why not? I thought you'd like it."

"I don't know," said Prudence, conjuring up a picture of herself dancing with Lord Feversham.

"Oh, I do think it would be splendid," said Alethea, who enjoyed balls and parties even though she attended very few of them. "And I must thank you, Lord Worcester, for asking for my advice on whom to invite. Just think, I shall have the ability to elevate or devastate my neighbors by including or excluding them. Why, the idea that I should have such power makes me quite dizzy."

Prudence laughed again and Worcester smiled for the first time. They continued to talk about the ball until Alethea noticed the clock and declared that the marquess had stayed up far too long and should retire to bed. Worcester, who had been enjoying himself, was reluctant to go, but under pressure from the ladies, agreed.

Chapter 11

After breakfast the next morning, the ladies went to the library to begin work on the list of guests to invite to the ball. Alethea sat at the large mahogany desk with Prudence sitting next to her. Dipping her pen into the ink, she began a list of all the county families.

"I don't want to miss anyone," said Alethea, adding another name. "Those who are forgotten will demand my head, I assure you." She smiled at Prudence. "Did your brother say how many you might ask?"

"He told me that all respectable members of society are to be invited."

"Of course, who his lordship deems respectable may differ a bit from my point of view," said Alethea with a smile.

Prudence smiled. "The ballroom here at Hartwood is quite large."

"I don't remember seeing the ballroom," said Alethea.

"Would you like to see it now?"

"Yes, very much," said Alethea, putting down her pen.

The young ladies left the library and proceeded up to the ballroom, which was on the third story. While not large by the standards of some of the great country houses, it was a spacious room that would accommodate a good many couples dancing.

"This is quite wonderful," said Alethea, casting her eyes around the room. There were large windows on opposite walls. She walked over to one of them and looked out at the park that stretched in front of the house. "It is an excellent view."

Prudence, who had followed Alethea to the window, looked out. "It is pretty," she said. Suddenly she turned to Alethea. "Did you feel that, Alethea? A cold draft as if a window had been opened?"

"No, Pru, I didn't feel anything," said Alethea, continuing to gaze out the window.

Prudence hugged her arms to her chest and shivered. "It seems rather cold to me."

"Oh, I hope you aren't catching a chill," said Alethea, turning toward her younger friend with some concern. The idea that Prudence might come down with the same fever that had struck the marquess was worrisome at best. "Perhaps it is rather cold here. Let us return to the library at once."

Prudence was only too happy to do so. They left the ballroom and started down the stairs. Prudence seemed in a very great rush. Several paces ahead of Alethea, she hurried down the stairs. Suddenly she seemed to lose her footing. Letting out a cry, Prudence fell forward and stumbled down several steps, until she landed with a thud on the hard marble of the second floor landing.

"Pru!" cried a horrified Alethea, following down the stairs after her.

Prudence appeared very much shaken.

"Are you hurt?" said Alethea, kneeling down beside her.

"I don't know," said Prudence. "I don't believe so."

"Catch your breath for a moment," said Alethea, placing her arm around her. The sound of the fall had brought a maid from one of the rooms. "Fetch his lordship," said Alethea.

The servant nodded and hurried away. "Oh, I feel so foolish. What a clumsy thing to do," said Prudence, tears coming to her eyes.

"What nonsense," said Alethea. "Anyone might slip on stairs. Do you think that you can stand?"

"I think so," said Prudence.

"Lean on me then," said Alethea, helping her up.

By this time Worcester had arrived. "Prudence!" he cried.

"I am all right," said Prudence, taking a tentative step. Then, moving her arm, she winced. "Oh, my arm!"

The marquess and Alethea helped Prudence to her room, where she sat down in a chair. "Does it hurt very much, Pru?" asked Worcester solicitously.

"It is rather painful," said Prudence, pressing her wrist gingerly.

Talbot, who had been informed of the incident, entered the room. "Dr. Chandler is here to see you, my lord. Shall I have him come up?"

"I must give the man credit for appearing at an opportune moment," said the marquess. "Have him brought here at once, Talbot."

The butler gestured to a maid who was standing near the door and the servant vanished, returning in a few moments with Chandler. "I was told Lady Prudence was injured," he said.

"I fell on the stairs," said Prudence. "I fear I've hurt my arm."

"Can you bend it, ma'am?"

Prudence nodded, bending her arm in illustration. "It is my wrist, I think."

"I shall have to take a look," said Chandler, kneeling down beside her. "If I may, Lady Prudence?" The doctor unbuttoned the tiny mother of pearl buttons on Prudence's cuff and pushed the sleeve up to reveal her wrist. It appeared swollen and bruised.

Taking Prudence's wrist carefully, he pressed it. "Is that painful?"

"Yes, very much so."

"I am sorry. I shall try not to hurt you, Lady Prudence." Chandler examined the injury as gently as possible, and then he smiled at Prudence. "I'm glad to report that there are no broken bones. Your wrist is badly sprained and it will be painful for some time. But I believe it will heal well enough."

"Thank heaven," said Worcester.

"And you had no other injury?" said the doctor, looking up at his patient. "Your other arm?"

Prudence shook her head. "No, it doesn't hurt."

Getting to his feet, he opened his medical bag. "I must bandage Lady Prudence's wrist." As he started to unravel a bandage, he regarded her questioningly. "But how did this happen, Lady Prudence? Did you feel faint or dizzy?"

"No, nothing like that," replied Prudence. "I was showing Alethea the ballroom. And then I had a strange feeling. A sort of chill. I know it's very silly of me, but I was in a very great hurry to leave there. I started to run down the stairs. I somehow lost my footing and fell forward. I put up my hands to break my fall."

"It was lucky you did so," said the doctor, "or you might have broken that pretty nose of yours."

Prudence blushed and Worcester frowned. "You ought to know better than to run down stairs," said the marquess. "You must be more careful. And what is this nonsense about a strange chill in the ballroom?"

"It makes me shudder just to think of it," said Prudence. "It seemed an unearthly chill. I was very much frightened."

"Do you know what she is talking about?" said the marquess, turning to Alethea.

Alethea shook her head. "I felt nothing, my lord. But I know that Lady Prudence seemed very eager to leave the room."

Prudence frowned at her brother. "There was a feeling as if something were telling me I didn't belong there."

"Good God," muttered Worcester. "Next you'll be telling me you've seen a ghost."

"I didn't see a ghost," said Prudence. "It was only a strange feeling."

"Well, it is the same sort of humbug."

Prudence, who was very much affronted by her brother's words, made no reply. Chandler began to wrap Prudence's wrist. "You will continue to have some pain, Lady Prudence," he said, "but you will find that it will improve rapidly." He smiled at her. "And don't worry. There are often cold drafts in large rooms."

Prudence smiled in reply. She thought the doctor exceedingly handsome and a very kind man.

When Chandler was finished, he turned to the marquess. "So you are up and about, my lord. You are looking quite well."

"I suppose you will suggest I go to my bed."

"I shouldn't dare to suggest that," replied Chandler with a smile. "But do stay in and near the fire. And don't neglect your rest. You ladies must see that his lordship doesn't attempt too much."

"We will, Robert," said Alethea.

"And, Lady Prudence, you must take care not to move that wrist or you will injure it further. I shall come tomorrow and see how you are faring."

"Thank you, Dr. Chandler," said Prudence, smiling at him. After the doctor took his leave, Worcester left the ladies in Prudence's room.

"I'm sure you'll feel much better in a short time, Pru," said Alethea. "I am glad that Robert called when he did."

"He is very nice," said Prudence.

"Yes, he is," agreed Alethea, "and he is an excellent physician."

While Prudence might have commented that she also found Chandler very handsome, she refrained from mentioning it. "I'm wondering, Alethea, if it's a mistake for Geoffrey and me to stay here at Hartwood."

Alethea regarded her in surprise. "What do you mean? I thought you liked it here."

"I do like it here, Alethea, but perhaps we don't belong here. First Geoffrey falls very ill and then I nearly break my neck in a fall. I felt something in the ballroom, Alethea. I believe your ancestors want us to be gone from here. I believe there *is* a curse."

"That's quite ridiculous, Pru. You can't blame these unfortunate occurrences on some silly old curse. I don't believe it, nor should you."

"Alethea, I feel that if I stay in this house something very bad will happen to me and to my brother."

Alethea regarded her young friend in some frustration. Prudence had been very understandably upset by the fall, which certainly had been an unnerving experience. If only Prudence had never learned of the nonsensical curse of the Beauchamps, Alethea told herself. "Nothing bad will happen," said Alethea. "You must believe me. Do put your misgivings aside."

Prudence hesitated before replying. "I shall try, Alethea."

"Good," said Alethea, who then changed the subject in hopes of getting her friend's mind off the absurd curse.

Chapter 12

Alethea stayed two more days at Hartwood and during that time grew better acquainted with both Worcester and his sister. She spent a good deal of time helping Prudence plan for the guests who would be arriving in a few days. Alethea also assisted Prudence with the invitations for the ball.

There was little time for Alethea to work on her own writing, but she didn't seem to mind. She was glad to help Prudence, for during her time at Hartwood Alethea had grown very fond of her.

Worcester's demeanor to his guest was rather cool and formal, but he wasn't really unfriendly. In fact, he seemed to enjoy talking with her. They had some rather spirited discussions about politics in which it was revealed that they had radically different opinions.

Prudence, who had little knowledge of current affairs, was surprised to find that Alethea was very well read on a good many subjects. She could more than hold her own in discussions of such matters as the Corn Laws and the Irish question. While Prudence had been rather worried the first time Alethea had expressed views contrary to Worcester's, she soon found that her brother enjoyed the verbal sparring that had ensued.

While Alethea thought the marquess terribly wrongheaded in most of his opinions, she had to admit that he could hold his own in an argument. He was not unintelligent, she decided, only woefully misguided.

Worcester, for his part, was growing to like Alethea very much. Yet he was so careful to hide this partiality, that she would have been very surprised to learn of it. The marquess was rather disturbed to find himself so favorably disposed toward her. After all, he had always thought he disliked clever women, especially those affecting knowledge of masculine subjects like politics.

But Worcester couldn't help liking her. In fact, one day while she was playing a song on the piano, he had found himself wondering what it would be like to be married to Alethea Brandon. Of course, he immediately dismissed the idea as absurd.

Yet it resurfaced that evening while he lay awake in bed. He found himself imagining Alethea there beside him, smiling that charming smile of hers. Fortunately, Worcester was a man of considerable self-control and he was able to meet Alethea the next day without betraying a hint of his feelings.

Each day Dr. Chandler called to see if Prudence's wrist was improving. Thinking such daily attentions unnecessary, the marquess had begun to suspect that the physician's calls were more social in nature.

It was Chandler's visit on the second day that put a stop to the increasing regard Alethea was beginning to feel for Worcester. Alethea, Prudence, and the marquess were in the drawing room when Talbot announced that the doctor had arrived.

"I suppose we must see him," muttered Worcester.

"Good afternoon," said the physician, coming in and bowing first to the ladies and then Worcester. "Lady Prudence, I hope your wrist continues to improve."

"It does, sir," said Prudence. "It feels much better today."

"I shall check it and redo the bandage," said Chandler, coming to sit beside her on the sofa.

Alethea could tell that Worcester wasn't very happy with the doctor's attentions to his sister, for he had adopted the look of a displeased monarch. "Come, come, Chandler," said the marquess, "is all that fuss necessary?"

"Yes, one must see if it is healing properly," replied Chandler, smiling pleasantly at Worcester. "And I do hope you are feeling well, Lord Worcester."

"I have never felt better," said his lordship.

"I am glad to hear it," said Chandler. When he had rebound Prudence's bandage, he seemed in no hurry to leave.

"You mustn't allow us to keep you from your rounds, sir," said the marquess, cutting short the doctor's small talk. "I know that you are a very busy man."

"Yes, I should be going," said Chandler, "but before I go, I was wondering if Lady Prudence might like a kitten. You see, a farmer has just given me one. I thought she'd be good company for her ladyship."

"Oh, a kitten!" cried Prudence. "I should love a kitten!"

"I don't like cats overmuch," said the marquess, frowning in disapproval.

"Couldn't I have the kitten, Geoffrey? Oh, please say that I might have it."

"Oh, very well," replied Worcester. "Go fetch it, Chandler, and have done with it."

"I shall be happy to do so," said the physician, breaking into a grin and leaving the room. He returned in a few minutes with a small gray-striped kitten, which he handed to Prudence.

"What a little darling," cried Prudence, pressing the small creature to her breast. "Does she have a name?"

"Oh, you must name her," said Chandler.

"Oh dear, what shall I call you?" said Prudence, addressing the kitten, who was mewing softly. "I know, I shall call you Poppet."

"That is an excellent choice," said Alethea.

"It is dashed silly," said the marquess.

Prudence ignored her brother. "Do you think she's hungry?"

"I shouldn't doubt it," said Chandler.

"I must take her to the kitchen."

"Oh, allow me," said Chandler, taking up the kitten. "I must be going, but I'll carry Poppet to the kitchen for you, Lady Prudence." He smiled at Alethea. "Good day, Alethea. Good day, my lord." He made a formal bow to the marquess before departing with Prudence.

When they were gone, Worcester rose to his feet. "Of all the damned impudence. Can you imagine the fellow bringing Prudence a cat?"

"I thought it kind of him," said Alethea.

"Kind of him?" The marquess folded his arms in front of him. "And the effrontery of him going off with her like that. Egad, the fellow is trying to ingratiate himself with my sister. He is nothing but an opportunist, a fortune hunter."

Alethea regarded Worcester in surprise. "He is nothing of the kind. Dr. Chandler is only a kind man performing his profession in a competent manner. I assure you, sir, he has no designs upon Lady Prudence."

"Don't you see how he looks at her and smiles?"

"It is only common courtesy. Indeed, my lord, I have known Robert Chandler for many years. He is a sensible man and, as such, he is well aware that Lady Prudence is above his touch."

"An ambitious man considers no lady above his touch," said the marquess. "He has the look of an ambitious man to me. And my sister is very young and very naive."

"But he is a very respectable gentleman, my lord," said Alethea indignantly.

"Gentleman, is he? Your definition of gentleman is apparently broader than mine. Why, he is little better than a tradesman. Who are his parents? Who are his grandparents?"

Alethea bristled at the remark and the haughty manner in which it was made. "Robert's father is a solicitor in Towmouth. And I don't know why one must be concerned about his grandparents. Isn't it more important that a man be good and honorable than have a fine pedigree?"

"A man's birth is of paramount importance. And I cannot say if he is good or honorable."

Flushed with anger, Alethea rose from her chair. "I am sorry you think so little of him. But you do him a grave injustice to think he is a fortune hunter."

"I am only concerned about my sister's happiness," said the marquess.

"Are you, my lord? Is that why you wish to marry her to a man she detests?"

"What are you talking about?"

"Lady Prudence said you wish her to marry Lord Feversham, whom she finds completely odious. Whatever his rank and fortune, it isn't enough if she will be miserable."

The marquess fixed an icy gaze upon her. "You presume too much, Miss Brandon, to speak about this."

"And you presume too much to slander Dr. Chandler in such an infamous manner, my lord," said Alethea, regarding him with indignation.

"Slander him? By heaven, I'm only saying that the fellow has no business bringing my sister a gift, even if it is one as worthless as a cat. I found that most inappropriate. Why, he is too familiar by half."

Alethea frowned at Worcester, thinking him the worst sort of pompous snob. "If you will excuse me, my lord, I shall go to my room."

"Come, come, Miss Brandon, there is no reason for you to get your back up."

Alethea directed an icy gaze at him before turning and abruptly leaving.

The marquess frowned as he watched her go. He hadn't realized that she was such a temperamental female. To take offense at his remarks seemed ridiculous. Of course, she was obviously very fond of this Chandler person, a fact which rather irritated his lordship.

When Prudence reentered the drawing room, she appeared surprised. "But where is Alethea?"

"Miss Brandon has gone to her room."

"Oh? Well, I shall join her." Prudence hurried off. When she arrived at the door to Alethea's room, she knocked on it before entering. Alethea was standing at the wardrobe, taking clothes from hangers.

"Oh, Alethea, you should have seen dear little Poppet drinking milk. It was so adorable. I wanted to bring her with me, but Cook said I must allow her time to sleep. The servants found her a nice little basket."

"That is very good," said Alethea, turning from the wardrobe to place the clothes on the bed.

"But what are you doing, Alethea?"

"I have decided that it is time I returned home, Pru. I have taken advantage of your hospitality far too long."

"Why, you haven't been here very long at all," said Prudence, appalled at the prospect of Alethea leaving.

"Well, I do have work to do on my book. And while I have been able to do a little writing here, I know I should accomplish far more at home. I was to be finished by the end of the month, you see. And besides, Nelson is unhappy when I'm gone."

"But I shall miss you dreadfully," said Prudence.

"Well, you must call on me at Crow's Nest Cottage. And I'll visit you as well."

"But why have you decided to leave now?" A look of enlightenment came to her face. "Was it something Geoffrey said to you?"

"No," said Alethea, who had no wish to instill any bad feeling between sister and brother, "it is simply time for me to return home."

After making repeated entreaties, Prudence was finally convinced that nothing she could say could persuade Alethea to stay. Finally reconciled to the unfortunate news, she called for her maid to assist Miss Brandon make ready for her departure.

Chapter 13

When she awakened the next morning in her bed at Crow's Nest Cottage, Alethea was very glad to be back home. It was wonderful to find herself at her well-beloved home, attended by the devoted servants she had known since her girlhood. She had especially missed Nelson, who pined when she was away.

After breakfast,, Alethea began work on her book. She was able to get a good deal accomplished even though her mind occasionally wandered back to Hartwood.

She was certain that Worcester was glad to be rid of her, since he undoubtedly felt that she was far too lowly a person to entertain at Hartwood. Yes, thought Alethea, the marquess was probably very happy to separate his sister from such an unsuitable companion as herself.

Yet Alethea didn't spend much time thinking about Worcester, for she was too busy concentrating on her book. In the afternoon, she continued to write until three o'clock, when her maid appeared in the doorway. "Dr. Chandler is here, miss. I showed him to the drawing room."

Alethea put down her pen, happy at the interruption. When she arrived in the drawing room, she found the physician surveying a ship's model that sat on a shelf at one end of the room. "Robert, how good of you to call."

"Good afternoon, Alethea," he said, turning toward her. "I called at Hartwood and found that you'd gone home."

Alethea motioned for him to be seated. "Will you have tea?"

"I should like that very much."

"Good," said Alethea, ringing for Molly. When the maid appeared, Alethea ordered tea. Then she smiled at Chandler. "How is Lady Prudence? I hope her wrist is better."

"Yes, it is. She is doing very well. She wasn't in very good spirits though. She said she wished you had stayed longer at Hartwood."

"Poor girl. But I could hardly stay on there indefinitely."

"So did you enjoy your visit at your ancestral home?"

Alethea laughed. "Yes, I did."

"And it appeared you got on famously with Lord Worcester. I must confess, I found that surprising. After all, aren't you Brandons sworn to despise Worcester and all his ilk?"

Alethea laughed. "Well, I certainly don't despise Lady Prudence. She is a very sweet girl."

"Yes, she is," said Chandler.

There was a trace of wistfulness in his voice that made Alethea regard him curiously. "So you liked Lady Prudence?"

"I fear it is more than that," said Chandler. "I know you will think me a proper fool, but I believe I've fallen in love with her."

"What!" cried Alethea, regarding him with astonishment. "Oh, Robert, you scarcely know her!"

"I always thought the notion of love at first sight utterly ridiculous. But when I first saw Lady Prudence, I had the oddest feeling. And then when she first spoke to me, I thought that I had never heard such a melodious voice. I thought I had met an angel."

"Oh dear," said Alethea.

Chandler laughed. "Oh, I am well aware that I have no chance with her. Not only am I her social inferior, but I haven't any money. Can you imagine what her brother would think of the idea of his sister marrying someone like me?"

"She could do far worse," said Alethea.

"I doubt his lordship would think so."

"Well, I know he wouldn't be very pleased about it."

He laughed again. "That is putting it mildly, I'm sure. But in any case, I shall try to set aside my feelings for Lady Prudence. I expect it won't be too difficult once I am away from here."

"Away from here? What do you mean?"

"I'm going to London. You know that my uncle Henry has been wanting me to join his practice in town for some time."

"Yes, but you always said you preferred to stay here."

"There are much better opportunities in London. My uncle is doing very well there and I must think of my future."

"But are you certain you wish to go?"

"I have made up my mind," said Chandler resolutely. "I hope to leave within a month if I can settle my affairs here."

"But who will take your place?"

"That is all arranged. There will be a new man. By all accounts he's very good."

"Oh, Robert, this is terrible. What will I do without you?"

"You'll get on very well. And London isn't Australia. You may come visit me whenever you like."

"But I hate London," said Alethea.

"What stuff!" said Chandler with a laugh. "You always love London."

She smiled. "Oh, perhaps I do like it. But I wouldn't want to live there. And I won't like it at all when you're gone. Indeed, I'm quite vexed with you for deciding to go off and leave us."

At that point Molly entered the room with tea. Alethea poured a cup, handed it to Robert, and they continued to discuss his plans for moving to London.

Worcester had spent a good part of the afternoon walking about the area surrounding Hartwood. There were several paths leading through picturesque meadows and woods and the marquess walked for miles.

The weather was particularly good that day, cool, but bright and sunny with only a hint of wind. Since Worcester was feeling entirely recovered from his bout of illness, he was glad to be out getting some long-needed exercise.

When he returned to the house, he handed his topcoat and hat to the butler. "Where is Lady Prudence, Talbot?"

"In her room, my lord. She's been there all afternoon."

Frowning slightly, Worcester went to the drawing room, where he settled himself on the sofa. That morning his sister had been in a particularly gloomy mood. She had only perked up when Dr. Chandler had arrived to pay another of what the marquess considered totally unnecessary calls.

His lordship's frown grew deeper. Thinking of the doctor brought Alethea to mind again. He had devoted a good amount of his walk to thinking about her. Glancing around the room, he found himself wishing she hadn't gone. She had been good company despite her crack-brained notions about so many things.

Worcester folded his arms in front of him and appeared thoughtful. "I beg your pardon, my lord," said Talbot, entering the drawing room. The butler carried a silver salver on which were several letters. "The post, my lord," he said.

"Thank you, Talbot," said the marquess, taking the letters. He opened each one and read them. Once he had finished, he stood up and rang for a servant. Talbot appeared quickly. "Would you tell Lady Prudence that I wish to see her?"

The servant bowed and retreated, leaving his master to peruse one of the letters again. It was some time before Prudence appeared carrying the tiny gray kitten. "I'm told you wished to see me, Geoffrey," she said.

"Yes, do sit down, Prudence," he said.

She nodded and sat down on the sofa. Placing the kitten in her lap, Prudence stroked her gently.

The marquess, who had never liked cats, frowned at the little creature. "This is a letter from the Duchess of Cranworth. She and her party will be arriving soon."

Prudence continued to pet the kitten. "I wish Miss Brandon had stayed. If she were with me, I shouldn't mind the others so much."

"Mind them?" He regarded her in frustration. "What a difficult girl you are. One might think you would be please that I have assembled such distinguished guests. All of them are fashionable people from the first circles of society."

"I don't like fashionable people," said Prudence.

"Well, you will have to make the best of it," said the marquess, who was becoming irritated with his sister.

Prudence looked down at the kitten. "I'm worried about Poppet," she said. "She seems rather listless. Yesterday she was so playful, but today she doesn't seem very well."

"She looks well enough to me," said the marquess. "She probably needs to sleep. Leave her in her basket for a time."

Prudence rose from the sofa and pressed the kitten against her breast. "I'll do that, Geoffrey. Come, my poor dear Poppet. I'll see what Cook has to say. She knows all about cats."

Prudence hurried off, leaving Worcester with his letters.

Chapter 14

Alethea spent the next two days busily working on her book on herbal medicine. Occasionally she would stop and take a break for food or a short walk. Pleased that her writing was going very well, she was confident that she would make a good deal of progress if she could be spared interruptions.

However, on the following morning, there was a distraction in the form of an unexpected visitor. Alethea, who was sitting at her desk deep in concentration, didn't notice when Molly entered the room.

"Excuse me, miss," she said, "but there is a gentleman to see you."

"A gentleman?" said Alethea, looking up from her work to see that Molly's round face was flushed with excitement.

" 'Tis the Marquess of Worcester!" she said.

"Here?" said Alethea, eyeing the servant with a look of amazement. She had never expected him to call on her.

"Aye, miss."

"Is Lady Prudence with him?"

"No, miss, his lordship's alone."

Although Alethea thought this very odd, she did her best to react as if it weren't in the least extraordinary that Worcester should appear alone at Crow's Nest Cottage. She rose from her chair. "I suppose one shouldn't keep a marquess waiting."

"Indeed not, miss," said Molly. "I have shown him to the drawing room."

"Very good Molly. I'll join him there." Alethea pushed a wayward curl from her face. Aware that she was wearing an old mauve dress, she hesitated, wondering if she should go and change into something more presentable. Then, deciding that she didn't care in the least what he thought of her, she went directly to the drawing room.

She found the marquess standing there. He was dressed in an excellently cut coat of olive superfine, ivory breeches, and riding boots. As always, he was dressed carefully, but without any pretense of dandyism. His face bore the serious expression she knew so well from her time at Hartwood.

"Lord Worcester," said Alethea, curtsying politely.

He bowed in reply. "Miss Brandon."

"Do sit down, my lord," she said, pointing to a chair, beside which was a tall wooden carving of a rather grim-looking pagan god. Seeing him cast a questioning look at the carving, she smiled. "It is Hawaiian," she said.

"Indeed?" he said, frowning at it for a moment before turning to her. "Miss Brandon, I have a matter of some seriousness to discuss with you. And I should be grateful to you if you would return to Hartwood with me."

"What's wrong?" cried Alethea, alarmed at the remark. "Is Lady Prudence all right?"

"Yes, she is well enough." He paused. "In truth I'm concerned about her."

"But you said she was well."

"It's her state of mind that concerns me. Since you left, she's been rather unhappy. And now her kitten has taken ill. She has been very upset, for she believes that this ridiculous curse has caused the animal to sicken.

"And this morning she refused to leave her room. She sits with the kitten, crying over it as it grows weaker. She told me that she won't stay at Hartwood. If the animal dies, and I'm certain it will, she will be inconsolable."

"Oh dear, I'll go to her at once."

"Thank you, Miss Brandon."

Alethea lost no time in fetching her bonnet, pelisse, and her bag of herbal medicines. Worcester escorted Alethea outside and handed her up into the awaiting carriage.

When the vehicle started off, the marquess sat in silence for a time. "It is good of you to come," he said finally.

"Oh, I'm happy to do so."

He frowned. "I was afraid you wouldn't wish to come. I know you were angry with me."

"I do have a temper, my lord," said Alethea. "It's one of my many failings. I was exceedingly vexed with you, but I have cooled since then. And if I can be of assistance to Lady Prudence, I'm only too glad to do so. I'll try to help poor Poppet."

Worcester shook his head. "From the look of the creature, I don't think anyone could do anything for it. But I shall feel much better if you're there to help Prudence cope with its loss. And I'd be grateful to you if you'd try to convince her that this curse is nothing but silly superstition."

"I shall try my best," said Alethea, although she was starting to wonder if there might be something to it. After all, the marquess and his sister did seem to be having very bad luck.

It wasn't long before they arrived at Hartwood. After entering the house, Worcester led Alethea to Prudence's room. There they found her sitting in a chair near the bed, a forlorn expression on her face. On the bed lay the tiny kitten, motionless.

"Prudence," said Alethea.

"Oh, Alethea!" cried Prudence, rising from her chair. "Poppet is dying! Is there anything you can do to help her?"

Alethea stared down at the tiny gray bit of fur on the bed. The kitten was still breathing. She could see the tiny chest rising and falling.

"I know it is the curse of this house," said Prudence. "She was fine when Dr. Chandler brought her to me. Then she started to look sick. She hasn't eaten anything for two days."

"Has she taken any water?"

Prudence shook her head. "We couldn't get her to drink. And now she is so weak."

"She must take some water," said Alethea. "I'll need a rag and some water poured into a bowl." Once the requested items were obtained, Alethea dipped the rag into the water, and, forcing the tiny animal's jaws open, she placed drops of water into her mouth. The kitten licked feebly at the water. "Good girl, Poppet, you must drink all you can. And you must fight as hard as you can. Yes, fight very hard, my girl."

Alethea continued to drip water into Poppet's mouth, all the while murmuring words of encouragement to the tiny creature. "Do you think she might get better, Alethea?" said Prudence, a bit more hopeful now that her friend was there.

"I don't know, Pru, but you mustn't give up."

"I have been praying so very hard," said Prudence. "But Poppet

was growing worse. I do think she looks a bit better now. Don't
you think so, Alethea?"

"Perhaps a little," said Alethea. "Yes, I do think she needed
water badly. We'll have to see that she takes more of it." She continued to work with the kitten.

Worcester stood there watching Alethea, who was intent upon
her tiny charge. He didn't notice when Talbot entered the room.
"I beg your pardon, my lord, but Dr. Chandler is here. He is inquiring after Lady Prudence."

"Chandler? Tell him Lady Prudence is much improved and in
no need of his services," said the marquess.

"But, Geoffrey," cried Prudence, "perhaps he might help Poppet. Oh, do have him brought up, Geoffrey."

"Oh, very well. Bring him here, Talbot."

When the butler returned with Chandler, the physician entered
the room. "I heard the kitten is ill."

"Dr. Chandler." said Prudence, rising to her feet, "can you help
Poppet?"

"I'm sure Alethea is far better able to do that than I," said
Chandler. "She is the one who nurses sick animals. Poor little
Poppet. What is wrong, Alethea?"

"I don't know, Robert. She seemed so healthy when we first
saw her, but young animals often get sick."

"She was so active and playful," said Prudence, a tear rolling
down her cheek. "And then suddenly she became ill. It's because
of this house and that dreadful curse."

"Prudence," said the marquess, "stop talking nonsense."

"Pru," said Alethea, "I believe Poppet is a bit stronger. See
how she licks at the water now. Indeed, I believe it might be best
if we left her for a time and allowed her to sleep. Often animals
are best left to themselves. Why don't we have a cup of tea? It
would do you good, Prudence."

"I don't like to leave her," said Prudence, reaching down to
stroke the kitten.

"Come, Pru," said the marquess. "If Miss Brandon thinks Poppet should rest, we should do as she says."

Prudence took one last look at Poppet before nodding and leaving the room. When they got out into the corridor, Prudence
turned to the physician. "Will you have tea with us, Dr. Chandler?
Oh, do say yes."

While Chandler knew he should refuse, he had no wish to leave. "Yes, that would be very nice. Thank you, Lady Prudence."

Alethea glanced over at the marquess. His face betrayed no emotion, even though Alethea was sure that the idea of Chandler staying to tea didn't please him.

As they walked into the drawing room, Prudence seemed to feel faint. Chandler, who was walking next to her, hastened to take her arm. "Lady Prudence, are you unwell?"

"Oh, no, but I do feel a little weak."

The marquess regarded his sister in some alarm. She looked terribly pale. He and the doctor assisted her to a chair. "She has hardly eaten since you left us, Miss Brandon," said Worcester. "She has been too worried about the cat."

"Oh, Prudence," said Alethea, "you mustn't make yourself sick."

"No, you mustn't," said Chandler.

"I'm sorry to be such a nuisance," said Prudence.

"You aren't a nuisance," said the marquess, ringing for a servant. Talbot appeared quickly. "Have tea brought at once."

"Are you feeling better, Prudence?" said Alethea.

"Yes, a little. It's only that I'm very tired. You see, I haven't slept well. I've had very bad dreams."

"Bad dreams?" said Chandler.

Prudence nodded. "Last night I dreamed that something horrible was chasing me from this house." She looked up at her brother. "I do wish we could go back to London. I don't wish to stay here any longer. Oh, do say we could go back to town, Geoffrey. Poppet will be better if we leave here. I'm sure of it. No Beauchamps should live at Hartwood."

"This curse business again," said the marquess. "She has thought of nothing else since her fall."

Alethea looked over at the marquess. "I believe it is time we rid the house of the curse."

"Is that possible?" said Prudence, regarding her in surprise.

"Oh, come now, Miss Brandon," said the marquess. "Let's have no more of this superstitious nonsense."

"Oh, I'd thought it nonsense, my lord," said Alethea, "but now I'm not so certain. The day that Prudence fell on the stairs I sensed something out of the ordinary."

"Did you?" cried Prudence.

"Yes," said Alethea, hoping she sounded convincing. "There

was a sort of a presence. It wasn't very frightening to me, but then I am a Brandon. Yesterday I found myself thinking about the curse. I wondered if there was anything that might be done to alter it. I consulted some of my books to see if the matter of curses was discussed.

"There was one very old volume that did discuss how one might try to remove a curse. I thought that I might attempt it when I came to Hartwood." She opened the reticule she was carrying and pulled out a piece of paper. "I copied some of the words down. Oh, I cannot say for certain that it would work."

"But it sounds worth trying," said Chandler, casting a conspiratorial look at her. "And since you are a Brandon, you might be able to do it."

"Precisely," said Alethea. "It is necessary that one of my family take away this curse." She glanced over at the marquess. "If his lordship has no objection, I would like to try." When he hesitated, she continued. "Yes, do allow me to do so, Lord Worcester."

Finally realizing that Miss Brandon was engaging in a charade for Prudence's benefit, he nodded. "Yes, yes, by all means try, but I still think it nonsensical."

"But what is to be done, Alethea?" said Chandler.

"Well, first of all, I believe it would be a good idea to remove the portrait of the first marquess from the house." She motioned toward the large portrait hanging over the fireplace. "It must be taken down."

"Come now," said Worcester, "I'm sure that isn't necessary."

Alethea nodded gravely. "He is the guilty party, my lord."

"I don't know if that's true or not," said Worcester, looking up at the picture of his ancestor.

"Oh, Geoffrey," cried Prudence. "Do remove it from the house. I'm sure that would help."

"Oh, very well." Worcester rang the bellpull again and Talbot reappeared.

"Tea will be ready very soon, my lord."

"I wasn't ringing about that," said Worcester. "Talbot, get some of the men and have the portrait of the first marquess taken down." He pointed at it. "That picture there. It's to be taken from the house."

Talbot allowed a look of slight surprise to come to his usually impassive face. "Taken from the house, my lord?"

The marquess nodded. "Take it to the stables immediately. And have it wrapped and sent to London."

"Very good, my lord," said Talbot, "I shall have it done as soon as you have your tea."

"Oh, do take it down at once," said Prudence.

The butler looked at the marquess, who nodded. "Yes, have it done immediately. We'll have tea when it's gone."

Talbot bowed and then went off to do his master's bidding. He returned a short time later accompanied by two servants who carried a ladder.

They watched as the men took down the painting. "Now I want it taken from the house," said Worcester.

"Go on then," said Talbot, directing his subordinates to carry the picture away. They returned in a short time to fetch the ladder.

"Yes, that is much better," said Alethea with a smile.

"Yes, I feel something has changed already," said Prudence.

"It does rather leave an empty space," said Chandler. "Perhaps Alethea might bring the portrait of Giles Brandon from Crow's Nest Cottage to take its place."

Alethea laughed. "I think he is best left at home."

At that moment the servants entered with tea. Prudence, who appeared considerably heartened by the idea that the curse was to be removed from the house, had no difficulty drinking a cup of tea and eating some cake. When they had finished their refreshments, Prudence seemed eager for Alethea to proceed. "What must be done now, Alethea?"

"First we must have his lordship declare that, as the head of the Beauchamps, he apologizes for the evil deed perpetrated by the first marquess."

"Come, now, Miss Brandon," said Worcester, putting down his teacup and regarding her with a frown.

"Oh, yes, that is essential." She stood up and took an embroidered pillow from the sofa. Placing it on the floor, she smiled. "I think it would be prudent for you to kneel when you apologize."

"Kneel?" said the marquess, rising to his feet and regarding her indignantly. "Really, Miss Brandon, you go too far!"

Chandler had great difficulty to keep from bursting into laughter. He exchanged a glance with Alethea.

"I shall be happy to kneel down and apologize for my family," said Prudence.

"Oh, I think it would be better if his lordship did that," said Alethea. "As the heir of the first marquess, it is his duty."

"Geoffrey, will you do it?" said Prudence.

Looking from his sister to Alethea, Worcester frowned. Despite her solemn expression, he was sure she was enjoying this. "Oh, very well," he said, kneeling down on the pillow. "I must be completely addle-pated to do this."

"And now you must apologize, my lord," said Alethea.

"Yes, yes," he said irritably.

"And perhaps it would be good if you placed your hand on your heart," suggested Alethea.

"Madam, you are trying my patience," said the marquess.

"Oh, do as Alethea says, Geoffrey," said Prudence.

Frowning again, Worcester placed his hand over his heart and looked at Alethea. "What do you wish me to say?"

"Repeat these words, my lord. 'I, Geoffrey Beauchamp, Marquess of Worcester . . .' "

"I, Geoffrey Beauchamp, Marquess of Worcester . . ."

"Do apologize for the evil and despicable deeds of my ancestor, the first Marquess of Worcester."

Worcester raised his eyebrows at her, but obediently repeated the words.

Alethea continued. "And humbly beg forgiveness for the heinous crimes of my ancestor."

"And humbly beg forgiveness for the heinous crimes of my ancestor."

"So help me God," said Alethea.

"So help me God," said the marquess, rising to his feet.

"And now, if you would open a window, my lord," said Alethea. "Then the curse will fly out if we are successful."

At this remark, Worcester raised his eyebrows once again, but made no comment. Going over to one of the windows, he opened it wide to admit some cold air.

"I, Alethea Brandon, speak for my family," began Alethea in a loud, commanding voice. "As the present marquess has humbly begged forgiveness for the sins of his ancestors, I ask that the curse be removed from the Beauchamp family." She paused, and taking up the paper in her hand, began to recite some words in an unintelligible language. When she finished, she tossed the paper into the fireplace and watched it burn. Then turning to the others, she smiled. "I feel that it has worked. Yes, I am sure of it."

"Oh, Alethea, I believe you are right," said Prudence.

Walking over to the window, Worcester pulled it shut. "I sincerely hope so."

"I, too, feel a change in the house," said Chandler, smiling at Worcester's sister. "Now do get some rest, Lady Prudence."

"I shall, Dr. Chandler," she replied.

Alethea could not fail to note the way Prudence was smiling at the physician. She frowned slightly. It was lucky that Robert was leaving for London. Once in the city, his path would never cross Prudence's, and he would forget her in time.

It was a pity, thought Alethea, that differences in station and wealth made a match between Robert and Prudence impossible. They seemed to be so well suited in other ways. Robert was a fine man, kind and intelligent. He would make someone a wonderful husband. And Prudence was sweet and considerate. Alethea looked away, deciding that there was no point in dwelling on such things.

After Chandler took his leave, Prudence said that she wished to go to her room. Alethea, fearing that Poppet might have taken a turn for the worse, accompanied her.

When they entered the bedchamber, Prudence let out an anguished cry. "Poppet! Where has she gone?" The little gray striped cat was no longer lying on the bed.

"Oh, she must be nearby," said Alethea, entering the room and looking around.

"Poppet! Here, kitty!" said Prudence.

Suddenly there was a meow and Poppet appeared from under the bed. She stood there twitching her tail and looking perfectly healthy.

"Poppet!" cried Prudence, sweeping up the kitten into her arms.

Alethea regarded the animal in surprise. "Good heavens, she is so much better."

"Yes, she seems completely well! Oh, I must show Geoffrey at once. I know what has happened! The curse has been removed and now Poppet is well!" Prudence hurried out of the room. Alethea stood there for a moment with a look of astonishment on her face before following after her young friend.

Chapter 15

Although Prudence begged her to stay for dinner, Alethea thought it best that she return home. The following morning a messenger arrived from Hartwood, bringing a letter from Prudence in which that young lady reported that she had had a good night's rest and that Poppet was apparently totally recovered. Prudence thanked Alethea profusely for removing the curse from Hartwood, saying she knew that was the reason the kitten was now doing so well.

The letter also included a request. "I do hate to ask you, Alethea," Prudence had written, "but Geoffrey insists I send the invitations to this ball he is having. The invitations have come from the village and must be addressed. I still cannot write in a legible fashion and I should be so grateful if you could help. You have already done so much that I feel horrid asking you for something more. And you must stay for dinner as well. We will send the carriage for you at eleven o'clock if that is acceptable to you."

After reading the letter, Alethea took up her quill pen to write a reply. It seemed she was doomed to have interruptions that would prevent her from finishing her work on schedule. Still, Alethea wasn't so displeased at the idea of going to Hartwood. She had been wondering about Prudence and the kitten. And she had to admit she had also been thinking about Worcester.

As she sat at her desk in the library with Nelson at her feet, Alethea stared out the window at the sea. Smiling, she remembered the marquess repeating the apology while kneeling on the cushion. He wasn't really so bad, she told herself. After all, he had been willing to take part in her little subterfuge for the sake of his sister.

Alethea wrote an acceptance to Prudence's invitation. After blotting it, she folded the paper and took it to the messenger, who stood waiting in the entry hall. Then she returned to work on her book.

In the afternoon, she grew tired of writing. Rising from the desk, she decided to get some fresh air. Nelson was eager to accompany her.

Outside, Alethea found the weather chilly and the sky overcast, but she was warm in her wool cloak and bonnet. As she and the mastiff walked along the path that provided many outstanding sea views, Alethea paused now and again to stare out at the waves.

After she had walked for a while, she came to the road that led to the village. Deciding to go a bit farther, she turned onto the road. Suddenly a rider appeared in the distance.

When he came into view, Alethea was very much surprised to recognize Worcester. He was astride a fine chestnut horse that he rode with the ease of an expert horseman.

Having never expected him to appear, she stopped. He was soon pulling his horse up beside her. "Lord Worcester," she said.

"Miss Brandon." The marquess lifted his tall hat politely.

"What a fine horse," said Alethea, patting the animal's neck.

"Do you ride, Miss Brandon?"

"Oh, yes," she said. I have a mare named Kate whom I ride most mornings. She is a poor old dear, not a fine one like this fellow."

The marquess looked down at the enormous dog standing beside her. "So this is Nelson?"

"Yes, I must introduce you. Lord Worcester, I have the honor of presenting Nelson."

Worcester nodded to the mastiff. "I am very pleased to meet you, Nelson. Prudence has sung your praises." The big animal responded by fixing his brown eyes on the marquess and wagging his tail. Dismounting from his horse, Worcester patted the dog's head.

As he did so, a light drizzle began to fall. "Oh, it begins to rain. You should return home, Miss Brandon."

"Oh, I'm fine, I assure you, my lord."

"Allow me to escort you back, Miss Brandon."

"That is very kind, Lord Worcester, but it isn't at all necessary."

"Oh, I don't mind in the least," he said.

As they started walking back toward Crow's Nest Cottage, she looked over at him. "And do you believe the curse has vanished from Hartwood?"

A smile crossed his usually solemn countenance. "It appears so."

"Well, I shouldn't be surprised since your lordship pleaded for forgiveness with such forcefulness."

"I do think you were doing it a bit brown, Miss Brandon," said Worcester. "What was it you said, 'heinous crimes of my ancestor'?"

"Well, one cannot dispute that they were heinous."

"Oh, very well, I suppose they were, if true."

"Oh, I have no doubt of that. More than two hundred years of family tradition can't be wrong." Alethea smiled. "Prudence said that Poppet is doing well."

"The dashed creature is running about chasing after balls of yarn. It is quite the picture of health."

"That is what happens when curses are removed," said Alethea. Worcester smiled again. "Prudence said you have agreed to come to Hartwood tomorrow."

"Yes, you will have me underfoot again, my lord."

"It is good of you to come."

"I am happy to do so." They walked along in silence for a time. When Crow's Nest Cottage came into view, the drizzle turned into a heavy rain. "Oh dear," said Alethea, picking up her pace. "Would you wish to come in and get out of the rain, Lord Worcester?"

"Yes, I would," said the marquess, surprising her with his answer. She hadn't expected him to accept. Indeed, she assumed he would have been eager to return to Hartwood.

Arriving at the house, Alethea called for her servant John to see to the marquess's horse. Molly met them inside the door and assisted Alethea with her coat and bonnet. The servant then took Worcester's hat and topcoat.

By this time the rain had become a downpour. "Oh, my," said Alethea, "you may be stranded for a time. Really, you should stay until it lets up. It hasn't been very long since you were ill."

The marquess didn't seem in the least perturbed about finding himself at Crow's Nest Cottage. In truth, he found the prospect quite appealing. He was thinking that Alethea looked very attractive with her face flushed from her walk and her dark curls damp about her face.

"There is a very good fire in the drawing room, my lord," she said, escorting him inside. "Do sit down near the fire."

"Thank you, Miss Brandon."

"Would you like a cup of tea?"

He nodded. "Yes, I would like that very much."

Molly stood in the doorway. "Would you bring tea, Molly?"

The servant bobbed a curtsy and hurried off, eager to inform the cook, Sarah, that the marquess was there and wanting tea.

Worcester took a seat and Alethea sat down in a chair next to him. Looking over at him, she imagined that he was probably thinking that Crow's Nest Cottage was a poor, inconsequential sort of place.

Yet the marquess didn't seem to mind his less-than-lordly accommodations. His face bore none of the haughtiness that he had exhibited when they first had met. No, he seemed quite amiable and content sitting there.

Glancing around the room, Worcester's eye fell upon a watercolor painting of flowers in a vase that was hanging on the wall. "What a lovely picture."

"Oh, thank you," said Alethea. "It is one of my poor efforts."

"You painted it?" said Worcester, getting to his feet and going to the picture to take a closer look. "It is very good, Miss Brandon. You are very accomplished." He turned from the painting to look at her. "I didn't know you were an artist."

"I don't know that I would call myself that, Lord Worcester," said Alethea, smiling at him. "Since I was a girl, I have drawn and painted plants and flowers. I have illustrated some of my father's books."

"I should like to see one," said the marquess.

"Would you? Then I shall be happy to show you. As my Aunt Elizabeth often tells me, I've never been one to hide my light under a bushel. If you would come with me to the library, my lord."

Worcester and Nelson followed Alethea from the room. In the library, Alethea took a very large volume from a shelf and laid it on the desk. "This is one of Father's book," she said, opening it.

The marquess paged through it, looking for the illustrations. Pausing at each one he found, he studied them carefully. "Yes, these are excellent, Miss Brandon. You have considerable talent."

"How kind of you to say that, Lord Worcester," said Alethea, smiling. She bent down over the book and turned to one page. "This is my favorite, the columbines."

The marquess was standing there looking over her shoulder. He was suddenly very aware of the faint floral smell of her perfume. Worcester found himself looking at the back of her head. Alethea's hair was pulled into a topknot on her head and wisps of dark hair fell about her neck. He suddenly had a very keen desire to kiss her. It was with some difficulty that he refrained from putting his arms around her and burying his face against the whiteness of her neck.

While Alethea had no idea that his lordship was resisting such a surprising impulse, she found that she was very much aware of him. His proximity was strangely unsettling.

"I'm sure you find botanical prints rather dull."

"I wouldn't say that," said Worcester.

Feeling slightly discomfited, Alethea moved away from him. "This is another painting of mine," she said, pointing to a picture lying flat on the table. "I mean to have it framed one day."

Walking over to her, the marquess looked down at the painting. It was another still life of flowers, painted with the same delicacy of her other work, but with more vivid colors. "That is splendid. I do like that exceedingly well. Indeed, I should like to buy it, if you would be interested in selling it."

"Buy it?" said Alethea, looking very much surprised.

"Yes, I'd like to. I'll give you a fair price. What will you take for it?"

"If you are serious in wanting it, Lord Worcester," said Alethea, "I am more than happy to give it to you."*

"Oh, I couldn't take it as a gift. It's too much."

"Well, I shan't sell it to you, sir," said Alethea. "If you want it, you must accept it as a gift or not at all."

"Then I shall accept, but it is too generous by half."

Alethea laughed. "It isn't as if I'm giving you a Raphael, my lord."

"But it is very fine work nonetheless."

"I must say, Lord Worcester," said Alethea, directing a mischievous smile. "I am pleasantly surprised to find you such a good judge of art." He smiled in return and Alethea continued. "I shall bring this when I come to Hartwood tomorrow."

The marquess thanked her again and they returned to the drawing room. They had no sooner taken their seats when Molly entered with tea.

Alethea poured him a cup and handed it to him. Then taking her own teacup up from the saucer, she glanced over at the window. The rain continued to pour down. "I do believe it's raining harder."

Worcester nodded. "It seems so. I suppose there is no chance of seeing the famous Hector."

Alethea grinned. "I fear not. He is far too clever to come out in such a rain as this. But you must come again to see him."

"I'd like that," said the marquess, taking a drink of tea. He was very happy to be there. In fact, he found himself in no hurry at all to get back to Hartwood. It was very pleasant to be alone with her. The room was warm and cozy.

While he ate the piece of cake she had placed on his plate, he gazed at her thoughtfully. She was very attractive. What would it be like to take her into his arms and to place his mouth on hers? While he had never thought himself subject to the base desires that ruled so many of his class, he now understood how it felt to desire a woman.

Worcester did his best to put such unseemly thoughts from his mind. He took his eyes from Alethea and looked around the room. Alighting on a table with a chessboard, he nodded toward it. "That is a fine-looking chess set, Miss Brandon. I am very fond of the game."

"Are you, my lord? I confess I like it very much myself."

"You play chess, madam?"

Alethea nodded. "Oh, yes. Perhaps you'd like to play after we are done with our tea. It would pass the time until the rain lets up."

The marquess was very proud of his skill at chess. He was also of the opinion that the female mind was not suited to the rigors of the game. He therefore smiled patronizingly at her. "If you'd like to play, I shall be glad to oblige you. But I must warn you that I'm an accomplished player."

"I see," said Alethea, putting her teacup down. "I suppose you imagine it will be easy to best me."

"I don't often lose when I play," said his lordship, exhibiting a trace of his old arrogance.

"Well, I shall try not to be crushed when I am defeated," said Alethea with a smile.

When they finished their tea, they rose from their seats and took their places at the table where the chess game was set up. Worcester made the opening move. He was rather surprised when Alethea responded in less than a second, moving her piece and then smiling at him.

Having decided upon his strategy, Worcester played confidently. He continued to be surprised that Alethea seemed to need so little time to consider her moves, responding very quickly to whatever he did.

At first the marquess wasn't sure if she knew what she was doing. A serene smile on her face, Alethea moved her chess pieces in what he thought was a rather unorthodox fashion.

When she moved her bishop to what he considered a most ill-considered position, he smiled indulgently. "I fear, Miss Brandon, that you have made a grave tactical error. Would you wish to reconsider the move? I shall allow you to change it."

"That is very good of you, Lord Worcester, but I assure you that isn't necessary."

"Well then, Miss Brandon, I have no choice but to take your bishop," he said, moving one of his men to the square and taking her chess piece.

Alethea didn't appear in the least upset. She stared at the board for a brief moment before making her next move. The marquess suppressed a smile. Like all those of her sex, thought Worcester, Miss Brandon had no head for the game. It wouldn't be long now, he thought, moving his queen and taking another of her men.

Picking up one of her knights, Alethea placed it onto another square. "Check," she said.

The marquess was taken by surprise. He looked down at the board. He studied it for a time before moving his king. Alethea hesitated only a moment before taking her turn.

After staring at the board for a time, Worcester finally made his move. Alethea smiled at him and took her turn. "Checkmate," she said.

The marquess was dumbfounded. He eyed the chessboard with an incredulous expression, certain that she was mistaken. Surely it couldn't be possible.

Seeming to know his thoughts, Alethea nodded. "Yes, Lord Worcester, it is checkmate. But I must say you did fairly well." The look that he gave her caused Alethea to burst into laughter.

Worcester looked at her and then smiled. "Dash it all, Miss Brandon, you played rings around me."

"Well, you see, my father has two chief passions in life, botany and chess. He taught me to play when I was four and I have been playing ever since." She grinned. "And I'm very good at it."

"You are damnably good at great number of things, it seems," said Worcester.

"Would you like to have another game, my lord?"

"Not right now," said the marquess. "I must sufficiently recover from this blow to my manhood. But I will play you again. Perhaps tomorrow at Hartwood."

"I should like that," said Alethea. She was pleased that he had taken his loss at chess surprisingly well.

"And you must play my brother Ned when he arrives. He thinks himself a very good player, although I beat him most of the time. And you must give him as sound a thrashing as you gave me."

"I shall endeavor to do my best," said Alethea, starting to return the chessmen to their original positions. Worcester replaced his pieces as well, and then they rose from the table.

The marquess glanced out the window, noting that the rain had lessened. It was coming down lightly. There was no reason to stay longer, but he really didn't wish to go. "It isn't raining very hard now," he said.

"No," said Alethea, looking out the window.

"I should be getting back to Hartwood. Prudence will be wondering what has become of me. I thank you for tea and for the chess game, Miss Brandon."

"You are most welcome, Lord Worcester," replied Alethea, ringing the bell for Molly. When the maid arrived, she informed her that the marquess was leaving. "Do have John fetch his lordship's horse."

"Very good, miss," said Molly, bobbing a curtsy and hurrying out.

"I shall see you to the door, Lord Worcester." She walked with him from the drawing room to the entry hall, where Molly handed him his topcoat and hat. "It is very damp," she said as Molly assisted him with his coat. "You must be careful not to catch cold. Wait one moment."

Alethea hurried away only to return quickly with a green woolen scarf. "Put this around your neck, sir."

"Really, Miss Brandon, that isn't necessary."

"I insist, Lord Worcester. I don't want you getting sick again."

"I don't see much chance of that now that you have rid Hartwood of the curse of the Beauchamps."

Laughing, Alethea wrapped the scarf around his neck. "I gave this to my father one Christmas. He thought it decidedly unfashionable. Perhaps you might make better use of it."

"I expect you knitted it yourself, madam."

"I did, but I am better at chess than knitting."

He smiled. "The carriage will come for you in the morning."

She nodded. "I shall be ready."

Worcester took his leave. John had fetched his horse from the stable and it awaited him. Alethea stood at the open door as he mounted his horse and set off. After watching him for a time, she closed the door and made her way to the library.

Chapter 16

When Alethea arrived at Hartwood the following morning, Prudence was very happy to see her. Alethea was just as glad to find her young friend in excellent spirits. Poppet appeared healthy and full of energy and Alethea was soon laughing at her playful antics.

Alethea was surprised and a bit disappointed to find that Worcester wasn't at home. He had gone to the village, Prudence told her, and wouldn't be home until after luncheon. The two young ladies, assisted by Mrs. Graham, set about on the project of the invitations. They worked diligently, making excellent progress.

The marquess appeared briefly in the early afternoon, but he was called to the library to meet with his steward about estate business. When the ladies were finished with the invitations, one of the servants took them to be posted in the village.

Worcester did join them for tea. As he took a seat beside Alethea on the sofa, he seemed in a very good mood. He spoke about the chess game he had played with her at Crow's Nest Cottage, shaking his head as he related his astonishment at his defeat.

Prudence was rather amazed by her brother's demeanor. He had always been so reserved in company, yet there he was, talkative, smiling, and even laughing at himself.

Prudence found herself pondering the change. It seemed that Alethea Brandon certainly had a knack for keeping Worcester in a good humor despite the fact that Alethea didn't seem in the least deferential to him. And what really interested Prudence was the fact that even though Alethea often expressed opinions that differed from his, Worcester seemed to accept her comments with equanimity.

The three of them sat there enjoying their tea when the butler arrived with a handsome young man following behind him. Recognizing the newcomer as her brother Edward, Prudence jumped up from her chair and hurried over to embrace him. "Ned! I am so glad you have come at last!"

"My dear Pru," said Edward, kissing his sister on the cheek. "But what is wrong with your arm?"

"Oh, I fell and sprained it, but it isn't serious. Dr. Chandler said that I shall be quite recovered in a short time."

"I'm glad to hear it."

"I am so happy to see you, Ned. Come, you must meet Alethea."

Edward directed his gaze to the dark-haired young lady sitting beside his brother on the sofa. She was a very good-looking woman, he found himself thinking.

Alethea, in turn, studied Edward. He didn't look much like Worcester, she told herself. He was more like Prudence with her fair hair and more delicate looks. Dressed at the height of fashion, Edward looked very handsome as he smiled at Alethea.

"Miss Brandon," said Worcester, "may I present my brother, Lord Edward Beauchamp. Edward, this is Miss Brandon."

"Your servant, Miss Brandon," said Edward, taking Alethea's proffered hand and bowing over it politely.

"Lord Edward," said Alethea, "I am very happy to meet you."

"The pleasure is entirely mine, Miss Brandon. I must stay I didn't expect to meet such an enchanting lady upon my arrival here. Do you live nearby or are you one of my brother's guests from town?"

"I live nearby," said Alethea.

"Well, if I had known that the neighbors were so charming, I should have tried to set off from town earlier."

"Miss Brandon wants none of your bottle-headed flummery, Ned," said the marquess, frowning at his brother.

"But I do, indeed, Lord Worcester," said Alethea with a smile. "I am fond of bottle-headed flummery."

The marquess raised his eyebrows at her and then turned again to his brother. "Well, sit down and have some tea," he said gruffly.

"I hear and obey, my lord brother," said Edward, taking a seat in a chair across from Worcester and Alethea. Prudence poured him a cup of tea and handed it to him.

"We have so much to tell you, Ned," said Prudence. "A good many things have happened. I would have written, but I thought you would be here soon."

"Yes, you were rather late in coming," said the marquess, eyeing his brother with disapproval.

"Well, there was one thing and then another. It was very hard to leave London. But I'm glad to be here, curse of the Beauchamps or no. Oh, I shouldn't have mentioned it. I don't want to upset Pru."

"I know all about it," said Prudence with a smile.

"And you think it nonsense," said Edward.

"Not at all," replied Prudence. "It was very real. I believe it was the curse that made Geoffrey so gravely ill."

"You were gravely ill?" said Edward, startled at this admission.

"Prudence exaggerates," said Worcester.

"I do not exaggerate," said Prudence. "If it hadn't been for Alethea, I don't know what I might have done. Miss Brandon came to our aid. I believe we owe Geoffrey's recovery to her."

"Then I must thank you with all my heart, Miss Brandon," said Edward.

"I wasn't at death's door, I assure you," said Worcester, "but I will admit Miss Brandon's potions did me good."

"I was very worried about him, Ned," said Prudence. "I thanked Providence for Alethea and also for Dr. Chandler. He is a wonderful physician. He is also very kind. He gave me Poppet."

"Poppet?" said Edward.

"Here she is now. Come here, my darling Poppet."

Edward turned to see the small gray striped cat come into the room. "A cat?" He looked over at his brother. "I thought you detested cats, Geoffrey."

"I do."

"Geoffrey!" cried Prudence.

"I'm sure his lordship doesn't detest Poppet," said Alethea, casting a mischievous look at the marquess.

"No, I love her dearly," said Worcester.

Alethea laughed. "There is no need to go so far, my lord."

Poppet walked over to Prudence and jumped up into her lap. "Isn't she wonderful, Ned?" said Prudence, stroking the animal's soft fur.

"She is a very handsome cat," said Edward. "It seems you have had a very interesting time here at Hartwood."

"Yes, we have had a most interesting time," said Prudence.

"It appears as though you've had much more excitement than I've had in town. So you like it here at Hartwood, do you, Prudence?"

"Oh, very much. Of course, I was very much afraid to be here until Alethea removed the curse. Now it is gone, and we have nothing to fear, thanks to Alethea."

"You removed the curse?" said Edward, taking up his teacup and smiling at Alethea. "First you save my brother and then you remove the family curse. Are you some sort of sorceress, Miss Brandon?"

Alethea smiled in return. "No, I am no sorceress, Lord Edward."

"Then how did you lift the curse?"

"I make a study of such things," said Alethea, "and I am also a descendant of the lady who placed the curse on your ancestors. I was, therefore, able to lift it."

"This is truly remarkable," said Edward with a grin. "I must say I'm very much relieved. I wasn't eager to stay here with the curse of the Beauchamps and all that. But now it appears I'm perfectly safe. I thank Providence and Miss Brandon for my good fortune." He cast a grateful look at Alethea, who smiled in return

Noting that Alethea seemed to be quite charmed by his brother, Worcester was mildly irritated with Edward. His brother had an ease in talking to ladies, which the marquess had always envied. And Worcester considered Edward a good deal better-looking than he was himself. His brother's charm made the marquess seem stiff and awkward in comparison.

"I am happy that the curse of the Beauchamps is a thing of the past," said Alethea.

"But how did the curse originate?" said Edward. "I couldn't remember. My Aunt Charlotte wasn't quite sure either. I wrote asking her about it and she was rather vague. But she was quite clear in saying that we shouldn't attempt to stay at Hartwood."

"I pray you don't have Miss Brandon tell the story," said Worcester. "I've heard quite enough about it and I don't wish to be reminded of the treachery of our ancestor."

"Treachery? Oh, you must tell me, Miss Brandon."

"Indeed, I must, Lord Worcester," said Alethea, smiling mischievously at the marquess. "I shall be brief. Your perfidious ancestor, the first marquess, took a fancy to Hartwood, which was owned by my illustrious and virtuous ancestor. The first marquess, a certain Geoffrey Beauchamp, conspired to have my ancestor arrested for treason so that he might have Hartwood."

"And the poor man was beheaded in the Tower," said Prudence.

"Oh dear," said Edward.

"But it was a long time ago and there is no point in holding a grudge. So I removed the curse."

"That was dashed good of you, Miss Brandon," said Edward with a bright smile. "Don't you think it dashed good of her, Geoffrey?"

"I do so indeed."

"Well, I think it quite noble of you, Miss Brandon," said Edward. "Indeed, I have an idea. Why don't you return Hartwood to her, Geoffrey?"

"That is a good idea," said Prudence with a laugh.

"Indeed, it is not," said Alethea. "I can scarcely manage Crow's Nest Cottage. Hartwood is far too grand for me, I assure you, Lord Edward. No, the Beauchamps are welcome to it. But I'm glad you are here, for the house has been too long empty. It's time someone came to stay."

"Now that I know I won't be chased by ghosts, I shall be happy to stay here," said Edward. "I only wish I'd come earlier." He looked at his brother. "When will your guests arrive, Geoffrey?"

"I expect the Duke and Duchess of Cranworth the day after tomorrow. Feversham will accompany them."

At the mention of Feversham's name, Alethea saw a shadow cross Prudence's face. Her young friend had been looking happy and animated, but now she grew solemn.

"And when will Lady Catherine arrive?" asked Edward.

Worcester frowned slightly. "She and her parents are expected the day after tomorrow as well."

"I am sure it will be very nice to have company," said Alethea. "Hartwood is such a large house. It needs a good many people to fill it. And, Lord Edward, there is to be a ball here."

"A ball? Good God! Geoffrey, you astound me."

"I don't see what's so astonishing," said Worcester, regarding his brother with disapproval. "Why shouldn't I have a ball to meet the local society?"

"I have no argument with your doing so," said Edward. "No,

indeed, I think it quite splendid of you. It's only that I thought you detested balls."

"They are necessary at times," returned Worcester.

"It will be very exciting attending a ball here," said Alethea. "Indeed, the invitations were just sent. I know that everyone will talk of nothing else. And when the word is passed about all the noble company staying at Hartwood, the county will be in an uproar. It will be a very good thing for our local dressmakers, I must say."

They all laughed and the conversation continued about the ball.

Chapter 17

Alethea enjoyed her dinner that evening at Hartwood, since she found Lord Edward very amusing. He entertained them with droll stories about people he knew, and Alethea and Prudence laughed heartily. Edward was also very interested in Hartwood and the surrounding area and he asked Alethea a good many questions about local society.

Worcester remained fairly quiet, venturing a comment now and again, but he was far overshadowed by his gregarious younger brother. When the evening ended, Alethea was sent home in Worcester's carriage.

The following afternoon she stayed in the library, working diligently on her book, with Nelson sleeping on the rug in front of her desk. She accomplished a good deal despite the fact that she occasionally found her mind wandering back to Hartwood. Alethea thought of Worcester and how different he was from Lord Edward. Yet for all of the marquess's obvious faults, there was something about him that she liked. Indeed, she had, of late, realized that she was feeling a decided attraction to him.

Her musings were interrupted by Molly, who entered the library. "Beg your pardon, miss, but Mrs. Truscott is here. She is waiting in the drawing room."

Hurrying to join her aunt, Alethea greeted her warmly. "Aunt Elizabeth, how good to see you."

"Good morning, my dear. And there is Nelson. Good day to you, sir." Nelson rose up and wagged his tail.

As Alethea took a seat on the sofa, Elizabeth pulled a piece of paper from her reticule, and waved it at her niece. "I must say I was very much astonished to find this in the post this morning.

An invitation to a ball at Hartwood! And if I'm not mistaken, the hand that addressed this is yours."

"I confess I did address some of the invitations. Poor Lady Prudence sprained her wrist so Mrs. Graham and I helped her with them. I'm sure the invitations will cause a sensation."

"My dear girl, no one is talking of anything else. Since Worcester arrived, the town has been abuzz. When I heard that you had been staying at Hartwood, I was quite astounded. I do think you might have called on me to tell me about it."

"But I have been so occupied, Aunt, with being at Hartwood and working on my book."

"A short note would have sufficed to tell me that you had become acquainted with Lord Worcester and his sister," said Elizabeth. "Numerous callers have asked me what you think of them, and you can imagine my embarrassment when I must admit I know nothing of the subject."

"I am sorry," said Alethea, "but I've been so frightfully busy."

"Alethea Brandon, that is no excuse. You are apparently the only person in the county who has become acquainted with the marquess and his sister. Dr. Chandler has told me that you are on quite intimate terms with Lady Prudence and that she is an enchanting creature. Now you must tell me some news so that I will have something to say when I'm asked."

"Very well, I was summoned to Hartwood when Lord Worcester was very ill and Robert was away. I gave him some of my herbal medicine to help bring down his fever. Fortunately, he recovered rapidly.

"I did have the opportunity to become friendly with Lady Prudence. I like her very much. She's a lovely person, not in the least grand. Oh, I can tell you that I met Lord Worcester's younger brother, Lord Edward. He arrived yesterday."

"Oh, good, I hadn't heard of this," said Elizabeth, happy to have some tidbits of news she could relate to her friends. "What is he like?"

"Quite charming and very handsome. He has fair hair like his sister, and I shouldn't think he is much older than one-and-twenty. Yes, I daresay all of the young ladies in the area will find Lord Edward very dashing. I liked him very much. He is a very amiable gentleman."

"I do hope he'll be at the ball. I'd very much like to meet him."

"Yes, he'll certainly be there. The marquess has commanded

him to stay and assist with his guests. There are several titled ladies and gentleman who will soon arrive at Hartwood, including the Duke and Duchess of Cranworth."

"Indeed?" said Elizabeth, quite thrilled at the prospect of a duke and duchess in the vicinity.

"Yes, and there are others. Let me see. I believe there was the Earl of Huntingdon and Lady Huntingdon and their daughter."

"You cannot mean Lady Catherine!" cried Elizabeth.

"Yes, I believe that was her name. Do you know her?"

"Know her? I wish I could say I did. I saw Lady Catherine Percy in town last Season. She is considered the most beautiful girl in the kingdom. They say she had all manner of marriage proposals, but thus far hasn't accepted any of them. I can scarcely wait to tell Lady Middlebury about this. To think that such illustrious company will be at Hartwood."

"Yes, it is rather overwhelming," said Alethea with a sardonic smile. "I do hope we will all be able to stand the strain of meeting them."

Elizabeth didn't seem to hear her. "I wonder what I should wear to the ball. We'll all appear dowdy beside such personages."

"You will look splendid as always," said Alethea, who knew very well that her aunt had a good many fashionable ball gowns from which to choose. She smiled at her aunt. "I shall look dowdy, but I daresay I don't very much care."

"Alethea," said her aunt, casting a severe look at her wayward niece, "you mustn't be flippant. Of course you must care how you dress among such company. You must have a new gown made."

"I have neither the time nor inclination for new gowns, Aunt," said Alethea. "And with all of these grand people about, I don't think anyone will be looking at me. Oh, yes, there is one other gentleman arriving at Hartwood. Lord Feversham."

"Feversham!" cried Elizabeth. "Not Viscount Feversham?"

Alethea shrugged. "I'm sure I don't know. But who is this Viscount Feversham?"

"Who is he? You mean you haven't heard of him?"

"I have not."

Elizabeth shook her head. "Lord Feversham is one of the leading gentlemen of society. He is an intimate of the Prince Regent's. He is a consummate man of fashion. Although I've never met him, I did see him at Vauxhall Gardens and I must say there isn't a more handsome and elegant man in all of England. I'm quite amazed that you are unfamiliar with his name."

"Alas, my dear aunt, my knowledge of fashionable people is quite lamentable. I must say I would have preferred not knowing how celebrated and brilliant Lord Worcester's guests will be. Now I shall simply quake upon meeting them. Perhaps I shan't attend this ball."

Elizabeth appeared horrified. "You must attend it. Everyone is relying on you to introduce them to Worcester and his family. And while you say you don't want a new gown, I believe you are only gammoning me. I shall see you have a new dress. Indeed, I'll stop at Mrs. Tate's on my way home and see if she has any ideas. We can't have you looking like a provincial miss among such elite society."

Although Alethea protested again that she didn't need a new gown, her aunt would have none of it. Yet, eager to spread the news, Elizabeth didn't have time to argue. A short time later, Alethea's aunt took her leave.

While Alethea had been conversing with her aunt, Prudence and Edward climbed into a carriage and proceeded away from Hartwood. Earlier that day Prudence had expressed her desire to call upon Miss Brandon at Crow's Nest Cottage, and Edward had volunteered to escort her there.

Worcester, who would have liked to accompany them, had, unfortunately, made other plans. He had promised to meet with some of his tenants that afternoon, and although he could have easily put off the appointment, he didn't want to appear overeager to visit Miss Brandon.

Edward and Prudence had, therefore, set off without their elder brother. Seated beside Edward, Prudence looked over at him. "I'm so glad you are here, Ned."

"I must admit I wasn't altogether happy to leave London, but I missed you, of course. And now that I've seen Hartwood, I think it a dashed interesting place even without a curse on it. And I do like your Miss Brandon. She's very charming."

"I like her very much," said Prudence. "And you'll love Crow's Nest Cottage. The sea stretches before you and one can look out forever. And there are so many interesting things at Miss Brandon's home. Odd things, actually."

"Odd things?"

"Statues and masks from foreign places. There is a strange wooden carving from the Hawaiian Islands. And a god from India. I forget which one, but Alethea can tell you all about him. He has a good many arms."

"Well, I shall be eager to see these odd things," said Edward in reply. He smiled at her for a moment before continuing. "Prudence, I hope Geoffrey hasn't been in a bad temper while you've been at Hartwood."

"Why, no," said Prudence, "not at all. Of course, I was so worried when he was ill. If Alethea hadn't come, I don't know what I would have done. I like Hartwood very much, but I'm not looking forward to our guests."

"You mean Feversham."

Prudence's frown grew deeper. "Yes," she said softly.

"Well, I must say that I cannot understand Geoffrey foisting that fellow on you. Why he has got it into his head that Feversham is the man for you is quite incomprehensible. You don't wish to marry him, do you?"

Prudence shook her head glumly. "I don't, Ned, but Geoffrey says I must marry someone." She looked over at her brother. "Why must I marry? Miss Brandon isn't married and she is very happy. I wish Geoffrey would allow me to do as I please. If he believes it is so necessary to marry, why doesn't he take a wife?"

"My dear Pru, it seems he has every intention of doing so."

"What?" Prudence regarded her brother in surprise. "What do you mean, Ned?"

"Why, I thought he would have told you. He is planning to marry Lady Catherine Percy."

Prudence's blue eyes opened wide in surprise. "Lady Catherine?"

"Yes, that's why he's invited them here. He expects to discuss the marriage settlement with Huntingdon. And if the lady accepts him, Geoffrey will soon be wed."

"But he never said a word to me about her. I didn't even know that he liked her."

"Oh, I can't say whether he likes her or not," said Edward. "Affection has no place in such marriages according to our dear brother. Marriages among the great families aren't the same as those among lesser mortals."

"But will Lady Catherine accept Geoffrey? She has so many suitors."

"I fancy our brother's rank and fortune will suit the lady well enough."

Prudence sat for a moment trying to digest this surprising news. That her brother planned to marry Lady Catherine seemed fantastic. She was well acquainted with the lady. They attended all the same social functions and had often found themselves thrown together.

Catherine was one of the great beauties of society. Small and dainty, she had features of classical perfection, a lovely figure, and thick, chestnut hair that was always perfectly coifed. Although Catherine could be a very charming young woman, Prudence knew her well enough to know she was a mean-spirited creature who delighted in making sport of others.

Prudence had often heard Catherine laugh and say cutting remarks about people. In fact, she was widely popular for this trait. A sensitive soul, Prudence always sympathized with those who were the objects of Catherine's scorn. It was hard for her to believe that her brother would choose to make Catherine Percy his wife.

"I see you aren't very pleased at the prospect of Lady Catherine for our sister-in-law."

"I cannot imagine that they will be happy," said Prudence. "Just as I cannot imagine that I could be happy married to Feversham. I suppose there will be some satisfaction in knowing that Geoffrey will be as miserable as I shall be."

"Poor Pru," said Edward, reaching over to take her hand, "but don't worry, if you don't want to marry Feversham, you must stand firm. You must tell Geoffrey you won't have him."

"I have said I didn't wish to marry him, but he doesn't care."

Edward nodded gravely. "Sometimes I think that Geoffrey would like to have all of us unhappy."

"All of us? You as well?"

Her brother appeared thoughtful. "I shall tell you something, Pru, but you must swear that you'll not tell Geoffrey."

"Of course, I won't tell him, Ned. What is it? Is something wrong?"

"In some ways it's quite wonderful. You see, I've fallen in love."

"What!" cried Prudence. "With whom?"

"I met the most wonderful girl. Her name is Thomasina Whitfield."

"But, Ned, that is splendid."

Edward shook his head. "Geoffrey wouldn't think so. He has told me many times that I'm too young to marry. And when he feels I'm old enough to take a bride, he seems to think that he must have a hand in choosing her for me. You see, Pru, I don't think our noble brother will approve of Miss Whitfield. Her father is in trade. He owns a brewery."

"Oh dear," said Prudence.

"The Whitfields are very wealthy, but I daresay that won't signify in the least with Geoffrey."

"What will you do?"

"I don't know, Pru, but I shan't give up Thomasina. We love each other very much. I intend to marry her and if I can't have Geoffrey's blessing, then so be it. I know that he'll cut me off without a penny. Thomasina said she doesn't care and that we'll have enough from her father, but I don't like the idea of being estranged from Geoffrey."

Prudence squeezed her brother's hand sympathetically as the carriage continued on toward Crow's Nest Cottage.

Chapter 18

When Molly appeared at the door of the library at Crow's Nest Cottage, Alethea looked up from her writing. "I pray you won't tell me there are more callers, Molly."

"But there are, miss," said the servant. "I know you didn't wish to be disturbed, but 'tis Lady Prudence and a young gentleman called Lord Edward."

"Oh," said Alethea, "I shall be glad to see them. But isn't Lord Worcester with them?"

"No, miss," said Molly.

Noticing the curious look her maid was directing at her, she regretted the question. Alethea rose from the desk. "Would you see about tea? I'm sure they'll wish to stay."

"Very good, miss."

When Alethea joined her guests in the drawing room, she smiled to find Prudence and Edward examining the statue of the Hindu god. "Good afternoon. I see you are making Lord Shiva's acquaintance, Lord Edward."

"I have indeed, Miss Brandon," said Edward. "He is a very fine fellow indeed. I daresay all those arms are quite handy, but it would give one's tailor fits."

Alethea laughed. "Yes, I'm sure you're right."

"Do forgive us for barging in on you, Alethea," said Prudence. "I know you must work on your book."

"I'm nearly finished. I have only the chapter on the use of herbs in folklore, witches' potions, and that sort of thing."

"Oh," cried Prudence, "I forgot to bring the book you left at Hartwood. The one on spells. You probably need it."

"No, I have my notes. I'm in no hurry to have it back. Perhaps you and Lord Edward will want to read it."

Edward laughed. "I must say a book on witches' spells sounds rather fascinating, but don't you think it unwise to leave such a book with my sister? She's probably casting spells and getting into all sorts of mischief."

They all laughed. "But where is Nelson?" said Prudence.

"I'm afraid he isn't here. One of the servants has taken him out for exercise."

"I am disappointed at not seeing him," said Edward. "Pru tells me he's a wonderful dog."

"Ned adores dogs," said Prudence.

"Then you are obviously a man of good judgment, Lord Edward," said Alethea with a smile.

"I told Ned all about the fascinating things you have here, Alethea."

"I'm happy to show them to you." Alethea set about taking her guests around the house, pointing out the various interesting artifacts that her grandfather and father had brought back from their world travels.

Since the weather was very good, they proceeded outside, where they walked down the path that led to the sea. Since the tide was out, there was a wide expanse of sand and they walked along, watching the waves go in and out. "I can see why you love it here, Miss Brandon," said Edward. "I've never seen a more perfect spot."

"It is wonderful," said Prudence, looking out at the sea.

"I've ordered tea," said Alethea. "I hope you'll stay."

Both Prudence and Edward seemed more than happy to accept this invitation and the three of them started back. They had no sooner begun walking when a man appeared, coming down the path from the house.

"It's Dr. Chandler," cried Prudence. Alethea thought she detected a note of eagerness in her voice.

"What a lovely day," said Chandler, striding toward them. Knowing the doctor's feelings toward Prudence, Alethea watched him intently as he bowed to that lady.

"Dr. Chandler," said Prudence, nodding to him.

Alethea thought Chandler was doing a good job of hiding his feelings. He didn't appear in the least ill at ease. "I was coming past on my way from a patient and thought I'd stop. What good luck to find you here, Lady Prudence. And how is that wrist of yours?"

"Much better, sir," said Prudence, smiling at him.

When Chandler eyed Edward with a questioning gaze, Alethea hurried to make the introduction. "You haven't met Lord Edward, Robert. Lord Edward, may I present Dr. Chandler? Robert, this is Lord Edward Beauchamp. He is Lady Prudence's brother."

This information seemed to please Chandler, who smiled at Edward. Both gentlemen nodded politely to each other and murmured that they were extremely pleased to make the other's acquaintance. "I have heard a good deal about you, Doctor, from my sister," said Edward. "My sister thinks you an excellent physician, sir."

"And I think her an excellent patient," said Chandler.

"Lady Prudence and Lord Edward are staying to tea, Robert," said Alethea. "Perhaps you'd like to stay as well."

"I should like nothing better," replied the physician. The four of them started up the path back to the house. At one steep section, Chandler took Prudence's arm and assisted her up.

When they all sat down in the drawing room, Molly brought tea and soon Alethea was pouring steaming cups for her guests. Chandler was pleased to find Edward such a contrast with his elder brother.

As Alethea watched them talking, she remembered how Worcester had been so disdainful of the doctor. The marquess would never condescend to converse with so ordinary a person. Indeed, thought Alethea, Worcester fell very short when compared to his brother.

"And will you be attending the ball, Dr. Chandler?" said Prudence.

"Yes, I'm looking forward to it," he said.

"I shall be glad of seeing a friendly face," said Prudence. "I know so few people here."

"I'm sure everyone will be eager to meet you," said Chandler, regarding her with an expression that made Alethea rather uneasy. They talked of the upcoming ball for a time and then a number of other subjects.

Time passed very quickly. When Chandler finally noticed the clock, he hurriedly rose to take his leave. He had stayed far longer than he intended. After bowing to the ladies, he exited the room.

"He's a likeable fellow," said Edward, taking up another tea-cake and nibbling on it.

"Yes, he is," said Alethea. "I shall miss him very much when he goes to London."

"He's going to London?" said Prudence.

Alethea nodded. "He will join his uncle's medical practice in town. I'm sure he will do very well there, but I'll miss him terribly. He's a very dear friend." Smiling, she changed the subject. "Will your guests be coming soon?"

"Yes, they are expected tomorrow," said Edward.

"When I told my aunt that a duke and duchess were to stay at Hartwood, she was very impressed," said Alethea. "And then when I told her the names of the other guests, she was quite astonished at their brilliance. She could scarcely wait to tell all her friends and acquaintances. I'm so very ignorant of society that I had no idea you were having such illustrious company. I'd never heard of Lady Catherine Percy. My aunt informs me that she is a personage of great consequence."

"She has that opinion of herself," said Edward dryly. "Whether the judges of history regard her in such a light remains to be seen."

Alethea laughed. "Well, I shall be very eager to see Lady Catherine. My aunt says she is a great beauty."

"She is beautiful," said Prudence. "Perhaps that is why my brother wishes to marry her."

Alethea looked at Edward in surprise. "You wish to marry Lady Catherine?"

A laugh escaped him. "Good God, no. It's my brother Worcester who wishes to marry her."

The remark stunned Alethea. Worcester was planning to marry Lady Catherine? Although rather taken aback, Alethea nevertheless managed to maintain her composure. "Indeed?"

"I was surprised as well, Alethea," said Prudence. "Edward only just told me on the way here. I had no idea that Geoffrey was thinking of marriage. He never said a word to me about it. If I weren't such a slowtop, I might have guessed why he had invited Lord and Lady Huntingdon and Lady Catherine."

"My aunt said that Lady Catherine is a much sought after lady," said Alethea, still trying to recover from the surprising news.

"Oh, yes," said Edward, smiling at his sister. "Nearly as sought after as Pru."

"What nonsense," said Prudence. "She is far prettier than I am."

"Not in my opinion," said Edward.

"But you are prejudiced," said Prudence, smiling at her brother.

At that moment the sound of a crow's harsh call made them turn toward the window. Hector appeared on the windowsill. The shiny black bird hesitated only a moment before flying into the room. To Edward's and Prudence's astonishment the crow snatched the tea-cake out of Edward's hand before flying back out the window and vanishing from sight.

"Oh, I'm so sorry," cried Alethea. "Hector's manners aren't what they should be."

Edward laughed. "Why, the impudent rascal!"

"He is that," said Alethea. "I do apologize."

"Don't apologize, Miss Brandon," said Edward. "It isn't every day that a bird steals the food from my hand. Prudence told me about your pet."

"I think Hector is wonderful," said Prudence.

"Yes, but he can also be a nuisance," said Alethea. They talked about Alethea's mischievous crow for some time until the clock on the mantel chimed the hour.

"Five o'clock, Pru," said Edward. "We'd better take our leave of Miss Brandon. We have taken too much of her time."

"I've enjoyed it so very much," said Alethea. "You must come again."

"Yes, we will," said Prudence, rising reluctantly from her chair to take her leave. "Will you dine with us on Thursday?"

"Yes, that would be lovely," said Alethea. "But I must say I am rather daunted by the prospect of your company. I've never spoken to a duke before."

"Well, my brother is far grander than the Duke of Cranworth, I assure you," said Edward, "and I saw no sign of your shrinking before him. The only thing you need to fear, Miss Brandon, is being dangerously bored should you have the misfortune to be seated beside Huntingdon."

They all laughed, and then Prudence and Edward made their farewells and left Crow's Nest Cottage. When they were gone, Alethea sat down in the drawing room. So Worcester was planning to be married. For some unaccountable reason the idea dismayed her. Walking to the window, she frowned as the carriage containing Edward and Prudence vanished from sight.

Chapter 19

Worcester stood in the drawing room at Hartwood, gazing out the window at the park that stretched from the house. The grass was a brilliant green and leaves were starting to appear on the shrubs and trees that dotted the landscape.

It looked as if it would be a splendid day. The early-morning sun was shining brightly on the dew-covered grass and a pleasant breeze was blowing in through the open window.

Folding his arms across his chest, Worcester continued to stare out at the picturesque grounds of the estate. He thought of Alethea and wondered what she was doing at that moment.

Perhaps she was still sleeping, he decided. A picture of Alethea lying in her bed came to his mind. He envisioned her attired in a nightdress, her wonderful dark hair disheveled about her face.

"My lord?"

Shaken from his reverie, the marquess turned to see his housekeeper. "Yes, Mrs. Graham?"

"There will be a good deal of work going on this morning. I hope it won't disturb your lordship."

"No, certainly not," replied Worcester. When he had left his room, he had noted that a number of servants were about, busily dusting and polishing. "I know there are many final preparations to be made. I trust all will be in readiness for our guests' arrival."

"Yes, indeed, my lord," said Mrs. Graham.

"You and Talbot have done a fine job on short notice, Mrs. Graham," said the marquess. "All appears in good order."

The housekeeper beamed at the praise, for Worcester didn't hand out compliments lightly. "Thank you, my lord. All the servants are very excited at having such distinguished company. They will do their best to see that all goes smoothly."

"I'm sure they will," said Worcester absently, for his mind had once again wandered to Alethea.

"Then I shan't bother your lordship any further," said the housekeeper, bobbing a curtsy and leaving her master to his solitary musings.

Feeling restless, Worcester left the room and went outside. There he strode down the garden path for a short distance. He stopped in front of the large fountain that stood in the center of the formal garden.

This was the day that Lady Catherine Percy would arrive. A frown appeared on his lordship's solemn countenance. He felt no sense of eager anticipation at the idea of seeing the young woman who would become the Marchioness of Worcester. On the contrary, he was beginning to have misgivings about the idea.

Reaching into his waistcoat pocket, Worcester pulled out a small object and stared at it for a time. It was a miniature portrait of Lady Catherine. The marquess knew that the tiny picture was an exceedingly good likeness, admirably capturing the lady's renowed beauty. Lady Catherine's father, the Earl of Huntingdon, had given it to Worcester when they had first discussed the marriage settlement.

At that time the earl had expressed his great happiness at the idea of his daughter wedding the marquess. After all, the union would bring together two of the wealthiest and most powerful families in the land. And besides that, Lord Huntingdon had been a very close friend of Worcester's father. The thought of his daughter marrying his dear friend's son had seemed wonderful indeed.

Worcester put the miniature back into his pocket. He found himself thinking that if Alethea Brandon could magically change places with Catherine Percy, he would be very pleased at the idea of marriage. The notion of going to bed with her each night was very appealing.

The marquess frowned. He had lately been devoting far too much time to ungentlemanly thoughts about Alethea. He must rid himself of them, he told himself resolutely. After all, there was no point in dwelling on what could never be.

Worcester remembered how at the previous night's dinner his brother had annoyed him by talking on and on about Alethea and her house by the sea. Edward had said she was "the most clever, interesting female in the world and dashed pretty in the bargain."

His brother had further irritated the marquess by speaking of Dr. Chandler. According to Edward, Chandler seemed "a fine fellow and very much the gentleman."

"Good morning, Geoffrey," called a cheerful voice from the direction of the house.

Worcester looked over to see his brother approaching. "Good morning, Ned."

"You're up and about early," said Edward, smiling cheerfully. "It's a bang-up fine day, isn't it?"

"Yes," said the marquess.

"I say, Geoffrey, would you join me in a ride after breakfast? Prudence is very eager to get a bit of exercise as well. I thought we could ride over to Crow's Nest Cottage and see Miss Brandon. We'd be back well in time to greet your guests."

Worcester frowned. "You only just visited her yesterday afternoon. I don't see any reason to bother Miss Brandon at such an hour. She has better things to do than entertain idle fellows like you."

Edward's pale eyebrows arched in amusement. "Indeed? Why, I believe she would enjoy seeing us. She's very fond of Prudence."

"That may be, but she has work to do. She's an artist and an author. I'll not have her disturbed. And I don't want you to be riding off very far. One cannot be sure when the guests may arrive. No, you will stay nearby. If you're in need of exercise, I suggest a turn around the garden."

"My, you are cross this morning, my dear brother," said Edward. "Very well, I shall stay here. I suppose we'll be seeing Miss Brandon at dinner tomorrow evening in any case."

"What?" said Worcester.

"Tomorrow is Thursday and Miss Brandon has been invited for dinner. Didn't you remember?"

"I know nothing about that," said Worcester testily. "No one mentioned it last night."

"Well, Prudence asked her to come when we called on her, and she accepted."

Worcester frowned. "I don't think Prudence should offer invitations without my leave."

"What? Prudence can't even invite someone to dinner?"

"She should have consulted me," replied the marquess. "I don't believe Miss Brandon will be comfortable with our guests."

"What nonsense," said Edward. "Miss Brandon will do well in any company. Good heavens, don't you like her?"

"I neither like nor dislike her," said Worcester, his face reddening a bit. "And I shall ask you to cease speaking of her to me. Now I suggest you go in to breakfast."

Surprised at his brother's agitated response, Edward regarded him strangely for a moment. "Are you having breakfast?"

"I'm not hungry," said the marquess. "You go on."

"Very well," said Edward. As he turned to walk back toward the house, he reflected that his brother was behaving very strangely.

Lady Catherine Percy sat back on the plush leather seats of the lumbering coach and frowned at her parents, who were seated across from her. Traveling could be so tiresome, she thought as she turned her gaze to the window.

There wasn't much to see along the way to the Marquess of Worcester's estate. There were fields and stone walls and cows and sheep, as well as assorted country bumpkins hanging about dreary villages. Catherine frowned again. The road had been rough and the accommodations at the inn where they had stayed the night appalling. And when they arrived at Hartwood, they would find themselves in an out-of-the-way country house with little to amuse them.

Catherine ran her finger along the edge of the carriage window. She wasn't looking forward to her stay at Hartwood. Her parents seemed very enthusiastic about the visit, for Lord and Lady Huntingdon were desirous of concluding the marriage negotiations and seeing their daughter betrothed.

Unlike her parents, Catherine wasn't so eager to become engaged. Having been one of the most sought-after girls in town and having received numerous offers of marriage, she wasn't sure she was right in choosing Worcester. He was terribly rich, of course, and she conceded that he wasn't bad-looking. Yet, he wasn't at all dashing and many of her stylish friends thought him very dull.

Still, she supposed he would do as well as any of the other prospects and her parents were set on the match. And once she was married and had done her duty in providing him an heir, Catherine reasoned that she could do as she pleased. The other married ladies of society did so, having affairs and enjoying themselves while their husbands looked the other way.

Catherine thought Worcester the sort of man who wouldn't

mind what she did. He was such a cold fish and appeared devoid of passion. She doubted that he would make many demands on her and as long as he would allow her plenty of money, she would bear up well enough.

"I do hope we'll soon be there," said Lady Huntingdon. A formidable woman in her midforties, she had been a great beauty in her day. She had grown rather stout and her dark hair was graying, but she was still considered to be a handsome woman. A lady of fashion, she devoted a good amount of time and money to her stylish wardrobe. She sat there resplendent in a canary yellow pelisse and matching bonnet.

"It isn't far now," said Huntingdon, who was a distinguished-looking man, lean and well dressed. Nearly fifty, he had gray hair and handsome features. "Yes, I daresay we'll be there very soon."

"I do hope so," said Catherine in a languid voice. "It seems we have been traveling forever."

She had scarcely made this comment when the carriage turned into a lane. "We must be nearly there," said the earl, looking out the window. The vehicle continued along, passing through a wooded area. When they had gone beyond the trees, Hartwood came into view. "There it is," said Huntingdon.

Lady Huntingdon cast a critical gaze at the house. "Why, it is rather insignificant, isn't it? No wonder Worcester never comes here."

Catherine looked at the house as they approached. "It isn't very well situated, is it?"

"No, it isn't," replied her mother, continuing to gaze at the house. "It reminds me of that wretched place where my cousin George lives. Huntingdon, don't you think it is very like Poplar Grove?"

"It is nothing like it," said the earl, who was a rather sullen fellow who enjoyed disagreeing with his wife.

"I should say it is," persisted her ladyship. "I shall never forget the fortnight we spent there. Oh, what dreadful food."

"I don't remember the food being dreadful at all," said Huntingdon.

Lady Huntingdon debated the matter with her husband as the carriage made its way up the gravel drive to the entrance of Hartwood. As the visitors climbed down from their vehicle, Worcester, Prudence, and Edward came out to greet them.

After welcoming his guests, the marquess ushered them inside, where they were quickly escorted to their rooms to relax until tea. After a time, the Huntingdons joined their hosts in the drawing room.

"We are so glad to be here," said Lady Huntingdon, taking a seat upon the sofa. Lady Catherine sat down beside her. She was elegant in a pale blue muslin dress with long sleeves and a high ruffed collar.

"I hope the journey wasn't too fatiguing," said Worcester.

"It did seem a long way," said Lady Huntingdon. "Of course, we were quite comfortable in Huntingdon's new carriage."

"Damned fine coach, that," said Huntingdon. "Best sprung vehicle I've ever owned. You must take a turn in it, Worcester. It was made by Bingham, of course. I'd never have one made by any other carriage maker. You must see the curricle he made for me. What a beauty it is and very fast. I've bested any challenger in that one, I have."

Worcester managed a civil smile. His prospective father-in-law had what was in the marquess's view an unhealthy preoccupation with racing curricles. Worcester had never liked to dash about in the madcap way favored by so many aristocratic gentlemen.

"Pity you and Feversham won't have your curricles," said Edward. "He enjoys racing as well."

Huntingdon frowned. "Feversham," he muttered. "Is that popinjay here?"

"Not yet," said Worcester, surprised at the older man's tone.

"He bought a horse from under my nose," said Huntingdon. "That mare of Rutherford's. Black Star out of May Queen. You know the one I mean."

Since Worcester had no idea what the earl was talking about, he made no reply. "Oh, yes," said Edward. "I've seen Feversham riding her in the park. What a beauty."

Huntingdon scowled. "I wanted that animal and Feversham knew it."

"Oh, what does it signify?" said Lady Huntingdon. "Such a fuss to be made over a horse."

"Yes, Father," said Catherine, "you'll find another. I pray you won't go on about it when Feversham arrives."

At that moment a diversion appeared in the form of Poppet. The small gray cat crept silently into the room. Seeing Prudence, she hurried over to her mistress and jumped into her lap.

"Oh dear, a cat," said Lady Huntingdon, frowning at the animal.

"Prudence is very fond of little Poppet," said Edward cheerfully.

"While cats may be useful for catching mice, I don't favor making pets of them," said the countess.

"If the girl likes the cat, why shouldn't she make a pet of it?" said Huntingdon.

Catherine pulled a silk handkerchief from her sleeve and sneezed into it. She sneezed again. "It's the cat," she said. "They make me sneeze."

Prudence regarded her in alarm. "Oh, I am sorry," she said.

"You had best take the cat away, Prudence," said Worcester, frowning at his sister.

"Yes, of course," said Prudence, clutching Poppet to her as she rose from her chair. "I shall take her away so she won't bother you." Prudence hastily retreated from the room.

"Such a dear, sweet girl," said Lady Huntingdon. "And very like her late mother."

"I don't see the resemblance at all," said Huntingdon.

Worcester was glad when the servants arrived with tea.

Although Lady Catherine could find a great deal of fault with a number of things at Hartwood, she found nothing to complain about with the delicious repast that had been prepared for tea. The conversation at first centered on such pleasantries as the weather and how everyone was feeling. It then shifted to the earl's favorite subject, fox hunting, a passion shared by Edward and Lady Catherine.

Worcester, who was indifferent to the sport, thought it a dull topic, but listened politely. Time seemed to go rather slowly and then Talbot appeared. "My lord," he said, "the Duke and Duchess of Cranworth are here and Lord Feversham."

"Show them in," said Worcester, rising to his feet.

"Ah, Cranworth," said the earl, "I shall be glad to see him. He can tell you all about riding with the Wexford Hunt, Worcester."

After nodding in reply, Worcester approached the door to the drawing room, where his butler was appearing with the newcomers in tow. The Duke and Duchess of Cranworth strode into the room. The duke was a big, corpulent man who was dressed in a tight-fitting wine-colored coat and ivory pantaloons. More than

sixty years of age and nearly bald, he had a round, ruddy face
with heavy jowls, thick eyebrows, and a large, bulbous nose.

His wife, a plump and pretty woman many years his junior,
was attired in a pelisse of pea green velvet decorated with gold
braid and military-style epaulets. Her bonnet was adorned with
great white ostrich feathers that bobbed when she walked.

While it was obvious by their fine clothes that the duke and
duchess were personages of consequence, they were outshone by
their son, the Viscount Feversham. That gentleman walked into
the room with a regal air not equaled since the Sun King himself
had ruled France more than a century ago.

Feversham was a magnificent figure in his finely crafted coat
of dove gray superfine and gleaming white pantaloons. He wore
coal black Hessian boots polished to a dazzling shine. The viscount's linen was snowy white and his neckcloth artfully tied
about his neck.

Feversham was considered a very handsome man. He had been
blessed with finely chiseled features and dark, curly hair that was
well suited to the Corinthian style favored by society bucks. On
his face he constantly wore a slight smile more akin to a sneer
than an expression of amusement. Ladies thought him very dashing.

Looking at the man whom her brother wished her to marry,
Prudence had a sinking feeling. When he bowed over her hand
and murmured a few polite compliments, she felt her stomach
churning with dread. She could barely say a word to him and was
very glad when Lady Huntingdon began to talk in a loud voice
and all heads turned toward her.

Chapter 20

Thursday morning Alethea set off from her house with a basket on her arm. Now that April had arrived a good many of her medicinal herbs were growing in the woods and it was time to begin to replenish her supplies. Nelson followed after her, but often stopped to investigate the fascinating smells of the forest.

As she walked along, Alethea looked up at the overcast sky. The morning air was cool and she expected that it would rain later in the day.

She sighed. That evening she was expected at Hartwood, but she had begun to wish that she hadn't accepted the dinner invitation. Of course, she was curious about Lady Catherine Percy. She was, likewise, interested in seeing Lord Feversham.

Yet, all in all, she would rather stay at home than spend the evening with a group of fashionable aristocrats who would doubtlessly scorn her for her plain gown. Alethea frowned as she thought about the dress she would be wearing. She had worn it before at Hartwood and hadn't thought too much about it, but now she wished she had something new and fashionable.

Alethea walked off the path and started through the woods, looking carefully at the forest floor for herbs. Spying one of the plants she had been seeking, Alethea let out a triumphant exclamation. "Oh good," she said, temporarily forgetting about her dinner engagement. Stooping down, she cut off some of the herb and placed it into her basket. Then she rose to her feet and continued her search.

Alethea spent two hours wandering about the woods, collecting plants. When she was finished, she started back, making her way to the road. Well pleased with her herbal harvest, she seemed in a better mood. Why should she care about dinner at Hartwood, she asked herself. And why should she fret about her old dress? No, she concluded, she had been a goose to give one moment's thought to the matter.

She continued walking along, swinging her basket merrily and singing. Suddenly the sound of horses approaching made her move to the side of the road and look back. There were five riders, two ladies, and three gentlemen. "Oh blast," muttered Alethea. "Worcester!"

It was indeed Worcester riding on a chestnut horse. She recognized Edward and Prudence. The other lady and gentleman were unknown to her, but as she got a better look at the unknown young woman's face, Alethea was very certain it was Lady Catherine Percy.

The horses were upon her in a few moments and they pulled up beside her. "Miss Brandon!" cried Edward, grinning broadly. "What great good luck finding you. I'd wanted to call on you at Crow's Nest Cottage, but my brother thought we shouldn't bother you." He smiled at Nelson, who was regarding the horses and riders somberly. "This great fellow must be Nelson."

"Good morning, Lord Edward," said Alethea, smiling at him. "Yes, it is Nelson."

"He's a fine dog," said Edward.

"Good morning, Alethea," said Prudence, very pleased to see her friend.

"Miss Brandon," said the marquess, tipping his tall hat.

"My lord," replied Alethea, making a slight curtsy. She then looked at Catherine, who was regarding her appraisingly. Alethea had no doubt that Catherine Percy was the most beautiful woman she had ever seen. She noted her pale, flawless complexion and striking blue eyes. Catherine was wearing a plum-colored riding habit that snugly fit her fine figure. Atop her head was a narrow-brimmed hat set at a rakish angle and trimmed with a veil.

"Lady Catherine," said Worcester, making the introduction, "this is Miss Brandon. Miss Brandon, Lady Catherine Percy."

"How do you do?" said Alethea.

Lady Catherine nodded in a queenly fashion.

"And, Miss Brandon," continued Worcester, "may I present Lord Feversham?"

"My lord," said Alethea.

Feversham eyed her with a look of mild interest and touched the brim of his beaver hat. "Madam," he said.

Alethea tried to appear unconcerned that she was wearing an old spencer with an obviously mended sleeve and a worn straw bonnet she should have parted with long ago. Alethea's skirt was muddy from stooping on the damp ground, and bits of dead leaves clung to it.

Seeing the way Lady Catherine was regarding her friend, Prudence felt some explanation was in order. "Were you looking for plants, Alethea?"

"Yes, Pru," returned Alethea with a bright smile. "And I've had very good luck."

"Alethea knows ever so much about herbs, Lady Catherine," said Prudence. "She uses them for medicine."

"How very interesting," said Lady Catherine, fixing a look of faint disdain upon Alethea. She couldn't imagine why Prudence Beauchamp wished to talk to the unkempt person standing before them. Seeing the mud and leaves on Alethea's skirt, she was appalled. She was also horrified by the enormous dog at her side.

"We shouldn't detain Miss Brandon," said the marquess. "I'm sure she has work to do."

"Yes, I do," said Alethea, meeting his gaze. He was watching her with a noncommittal expression that revealed nothing of what he was thinking.

"We look forward to seeing you this evening," said the marquess.

"Yes, I look forward to it as well, Lord Worcester."

"I should like to send my carriage for you, Miss Brandon."

Her hazel eyes met his gray ones. "That is very kind of you. I'd appreciate that very much."

"Then we'll take our leave of you, Miss Brandon," said the marquess, tipping his hat once again. The other gentlemen followed suit and then the riders continued on down the road. Alethea stood for a moment watching them before continuing on toward Crow's Nest Cottage.

As she walked along, she thought about Lady Catherine. She certainly appeared to be a very grand young lady. Perhaps she would do well as the Marchioness of Worcester. Turning into the path that led to the house, Alethea found herself thinking about Worcester and Catherine. She was sure that the contrast between her and the elegant Lady Catherine wasn't lost on him.

While Alethea pondered the matter, Worcester was considering the difference between the two ladies. Yet, contrary to the conclusion Alethea had reached, the marquess did not find her at all wanting because of the mud on her skirt and her unfashionable clothes. As he rode away, Worcester thought that Alethea had never looked lovelier. In his mind it was Lady Catherine who suffered in comparison.

When they arrived back at Hartwood, Prudence and Lady Catherine went to their rooms to change from their riding habits. Worcester, Edward, and Feversham joined the other guests in the drawing room.

"Did you have a good ride?" asked the duke, addressing his son.

Feversham, who had carefully cultivated an aura of ennui, shrugged. "Good enough, I daresay," he said. "I didn't muddy my boots in any case."

"A fine accomplishment, Feversham," said Edward. "It was an enjoyable ride, your grace. The weather is excellent. You must go out yourself."

"Not I," said the duke. "I'm done with sitting a horse. I prefer a carriage. My bones are too old to be jarred atop a beast."

"I cannot imagine not riding," said Huntingdon, a scornful expression on his face. "I shall certainly wish to take a ride later. I imagine you're enjoying that new mare of yours, Feversham. The black."

Feversham allowed his usual slight smile to widen a tiny bit. "Oh, yes, she's a fine-enough creature. But, in truth, I'm a bit disappointed in her. And if you're interested, I might be persuaded to part with her."

"What?" cried Huntingdon. "You'd sell her now?"

Feversham shrugged. "For the right offer."

Huntingdon regarded him indignantly and Edward found it necessary to step in. "We had the good luck to meet Miss Brandon on our ride."

"Who is this Miss Brandon?" said Lady Huntingdon. "Is she from one of the local families?"

"Yes," said Worcester.

"You will meet her this evening, Lady Huntingdon," said Edward, "for she'll be joining us for dinner."

"I imagine one must become acquainted with some of the local families," said Lady Huntingdon.

"Thus far we have only become acquainted with Miss Brandon," said Worcester.

"And she is very nice," said Edward. "She's such an interesting lady. She and Prudence have become good friends."

"I hardly think Lady Prudence has resided here long enough to have made good friends," said Lady Huntingdon, regarding Edward with disapproval.

"Well, she has, ma'am," said Edward.

"I'm always happy to have another lady in attendance," said the duke, "if she's pretty." He looked at his son. "You've seen her, Feversham. Is she pretty?"

Feversham stood for a moment considering the question. "I don't know, Father. I confess I didn't have a good look at her. She was wearing the most appalling old straw bonnet. Egad, I said to myself, where has the girl found that old thing? And she was carrying a frightful straw basket and then when I saw the mud on her skirt I found myself averting my eyes."

The duke burst into laughter. He found his son a very amusing fellow.

Worcester frowned ominously at Feversham. "Miss Brandon is a most attractive young lady."

"Oh, I don't dispute you, Worcester," replied Feversham, taking his snuffbox from his pocket and flicking it open. "I shall take a good look at her when she arrives for dinner. Then I shall judge."

Worcester frowned again. At that moment Prudence and Lady Catherine entered the room. Having changed from their riding clothes, the two young ladies were attired in elegant muslin dresses. Catherine smiled. "And what have you been discussing in our absence?"

"Why, we were just talking about Miss Brandon," said Feversham, taking a pinch of snuff. "My father wanted to know if she was pretty. Worcester proclaimed that she was. What do you think, Lady Catherine?"

"Pretty?" said Catherine with a shrug. "I would not call her ill-favored, but she looked like a wild Gypsy to me. And she had a horrible brute of a dog with her. It was enormous! And her skirt was covered with mud."

"There is a good deal being made of the mud on her skirt," said Worcester irritably. "She was collecting herbs and that is what happens when one does such work."

"Then why would anyone do it?" said Lady Huntingdon with a perplexed expression. "Certainly that sort of thing is what servants are for."

"But Miss Brandon studies herbs," said Prudence, who was emboldened to come to Alethea's defense. "She is writing a book about them."

"Writing a book on herbs?" said Catherine. "What a very dull subject."

"I don't think it in the least dull," said Edward. "Miss Brandon does some deuced clever things with herbs. Makes them into medicines and the like. Why, Worcester was cured of an illness thanks to Miss Brandon."

"Really?" said Catherine, turning to the marquess.

"It seemed her draft helped break a fever," said Worcester.

"You were unwell?" said the Duchess of Cranworth, regarding him with a frown. Her grace had an inordinate fear of illness and she took care to avoid sick persons.

"I was, but now I am completely recovered," said Worcester.

"I am glad to hear it," said her grace, eyeing him with suspicion.

"You have said that Miss Brandon is coming to dinner, Worcester," said Lady Huntingdon. "You make no mention of anyone else accompanying her."

"She will be coming alone," said Worcester.

"Alone?" said Lady Huntingdon in a tone that implied this was quite extraordinary.

"She lives alone," Prudence ventured to say. "She had lived with her father, but he has gone to sea."

"Indeed?" said the duchess. "Gone to sea? Is he a naval officer?"

"He is a botanist," said Prudence. "He will be finding plants on faraway islands and bringing them back. He is a very respected gentleman. He has written books."

"I have always thought the writing of books a highly overrated accomplishment," said Feversham, stifling a yawn.

"Hear, hear," said the duke. "I detest bookish fellows. And there is nothing worse than a bookish female. I do hope this Miss Brandon isn't a bluestocking."

"Surely Worcester wouldn't tolerate her if she were," said the duchess, turning to the marquess for confirmation.

"I wouldn't call her a bluestocking," he said.

"Nor would I," said Edward. "She is perfectly charming."

"Then we will look forward to seeing her this evening," said Lady Huntingdon. "She will be your only other guest?"

"I fear I haven't yet become acquainted with any other members of local society," said Worcester.

"If only you might remain unacquainted with them," said Feversham. "My experience has told me that the society one meets in such country backwaters as this has little to commend it. When one is in the country one finds himself speaking with all manner of persons one would cheerfully ignore in town."

"How true, Feversham," said Lady Huntingdon.

Worcester listened to these remarks in stony silence. He had known the guests now assembled in his drawing room for years. Yet it seemed he had never realized until now how annoying they were. The duchess began to speak of something else and the company abandoned the topic of Miss Brandon.

Chapter 21

In the late afternoon Alethea began her preparations for the dinner party. Even though she was unaware that she had been the topic of conversation at Hartwood, she wasn't looking forward to joining Worcester's guests.

Alethea bathed in one of her herbal solutions that was known to soothe the skin as well as one's nerves. Thus fortified, she began to dress for the dinner.

Molly assisted her young mistress with her hair and when they were done, Alethea regarded her reflection in the mirror with approval. Her dark curls looked very pretty piled atop her head and trimmed with satin ribbons. Around her neck was a pearl necklace, a family heirloom that Alethea loved because it reminded her of her late mother.

Alethea continued to stare into the mirror. While she had no illusion about appearing like a lady of fashion, Alethea thought she had no reason to be ashamed. She had a very good figure that was shown to advantage by the high-waisted, low-cut gown. And the pale blue of the silk dress was an excellent color for her.

"You look very lovely, miss," said Molly.

"Thank you, Molly," said Alethea. Molly handed her her best paisley shawl and her gloves and Alethea went to the drawing room to await Worcester's carriage. It soon arrived and Alethea was on her way to Hartwood.

Alethea was met at Worcester's door by Talbot, who greeted her with polite deference. After divesting herself of her shawl, Alethea was ceremoniously escorted to the drawing room. "Miss Brandon," said Talbot, announcing her in a sonorous voice.

All heads turned in her direction. Smiling, Alethea entered the room. "Oh, Alethea," said Prudence, hurrying to her. "I'm so glad you are here. And how lovely you look."

"How very kind, Pru, but it's you who looks lovely. What a stunning gown."

Prudence acknowledged the compliment with a smile. She looked very pretty in a lavender silk gown with tiny puff sleeves trimmed with lace. Her reddish blond hair was adorned with silk flowers. "Come, I shall introduce you to our guests." Taking her arm, Prudence led her first to the duchess, who was seated upon the sofa. "I should like to present Miss Brandon, your grace. This is the Duchess of Cranworth."

"How do you do, your grace?" said Alethea, making a graceful curtsy.

"And Lady Huntingdon." Alethea murmured her, "How do you do?" and curtsied again. Prudence made the other introductions.

As she greeted Worcester's guests, Alethea was very much aware that she was among society's elite. She thought that the duchess and countess were very grand in their splendid dresses and jewels. And the gentlemen standing before her were likewise magnificent in their well-tailored evening clothes. Feversham in particular was a magnificent specimen of a society buck.

Yet it was Lady Catherine who commanded most of Alethea's attention. Seated in an elegant French armchair, she was dazzlingly beautiful. Dressed in a white silk gown, she was the picture of an elegant lady of fashion. Alethea eyed the dress appreciatively, suspecting that the Empress Josephine herself couldn't have been more splendidly attired. On her head Catherine wore a stylish toque that matched her dress, and around her neck was a glittering diamond necklace.

Looking at Catherine, Alethea felt very dowdy and insignificant. Then, glancing about the room, her eye fell on the wall, where the portrait of the first Marquess of Worcester had been hanging. In its place hung the watercolor painting she had given Worcester.

She looked at him in surprise. Having seen her look at the painting, Worcester allowed a slight smile to appear on his face.

"We are told your father is at sea, Miss Brandon," said Lady Huntingdon.

"Yes, he is, ma'am," replied Alethea. "He is sailing to the islands of the Pacific."

"Whatever for?" said the duchess.

Alethea smiled. "It is a voyage of scientific discovery, your grace. My father will study the flora of the area."

"How interesting, I'm sure," said Feversham, languidly swinging the quizzing glass that hung from a ribbon around his neck back and forth.

"Miss Brandon's grandfather sailed with Cook," said Worcester.

"Isn't that wonderful?" said Edward. "How exciting it must be to explore new worlds and that sort of thing."

"I suppose some might think so," said Feversham.

"I only wish that I could have gone with my father," said Alethea. "It doesn't seem fair that men may have adventures while we ladies must stay at home."

"I do agree with you, Miss Brandon," said the duchess. "Gentlemen do have much more interesting lives, sailing on ships and being soldiers and things like that."

Alethea smiled. "Yes, that is true, ma'am, although I confess that I have no desire to face cannon fire."

"Nor do I," said Lady Huntingdon. "I am content to stay at home as all ladies should be."

As Worcester watched Alethea, he thought she looked very attractive standing there in her pale blue gown. He found himself wishing he could be alone with her.

Alethea would have been very surprised to learn what Worcester was thinking. She was certain that his thoughts were on the beautiful Lady Catherine.

Talbot entered the room to announce that dinner was served and all rose from their seats to proceed to the dining room. There was a procession from the drawing room with Worcester and the duchess in the lead.

Edward smiled at Alethea. "May I escort you in, Miss Brandon?"

"Thank you, Lord Edward," she replied, taking his arm.

As they followed the others toward the door, Edward spoke in a low voice. "And what do you make of our guests?"

"They are all very grand," said Alethea. "I am not accustomed to such august personages."

"Well, you are doing very well," said Edward.

"I am trying not to allow them to terrify me," said Alethea with a laugh.

"Well, I am terrified of Lady Huntingdon," whispered Edward. "She is a veritable dragon."

Alethea laughed again. She was very glad that Edward was beside her. She was even happier to find that she was to be seated next to him. He sat on her left and to her right was Lord Huntingdon.

Worcester occupied a position some distance away, at the head of the table between Lady Catherine and the duchess. From her vantage point Alethea had a good view of the marquess and his prospective bride.

Alethea noted that Worcester didn't look all that happy, but then most of the time he bore a serious expression. The marquess was very different from his lighthearted brother, who smiled and joked and seemed to have a perpetually sunny disposition.

Prudence, who was sitting opposite her brother at the far end of the table, appeared rather ill at ease. Feversham sat at her left hand, while, fortunately for Prudence, her brother Edward was directly on her right.

Dinner was a splendid culinary affair, for Worcester's cook was a talented and capable individual. Servants busied themselves serving and removing a wide variety of dishes.

Alethea found that she was enjoying the meal. Edward was an amusing dinner companion and they chatted amiably about a number of topics. And even though Alethea had taken Feversham for an empty-headed coxcomb, she had to admit that his remarks were diverting. He regaled the company with a number of interesting and usually uncomplimentary stories about members of society, provoking a good deal of laughter from the guests.

Lord Huntingdon, who was a rather dour individual, finally responded to Alethea's attempts at conversation when she commented on the fine roast beef being served. Huntingdon responded in his usual sour way that such food always gave him indigestion.

Alethea soon found herself discussing various herbal remedies recommended for stomach distress, a topic of keen interest to the earl. Soon they were deep in conversation, a fact noted by Worcester.

Although he was trying hard to keep himself from looking at Alethea, the marquess couldn't help himself. He found that his gaze kept falling on her. She appeared to be enjoying herself talking to Edward, Worcester had noticed. That was to be expected, for the marquess knew that his brother was a charming fellow, popular with the ladies. A frown appeared on Worcester's face. Alethea seemed very fond of Edward. Worcester felt a twinge of jealousy, for he was sure she found his younger brother far better company than himself.

Worcester continued to watch Alethea. He was somewhat surprised that she was getting on so well with the Earl of Huntingdon. After all, the marquess knew that his prospective father-in-law wasn't known for his conversation. Yet there he was chatting away to Alethea. The marquess frowned again, wondering what they were discussing.

"Miss Brandon seems like a very nice person," said Catherine, following the direction of his gaze.

Worcester looked over at her. "Yes, she is very pleasant."

"My father appears to find her interesting," said Catherine.

"She is an interesting and accomplished lady."

"I'm sure she is," said Catherine. "I admire her poise. I daresay it must be difficult for someone like Miss Brandon to find herself in such company. I must confess I couldn't act with such aplomb if I appeared in such an evening gown as that." When the marquess responded with an icy stare, Catherine hastily added, "Oh, I don't mean to criticize, but one doesn't see such dresses in town anymore."

"Fashion doesn't interest me," said Worcester testily.

Noting his irritation, Catherine found it best to change the subject. She wasn't very happy that the marquess seemed to find Miss Brandon so fascinating. Catherine saw nothing out of the ordinary about her and she resented that the man she was to marry seemed more interested in a provincial nobody than herself. Still, Catherine managed to smile and bring up another subject.

At the conclusion of dinner, the ladies left the gentlemen to their port, adjourning to the drawing room. There they settled into chairs and a sofa.

Prudence eagerly took the seat beside Alethea on the sofa. The duchess, Lady Catherine, and her mother occupied chairs nearby. "A very fine dinner," said Lady Huntingdon, nodding toward Prudence. "I did fancy the oyster sauce. I can scarcely remember having better, except, of course, at the royal pavilion in Brighton."

"Oh yes," said the duchess, "the food there is unsurpassed. His Royal Highness is quite the gourmand."

"I always enjoy dining with the prince," said Lady Huntingdon. "He is so very charming."

"Yes, he is," said Lady Catherine, directing a condescending smile at Alethea. "I don't suppose you have met His Royal Highness, have you, Miss Brandon?"

"I fear I haven't had that privilege," said Alethea.

"I daresay you wouldn't have the opportunity, living here as you do," said Catherine.

"That is true, and although I have visited London from time to time, I prefer to stay at my home year round."

"But you don't find that very dull?" said Lady Huntingdon.

"Indeed, ma'am, I am never bored," said Alethea.

"Would that I could say that," said the duchess.

"Miss Brandon has her work, your grace," said Catherine, smiling at Alethea. "Prudence told us you are writing a book on herbs, Miss Brandon. It seems we are in the presence of a scholar."

"A scholar?" cried the duchess. "I didn't think a lady could be a scholar. I'm sure I never wished to be one."

Alethea suppressed a smile. "I wouldn't call myself a scholar, your grace. But I have an interest in herbs. You see, my father is an eminent botanist. That is, a scientist who studies plants."

"How very interesting," said Lady Huntingdon in a tone that implied she felt just the opposite.

At that moment Talbot entered the room. "I beg your pardon, my lady," he said, addressing Prudence, "but there is a person here insisting to see Miss Brandon. His name is Tom Dixon. I told him Miss Brandon couldn't be disturbed, but he said that it was urgent."

Alethea was very familiar with Tom Dixon, who was a farmer and one of her closest neighbors. "Did he say what is wrong, Talbot?"

"Something about a cow taken ill, miss."

"A cow taken ill?" cried Lady Huntingdon. "Is the man mad? Why would he want Miss Brandon for that?"

"I often help farmers when their animals are sick," said

Alethea. She rose from the sofa. "I fear I must take my leave of you all. Tom wouldn't have come if it weren't serious. I am sorry to go so abruptly, Lady Prudence."

"Good heavens, Miss Brandon," said the duchess. "You can't mean to rush off with some farmer about a cow!"

"I fear I must, your grace," said Alethea. "Good night, ladies." And with those words she hurried away.

"I have never seen the like of that," said Lady Huntingdon. "Imagine Miss Brandon rushing off to tend a sick cow."

"Cows are very important to farmers," said Prudence. "Many are very poor and have so few of them."

"That may be," said Lady Huntingdon, "but that is hardly a reason to rush off with scarcely a 'by your leave.'" She shook her head disapprovingly. "Miss Brandon is a very unconventional young woman."

"I agree," said the duchess, who thought being unconventional a very serious fault indeed.

Prudence frowned, but said nothing. She wished Alethea hadn't had to go. The rest of the evening stretched out unpleasantly before her.

"Miss Brandon seemed a nice girl," said Lady Huntingdon, "and it was very kind of Lady Prudence to invite her to dinner."

"I will say she seemed well mannered enough," said the duchess, "and she wasn't a bad-looking young lady, not that I would call her a beauty. Indeed, both of these young ladies far outshone her. And her dress was decidedly unfashionable."

"But, your grace, perhaps we shouldn't apply our standards to persons like Miss Brandon," said Catherine with a disingenuous smile. "I daresay she has no pretentions of being a lady of fashion. She is a very commonplace young woman after all."

"She is not in the least commonplace," cried Prudence, very much offended. "She is clever and pretty and very kind."

"I'm sure she is," said Catherine, regarding Prudence with a patronizing look, "but I mean that her family is not in the least distinguished."

"Her father is quite distinguished. He has written an important book on plants."

"True gentlemen don't write books on plants," said Catherine.

"But he is a gentleman," said Prudence, her face flushed with indignation. "The Brandons are an old and honorable family. It was Alethea's ancestors who built Hartwood. It was taken from them years ago by the infamous conduct of the first Marquess of Worcester. Miss Brandon is my friend and I won't have her spoken of in such a fashion!" To hear the usually meek and mild Lady Prudence speak with such passion astonished her guests, who obediently said nothing more on the subject of Alethea Brandon.

Chapter 22

Tom Dixon's cow recovered thanks to Alethea's diligent care. After leaving Hartwood, she had returned to Crow's Nest Cottage to change her clothes. Then she had gone to Dixon's farm, where she had spent most of the night caring for the sick animal.

The following day an exhausted Alethea slept very late. When she rose from her bed she went promptly to work on her book. Nearing completion of the manuscript, she was anxious to finish so that it could be taken to her publisher in London.

For the next few days, Alethea labored long hours at her writing. She did find her mind wandering back to Hartwood every so often, but she was firmly resolved not to allow thoughts of Worcester to interfere with her work. After all, there was no point in thinking about him. He was to marry Lady Catherine Percy, and Alethea was sure that he gave no thought at all to her.

Alethea would have been rather surprised to find how wrong she was in her supposition. Not a day went by that the marquess didn't think of her. In fact, he found that she was occupying his thoughts with increasing regularity.

Worcester was becoming more and more unhappy at the idea of marrying Lady Catherine, for he discovered that she did not improve upon acquaintance. In fact, he found Catherine shallow, frivolous, and alarmingly uneducated. While he had formerly assumed that all women possessed those characteristics, his knowledge of Alethea had caused him to change his opinion.

He couldn't help but compare Catherine with Alethea In all things save wealth and family connections, Alethea was undoubtedly far superior. And in addition to that, he realized that he wasn't in the least attracted to Catherine. He wasn't sure why this was the case, for she was undoubtedly one of the beauties of society. But when he lay awake in his bed in the middle of the night, it was Alethea he fantasized about. It was she whom he wanted to hold in his arms there in the darkened room.

This unfortunate state of affairs put Worcester in a very ill temper, and as the days went on, he was finding his guests increasingly irritating. He realized that he didn't really like any of them. Feversham he found to be the worst of the lot. That gentleman was a pretentious boor who delighted in belittling others.

Ever since the invitations to the ball had been sent out, a number of the local gentry had been emboldened to call at Hartwood. The houseguests were always eager that Worcester receive them. After all, the duke and duchess and the Huntingdons were desirous of seeing new faces.

And besides that, Feversham made a point of ridiculing everyone who came to call, much to the amusement of his parents and the earl and countess. Once the visitors had left, he criticized their clothes and manners and sometimes did amusing impressions of them. Lady Catherine particularly enjoyed Feversham's lampoons and the more sarcastic and mean-spirited, the better.

Although Worcester didn't appreciate Feversham's mocking commentaries on his neighbors, he maintained a stony silence. He was also rather put out with his brother, for Edward was becoming more assertive in telling Worcester that he was wrong in thinking Prudence should marry Feversham. The marquess, who was readily coming to this conclusion himself, nevertheless resented his younger brother telling him what to do.

In short, life at Hartwood was growing increasingly intolerable for Worcester. His sister was miserable as well, for she was growing increasingly sick of the company. Early one morning some five days after Alethea had come to dinner, Prudence decided that she must see her friend. Rising before everyone else, Prudence dressed and crept out of the house. She then walked briskly toward Crow's Nest Cottage.

Alethea, who was by nature an early riser, was taking a brisk morning walk with Nelson at her side. The large dog was always ecstatically happy to be out with his beloved mistress. He kept running ahead and then turning back to dash back to her.

Suddenly, Nelson barked. A feminine figure was approaching,

striding quickly toward them. The dog stopped to regard the new-comer for a moment before rushing ahead.

"Nelson!" called Alethea. The dog stopped immediately and hurried back to her. "Why, look! It is Prudence." Alethea was quite surprised to see Prudence arriving alone and on foot. She waved to her.

Prudence smiled and waved back. Alethea and the dog went forward to meet her. "Pru!" cried Alethea. "What are you doing out at such an hour?"

"Oh, Alethea, I had to see you." To Alethea's considerable surprise, her friend burst into tears.

Alethea hurried to embrace her. "What is wrong, Pru?"

"Oh, everything," said Prudence, hugging Alethea tightly.

Nelson, who was disturbed at the visitor's sobs, regarded her with a worried look. "Come, come, Pru," said Alethea gently. "I'm sure it isn't as bad as that. Is anyone ill?"

Prudence shook her head. "It's nothing like that. No, it's just that I'm so unhappy. These days since I last saw you have been terrible."

"Let's go back to the house, Pru. We'll have a cup of tea and you will tell me what is the matter. Look, Nelson is very much upset."

"Oh, I'm sorry, Nelson," said Prudence, pulling away from her friend and looking down at the great tawny beast. She then knelt down and threw her arms around his neck. Nelson squirmed and licked her face, causing Prudence to laugh in spite of herself.

The two young ladies and the dog returned to Crow's Nest Cottage, where Prudence removed her bonnet and cloak and was led to a seat in the drawing room. "I'll have Molly bring us some tea," said Alethea. After requesting that Molly do so, she sat down next to Prudence. "Now tell me what is the matter."

"I am sorry to be such a baby," said Prudence.

"Nonsense, you're clearly upset. What has happened?"

"Nothing has happened, not really," said Prudence. "It is only that things are so awful. I can hardly bear staying at Hartwood another day. Feversham is horrid. He thinks himself so amusing and he makes fun of everyone. And Lady Catherine is detestable. I have never met a more unpleasant girl.

"And the duchess has been asking me how I like her son. I don't know what to say. And Lady Huntingdon is insufferable. And her husband is worse!"

"Poor Pru."

"Geoffrey grows more cross and disagreeable every day. I believe he quite dislikes me."

"Why, that is ridiculous. Lord Worcester loves you."

"I'm not sure of that," said Prudence. "And he and Edward aren't getting on. Edward wants to return to London and Geoffrey says he mustn't think of it. I cannot imagine a more unhappy place than Hartwood. I wish I could stay here with you."

"Well, that is unfortunately out of the question, my dear Pru," said Alethea. She reached out to pat Prudence's hand. "But I am so glad to see you. I've been hard at work on my book and I have scarcely seen anyone. Now my book is done."

"Oh, that is good," said Prudence, dabbing her eyes with her handkerchief.

"Yes, and now that I'm finished, I shall have more time to visit you. I shall call at Hartwood." She smiled. "Of course, I shall hope to be admitted."

"We will certainly receive you," said Prudence. "Oh, I'd be so glad if you would come."

"I shall call tomorrow without fail. And soon you will be having the ball. I shall be there for that."

"Yes," said Prudence, "the ball." She frowned. "I dread that more than anything."

"But why?"

"I shall have to dance with Feversham."

"You so dislike him?"

Prudence nodded. "I quite detest him. And I won't marry him!"

"My dear Pru, you don't have to marry him. Marquess or no, your brother cannot force you to do so. And Lord Worcester isn't a monster. You must tell him in no uncertain terms that you won't marry Feversham. It is as simple as that."

"But he'll be furious with me."

"Then so be it. Better a furious brother than Feversham for a husband."

Prudence looked thoughtful. "Yes, I suppose you're right."

"Of course, I am. And Lord Worcester will come round in time. He isn't an unreasonable man or at least I don't believe he is."

"Then you think I can refuse Feversham?"

"Of course. It isn't the Dark Ages after all. You will find someone far better than the Viscount Feversham to marry. Oh, here is tea."

Molly set down a tray with the blue-and-white teapot and a plate of tea cakes. Alethea poured the tea and handed a steaming cup to her young friend. "Thank you," said Prudence, taking the cup and saucer.

"Tea always makes one feel better," said Alethea. "Now you mustn't worry. All will be well. I'm certain of it. And I'm thought to have the gift of prophecy, you know."

Prudence smiled and took a sip of tea. "I do feel better," she said.

"And how is dear Poppet?"

"Oh, she is fine, although because cats make Lady Catherine sneeze, Poppet must stay in my room or with Mrs. Graham. I'm glad that Mrs. Graham is so fond of her. She quite spoils her."

"One can hardly help spoiling cats," said Alethea. She looked over at Nelson, who was sitting on the floor near them. "Or dogs. I am glad to hear that Poppet is well and she will be quite happy away from the company."

"As I am," said Prudence.

"When will they return to town?"

"Shortly after the ball," said Prudence. "Of course, I suppose the Huntingdons will stay until the arrangements are made for my brother's marriage. I don't believe a settlement has been reached."

Although Alethea didn't like thinking about Worcester's marriage, she succeeded in appearing indifferent. "I do hope they will be happy," she said.

"They'll be miserable," said Prudence. "How can it be otherwise? They aren't in the least suited. Of course, Edward has said that Catherine's marriage settlement will include an estate in Derbyshire that my brother wants very much. So perhaps that will make him happy."

"You can't believe he wants to marry her for an estate?"

Prudence shrugged. "I couldn't imagine why else he would wish to do so. I find her obnoxious. But sometimes I think Geoffrey deserves to be miserable since he seems so intent on making Edward and me unhappy."

"I'm sure that isn't true."

"It certainly appears to be," said Prudence.

Molly chose that moment to appear in the drawing room. "Dr. Chandler is here, miss."

"Oh," said Alethea, unsure what to do. Knowing how he felt about Prudence, it seemed unwise to receive him. Prudence looked expectantly at Alethea, who realized that it would seem very strange to refuse to admit him. "Oh, very well, Molly. Do show Dr. Chandler in."

When Chandler arrived in the drawing room, he was rather startled to see Prudence. Yet he managed to retain his composure. "Lady Prudence, this is an unexpected pleasure."

"Dr. Chandler," said Prudence, nodding to him.

Nelson had jumped up at the sight of his old friend. He hurried to Chandler, wagging his tail furiously. "Nelson, old fellow," said the physician, giving the big dog a friendly pat. "What a handsome lad you are." Nelson appeared pleased at the compliment.

"Robert, how good of you to call. You are about very early today."

"Yes, I had to see Martin Hodges this morning. And since I was passing so close to Crow's Nest Cottage, I thought I'd stop."

"Will you have a cup of tea?"

"I shan't refuse such a kind offer," said Chandler, smiling and taking a seat across from the ladies. Molly hurried to fetch another cup.

"I hope you are well, Lady Prudence. Your wrist isn't bothering you, is it?" said Chandler, doing a fine job of hiding his feelings. Alethea was sure that his pose of indifference required a good amount of effort.

"It appears to be completely better, sir," said Prudence. "And how do you do?"

"Oh, I am fine indeed. And Lord Worcester?"

"My brother is quite well, thank you."

"And little Poppet?

Prudence smiled. "She is well, sir."

"Good. Then it seems that the curse is truly gone."

"When I remove a curse, it is removed," said Alethea with a smile.

"I'm told that there are guests at Hartwood," said Chandler, taking a drink of tea.

"Yes, there are," said Prudence. "And they are all very disagreeable."

Chandler laughed. "Surely not all of them?"

Smiling, Prudence nodded. "Yes, all of them. You may ask Alethea. She's met them."

"And you concur with Lady Prudence's opinion?"

"Well, I have to admit that they *are* rather disagreeable, although one does enjoy listening to Lord Feversham. He says such perfectly nasty things about people. And I didn't mind Lord Huntingdon. Once we found a subject of interest to him, he was quite friendly. I sent him some of my remedy for indigestion."

"He'll be eternally grateful to you," said Chandler. "Well, after hearing your opinion of the Hartwood guests, I won't regret not meeting them."

"But you'll meet them at the ball," said Prudence.

"I fear, ma'am, that I won't be at the ball."

"What?" said Alethea. "You're not coming?"

He shook his head. "I shall be in London by then. I leave tomorrow."

"Tomorrow!" said Alethea, regarding him with a surprised look.

"Yes, my uncle is anxious for me to join him. And my successor, Mr. Worthington, has arrived in the village."

"But you cannot leave us so abruptly," said Alethea.

"Couldn't you stay for the ball?" said Prudence. "It is but two days away."

"Yes, you must attend the ball," said Alethea. "A ball at Hartwood isn't an ordinary occasion."

"I do wish you would come, Dr. Chandler," said Prudence, fixing her large blue eyes on the physician.

"I doubt that we will be able to change Robert's mind, Pru," said Alethea, thinking that it would be best if he didn't go to the ball. "He is a stubborn man, who makes a decision and stays with it." She then changed the subject. "Perhaps you'd like to see my primroses. They are especially fine this year."

"Oh, yes," said Prudence, "I should like to see them very much."

After allowing Chandler to finish his tea, they proceeded out to the garden, where Alethea's primroses were blooming in glorious profusion. Her guests had scarcely begun to express their admiration when Molly appeared.

"Yes, Molly?"

"I beg your pardon, miss, but Tom Dixon is here to see you. He said that his cow is much better but he needs some more of that medicine you gave her."

Alethea turned to Prudence and Chandler. "Do excuse me, I shan't be but a moment." She followed Molly from the garden.

Since Alethea was well aware that it wasn't a very good idea to leave Chandler and Prudence together, she hastened to the room where she kept her herbs. After fetching the needed medicine, she joined Tom Dixon in the entry hall, where Molly had left him standing.

"I do thank you, miss," he said, taking a bottle from Alethea's hand. "Do you think, miss, that you could take a look at that sore on old Peg's foreleg? She's just outside."

"Yes, of course, Tom, but I can only spend a minute. I have guests."

"Oh, I'm so sorry to disturb you, miss."

"That's all right, Tom," said Alethea, walking outside to see a white mare tied there. She also saw a carriage coming up the lane to the house. Alethea stared at the approaching vehicle, recognizing it as Worcester's. Knowing that Chandler and Prudence were in the garden, she thought the marquess was appearing at a most inopportune time.

The driver pulled the horses to a stop beside Alethea and Dixon. A groom jumped down to open the carriage door and let down the steps. Worcester stepped out.

"Lord Worcester," said Alethea, making a slight curtsy. "What an unexpected pleasure."

The marquess nodded to her. "Miss Brandon."

"I had just come out to have a look at Mr. Dixon's horse. She had a rather nasty sore on her leg, but it is much better." Alethea glanced over at the mare. "Yes, I can see it is." Walking up to the animal, she patted it before leaning down to examine the leg. "Yes, that's healing nicely, Tom. You've no call to worry."

"Thank you, miss," said Dixon. "'Tis good of you to take a look. I'll be off then." Noting that the marquess was staring at him with disapproval, he pulled at his forelock in a respectful gesture. "M'lord." Worcester acknowledged him with a slight nod. Dixon then mounted the horse and rode off.

"Dixon," said his lordship, watching the farmer. "Is that the man who called you away from Hartwood to see his cow?"

"I was very sorry to go," said Alethea, "but it was serious."

"His sort will always take advantage. You are too good-hearted, Miss Brandon."

"I don't know about that, my lord," said Alethea.

"But you are," said the marquess, "too good-hearted by half."
A slight smile came to his face. He thought Alethea looked very
lovely standing there in the bright sunlight, attired in a simple
frock of white muslin imprinted with tiny violets. "I'm looking
for Prudence," he said.

"She is here," said Alethea. "In the garden. I had to leave her
for a moment when Tom Dixon called. Dr. Chandler is here as
well.

"Is he?" said the marquess, frowning.

"Let us join them," said Alethea, ushering Worcester into the
house. "Dr. Chandler will be leaving us to go to London. We will
miss him terribly."

Making no reply to this remark, Worcester followed Alethea
through the house to a back entrance that led to the garden. They
walked outside into the brilliant sunlight and lush spring foliage
of Alethea's garden.

Alethea was surprised that Prudence and Chandler were no
longer standing there by the bed of primroses. "They were here
but a moment ago," she said.

"Good God!" Worcester's words startled Alethea, who turned
in the direction of his gaze. Down at the end of the garden stood
Prudence and Chandler. At their feet was Nelson, who sat there
looking up at them with keen interest. The doctor was holding
both of Prudence's hands in his and gazing down at her with an
earnest expression. "Prudence!" cried the marquess, striding off
toward his sister, with Alethea following behind.

Pulling her hands from Chandler's grasp, Prudence regarded
her brother with a horrified look. "Geoffrey!"

"What is the meaning of this, Chandler? How dare you take
liberties with my sister!"

Chandler reddened with indignation. "Lady Prudence and I
were merely talking."

"Merely talking? Do you take me for an idiot?"

"Geoffrey . . ." began Prudence, but he cut her off.

"I don't want a word from you, Prudence," he said. "I am addressing this . . . gentleman."

"Lord Worcester," said Chandler, "I have only the deepest re-
spect for Lady Prudence."

"Yes, that is abundantly clear," returned Worcester sarcastically. "Well, I will tell you this, Chandler. I will not permit you to
speak to my sister again. Do you understand?"

"I don't see that you have the right to keep me from speaking to her."

The marquess regarded him as if he hadn't heard him correctly. "I haven't the right? By God, I am her brother and guardian."

"Does that give you the right to dictate whom she may see?"

"It does indeed," snapped Worcester. "She must be protected from unscrupulous fortune hunters like you. Now leave here at once."

"I'm not your lackey, my lord," said Chandler, enraged by the marquess's words. "And this isn't your house."

"Robert," cried Alethea, taking his arm, "I think you should go."

"Very well, Alethea," he said. He nodded to her and then bowed to Prudence. Then after directing an angry look at Worcester, he walked away.

"Have you lost your senses, Prudence?" said Worcester. Prudence looked at him with a hurt expression before bursting into tears. "Oh, it isn't your fault," said the marquess. "That man is taking advantage of you."

"Lord Worcester," said Alethea, "you are making too much of this."

He stared coldly at her. "I don't wish to hear anything from you, Miss Brandon. It seems I misjudged you. I wouldn't have believed that you would arrange an assignation between my sister and that man."

"Assignation?" cried Alethea. "It was nothing but a chance meeting." When Worcester's only response was an icy stare, Alethea's hazel eyes opened wide in disbelief. "You think that I arranged a meeting between your sister and Dr. Chandler? Why, that is preposterous! I had no idea that either of them was coming."

"Alethea is right," said Prudence, tears streaming down her cheeks. "I didn't know Dr. Chandler would be here." Nelson, who was looking very distressed, nudged Prudence, who knelt down to bury her face against his neck.

"Come, come," said Worcester irritably. "Get up, Prudence. We are going home." He pulled her to her feet.

"Lord Worcester, you are very much mistaken about this," said Alethea.

"I think not," said the marquess. "You have been throwing this man in my sister's way since the time we arrived here."

"That is utter nonsense!" cried Alethea. "Truly, my lord, you are entirely mistaken."

"I think we will take our leave of you, Miss Brandon," said Worcester. "Come, Prudence." Gripping her arm, he led her away.

Nelson, who seemed very distressed by the entire business, whined and started after them. "Nelson," said Alethea in a commanding voice, "stay." The big dog stopped in his tracks.

Alethea stood watching as Worcester led his weeping sister across the garden and into the house. She shook her head. "How could he be so wrongheaded?" said Alethea, addressing Nelson, who had come back to stand beside her. The dog only cocked his head in reply.

Chapter 23

The ride back to Hartwood wasn't a pleasant one. Worcester was furious with his sister, but he was angrier still with Alethea. While Prudence sat sniffling in the carriage seat, the marquess stared grimly out the window, reflecting on the situation. He would never have thought Alethea capable of such a dishonorable deception.

"You are wrong about Alethea," said Prudence, wiping her nose with her handkerchief. "She didn't know I was coming to see her. I only just decided to do so when I woke up this morning."

"And why would you run off at such an hour, not telling anyone where you were going?"

"I wanted to see Alethea."

"And so you simply deserted your guests?"

"I wished to desert them," said Prudence, stifling another sob. "I detest them all."

"You are acting like a stupid child," said the marquess.

"And you are acting like an . . . like an ogre!" Prudence once again buried her face in her handkerchief and began to cry.

"I suppose you will tell me you are in love with this Chandler."

"Perhaps I am," sobbed Prudence.

Worcester folded his arms across his chest and eyed his sister with considerable frustration. "You could not think even for a moment that I would give you my permission to marry someone like him."

"No, you wouldn't allow me to marry anyone who would make me happy. You only want me to marry someone odious like Feversham."

"Well, odious or not, he is a man of wealth and position, not some penniless leech."

Prudence only sobbed harder at this, so Worcester decided to say nothing to further upset her. After all, his sister would have to pull herself together by the time they got to Hartwood. What would the guests think if they saw her in such a state?

They rode the rest of the way in silence, and Worcester was thankful that by the time they reached the house, Prudence was sufficiently recovered to enter it calmly. Fortunately, none of the guests saw her as she retreated to her room.

"My lord," said Talbot, approaching his master a bit warily. He had noted·that the marquess didn't seem in the best of moods. "Lord Huntingdon was looking for your lordship. He is waiting in the library for you. He said to tell you as soon as you returned."

Worcester wasn't too pleased at this information, but he only nodded in reply. "Very well, Talbot, I'll join him there at once."

When he entered the library, he found the earl seated in a leather armchair reading a newspaper. "Lord Huntingdon," he said.

"Ah, Worcester," said the earl, putting down the newspaper. "Where were you off to so early?"

"Oh, I had a trifling matter of business," said the marquess, sitting down near his guest. "I was told you wished to see me."

"Indeed, I did. You see, Worcester, I think it's time we discuss this business of Catherine's dowry. We've been here long enough. It's time the matter was settled."

"Yes, of course," said Worcester.

"You know you'll have my property in Derbyshire, of course."

"Yes," said the marquess absently. He was thinking about Alethea and how indignant she had looked when he left her.

Rising from his chair, Huntingdon walked over to Worcester's desk, where he picked up a paper. "These are the terms of the settlement I propose." He handed it to the marquess. "I think you'll find it very generous."

Worcester looked at the paper. "Yes, you are more than generous, sir."

"Good, then you find it acceptable?"

"Yes."

Huntingdon nodded. "Then we have an agreement. Now you had best speak to Catherine."

The marquess looked at him in surprise. "I'm sure that Catherine is well aware that you wish us to be married."

"Yes, of course," said Huntingdon with a trace of impatience, "but you haven't discussed the matter with her. I think it time you did so."

"Really, sir . . ." began the marquess.

"I'll have no more dillydallying," said the earl. "I didn't come here to waste my time. Indeed, there are a good many others clamoring for my daughter's hand. You must speak to Catherine so we may announce the engagement. Indeed, her mother has written to friends in town saying you were already engaged."

Worcester hesitated. For a moment he almost said that he had no wish to marry Catherine. Instead, he merely nodded. "Very well," he said.

That afternoon, Alethea sat in the library at Crow's Nest Cottage, checking over her manuscript. Often her mind would wander and she would think about Worcester and how angry he was with her.

It was certainly an unfortunate state of affairs that Chandler was in love with Prudence, reflected Alethea. "Poor Pru," Alethea said aloud to Nelson, who was lying at her feet. The dog looked up at her. "I fear Pru is in love with Robert. I saw how she looked at him." Alethea sighed. "If only Robert had a title and fortune."

At that moment Molly entered the room. "Mrs. Truscott is here, miss. She's waiting in the drawing room."

Alethea brightened, happy at the prospect of seeing her aunt. Rising to her feet, she went to join her. "Aunt Elizabeth," said Alethea, going over to her and greeting her with a kiss.

Nelson approached the well-known guest, wagging his tail eagerly. "Good afternoon, my dear."

"I'm so glad you called, Aunt Elizabeth," said Alethea.

"Well, I brought you something," said Elizabeth, pointing to the sofa across the room. Stretched out on it was a dress. "You refused to have a new gown for the ball. I decided to have one made for you."

"What!" cried Alethea regarding the dress in some surprise. It was a lovely creation fashioned from peach-colored satin. Its bodice and short puff sleeves were trimmed with lace. "Oh, Aunt, it is far too much. You cannot think to give it to me."

"It is of no use to me, for I assure you it won't fit," said Elizabeth. "I wasn't about to allow you to appear in some old faded dress before such exalted company as we will find at Hartwood."

"Oh, Aunt," said Alethea, sinking down into a chair near her aunt. "I don't think I'll be attending the ball."

"What!" cried Elizabeth. "Not attend the ball? I cannot imagine why you would say such a thing. Why, you're the only one really acquainted with Lord Worcester and his family."

Alethea nodded. "I am acquainted with them. That's certainly true, but I fear Lord Worcester is very vexed with me. I doubt he'd want me to attend his ball."

"What can you mean, Alethea?"

"There was a rather unhappy incident this morning."

Elizabeth regarded her attentively. "Unhappy incident?"

"Lady Prudence came to see me. Robert Chandler appeared as well. Aunt, you must promise you won't say a word to anyone about this."

"Alethea Brandon, you know very well that I am no tattlemonger."

"Yes, I know that," said Alethea. "You see, Aunt, we were in the garden seeing the primroses. I was called away for a moment. Lord Worcester arrived and when we went to join Prudence and Robert, they were holding hands and looking into each other's eyes."

"Oh dear," said Elizabeth.

Alethea nodded. "Lord Worcester was furious. He accused me of arranging an assignation between them."

"Then you would hardly have led him there to find them," said Elizabeth.

"I believe his lordship was too upset to think of that. Indeed, so was I." Alethea frowned. "I shouldn't have left them like that. I knew that Robert is very fond of her."

"Is he?"

"Yes, he told me so. Of course, he's well aware of the gulf between their stations. But his feelings are very strong. It appears that Prudence is fond of him as well."

Elizabeth shook her head. "Then it is good that Robert is going to London."

"Yes," said Alethea, "perhaps it is."

"Well, this does sound like a most unfortunate business, to be sure. But I don't see why it would stop you from attending the ball."

"But, Aunt, how could I attend under these circumstances?"

"My dear, you must forget all about it. In two days' time, it will have blown over. And Worcester will hardly bar you from his door. No, indeed, you've been invited and you must attend. If you don't go, everyone will think it devilish odd."

"But I don't want to go," said Alethea.

"And if you don't attend the ball, I shan't forgive you. After all, Mrs. Tate worked very hard on this dress. I believe it to be the finest she has ever made. You'll look stunning, my dear. Now, don't say you won't go, for I won't hear of it. You will attend the ball with us and that is final."

"Well, I shall consider it," said Alethea.

Elizabeth stood up. "Come, my dear, you must try on the dress. Mrs. Tate wasn't very pleased at making it without you coming in for a fitting, so I do hope it won't need much alteration." Going over to the sofa, she picked up the dress. "Do come on, Alethea."

"Very well, Aunt," said Alethea and the two of them left the room.

Chapter 24

Worcester frowned while his valet adjusted the folds of his snowy white neckcloth. "Quit fussing with it, Weeks," he said impatiently. "You've been at the damned thing long enough."

The valet, who was something of a perfectionist, nodded with a trace of reluctance. He wasn't quite satisfied with the way the cravat looked. Being in the same house with Feversham, who was such a figure of sartorial perfection, was making Weeks even more particular about his work. After all, he wanted his master to present a good appearance at the ball that evening. "Yes, my lord," said Weeks, abandoning the neckcloth. He then assisted Worcester with his well-tailored coat.

Worcester turned to look into the mirror while his valet carefully brushed a piece of lint off the garment. The marquess wasn't in the best of moods. He had never enjoyed balls and he hadn't been looking forward to this night.

In recent days he had often regretted the idea of giving a ball at Hartwood. Now that he and Prudence were on such bad terms, he regretted it even more.

Since coming back from Crow's Nest Cottage, Prudence had barely spoken to him. She was making no effort at all to be pleasant to their guests. Indeed, she was hardly civil to Feversham, who was halfheartedly attempting to woo her.

The marquess knew that his sister was very unhappy about the ball. Of course, he was hardly sanguine about it himself.

"Will there by anything else, my lord?" said Weeks.

Worcester was so lost in his thoughts that he had barely heard the servant. "No, that will be all, Weeks," he said finally.

The servant bowed and left him. Looking away from the mirror, the marquess walked over to the fireplace and stood watching the flames. He had certainly made a muddle of things, he told himself, for now he was engaged to marry Catherine Percy.

Worcester remembered how Catherine's father had dragged him to see her after they had talked about the marriage settlement. Huntingdon had eagerly informed his daughter that Worcester had something to say to her. The marquess had no choice but to propose.

Catherine had murmured her assent in a coy, maidenly way. She had then offered her hand, which Worcester had taken and kissed rather awkwardly.

Worcester shook his head at the memory. He was a fool, he told himself. Yes, he had thought marriage a business best entered in a cool, detached way. Yet now that he was engaged to a young woman for whom he felt not the slightest hint of affection, he realized that he might have been very much mistaken.

And to make matters worse, the marquess was increasingly convinced that the unthinkable had happened: he had fallen in love. Of course, reflected Worcester, Alethea Brandon thought him a blockhead for losing his temper and treating her in an infamous manner.

"Weeks said you were still here," said Edward, coming into the room. The young man looked dapper in his elegant evening clothes.

Worcester turned from the fire to regard his brother with a solemn expression. "Ned."

"I say, brother," said Edward, "you don't look very cheerful. I thought you'd be in high spirits, thinking of how much you'll enjoy dancing with your lovely fiancée."

The marquess thought he detected some irony in his brother's voice. "You know I don't like dancing," he replied glumly. "Indeed, I'll be glad when this accurst ball is done with."

"Accurst ball? That is an odd remark. It was your idea, wasn't it?" When Worcester only frowned in reply, Edward continued. "I think you should know that Prudence is utterly miserable."

"Well, miserable or no, she'll have to do her duty to her guests."

"Oh, she's well aware of that," said Edward. "But I cannot understand why you are so deuced horrible to her."

"I horrible to her? I only wish to keep her from that damned fortune hunter Chandler."

"You don't know he's a fortune hunter," said Edward. "He may sincerely love her."

"Are you a simpleton?" said Worcester. "The man is a fortune hunter with ambitions beyond his station. If Prudence fancies herself in love with him, that is unfortunate, but she will get over such an unsuitable attachment in a short time."

Edward, who had formed his own unsuitable attachment, frowned. "One doesn't necessarily get over these things easily. You might show some understanding, Worcester." Edward only called his brother Worcester when he was annoyed with him, a fact of which the marquess was well aware.

"Prudence is acting like a silly schoolgirl," he replied irritably. "I don't see why I shouldn't treat her as such," said Worcester.

Edward stifled an angry retort, for he really didn't wish to argue with his elder brother. "Well, I hope this ball won't be too difficult for Pru. She's worried that Miss Brandon won't come or that you'll be rude to her if she does."

"What?" said Worcester. "I do think I can be depended upon to be civil to guests in my house."

"Prudence is very upset that you're angry with Miss Brandon."

"And why shouldn't I be? She had that fellow Chandler at her house and allowed him to be alone with Prudence."

"You can't believe she schemed with him to do so."

The marquess shrugged. After he had considered the matter with a cooler head, he had concluded that Alethea hadn't really been at fault. "I think we'd best go down, Ned. Our guests will be arriving soon. You may tell Prudence that I'm not angry with Miss Brandon and that I will be glad to see her."

"Good," said Edward, happy to do so. He left the room, leaving Worcester to take one last thoughtful look at the fireplace before going to await his company.

Alethea had put off her preparations for the ball as long as possible. Finally, Molly had wrung her hands, saying that she had best hurry or she wouldn't be ready on time. Since Alethea didn't want to go to Hartwood, she didn't find that a terrible prospect.

Yet she finally heeded Molly's pleas, retiring to her room to get ready. When she emerged a short time later, wearing her new gown, Alethea looked stunning. The gown her aunt had given her had fit perfectly. It showed her excellent figure to good advantage and the color was the perfect compliment to Alethea's dark tresses. Alethea had to admit that she had never had a more magnificent dress.

When her aunt and uncle arrived at Crow's Nest Cottage, Elizabeth could hardly contain her enthusiasm when she saw Alethea. "Oh, my dear! You have never looked more beautiful!"

"It's this dress," said Alethea. "Anyone would look very grand wearing it."

"What nonsense. You are an exceedingly pretty girl."

"And you are a darling, Aunt," said Alethea. "I am so grateful to you for this wonderful gown."

"Oh, it was nothing." Elizabeth turned to her husband. George Truscott was a distinguished-looking gentleman with a solemn expression. Very taciturn, he seldom said more than a few words. "Doesn't Alethea look wonderful, Mr. Truscott?"

"Yes, yes, indeed," said Mr. Truscott, smiling at Alethea.

"Thank you, Uncle," replied Alethea. "And you both look wonderful. We will have nothing to be ashamed of despite the grand company at Hartwood."

"Oh, I'm so very excited," said Elizabeth. "But we mustn't stand here dallying. It grows late, my dears, and we must be off."

Molly hurried to fetch Alethea's wrap, and soon she and her uncle and aunt were on their way to Hartwood.

When they arrived there they found a number of carriages lining up in front of the entrance. Well-dressed ladies and gentlemen were descending from their vehicles and walking up the steps to the house.

When Alethea and the Truscotts entered the ballroom at Hartwood, it was already crowded with people. The herald announced them as they walked into the room, but the noise of so many people drowned out his words.

Alethea saw Worcester, who was standing with Prudence and Edward, greeting the guests as they arrived. She thought he looked tall and handsome in his dark evening clothes.

Worcester, who had not heard Alethea's name announced, suddenly caught sight of her. He stared at her, feeling an almost electric feeling of excitement. There she was, looking stunning in a peach-colored dress, her black curls piled atop her head in a charming fashion.

"Oh, it's Alethea!" said Prudence. "She did come! I'm so glad." The marquess made no reply, but continued staring at Alethea.

Alethea, noting his intense scrutiny, felt exceedingly uncomfortable. He was probably very irked with her for coming, she thought. Well, he would have to tolerate her presence, she decided, continuing toward him.

"Alethea," said Prudence, hurrying forward to take her hand. "I'm so glad you came. I worried that you wouldn't."

"Oh, I wouldn't miss this, Pru," said Alethea, pressing her friend's hand. "And you look lovely."

Attired in a delicate ivory satin gown, trimmed on the hem with lace and silk rosettes, with dainty silk flowers adorning her red-gold hair, Prudence looked beautiful.

"You put me to shame," said Prudence, smiling at her friend. "That's a wonderful dress."

"Thank you, Pru," said Alethea. "Do allow me to present my aunt and uncle." Alethea made the introductions and her Aunt Elizabeth expressed great pleasure at finally meeting the young lady of whom her niece had spoken so much.

Worcester watched them in silence. Alethea glanced over at him. When his eyes met hers, she regarded him with a questioning look. "Miss Brandon," he said, bowing slightly. "How good of you to come."

"Lord Worcester," she said, curtsying politely. "And Lord Edward."

"Good evening, Miss Brandon," said Edward, smiling brightly at her. "I'm glad to see you."

Alethea murmured that she was pleased to be there and introduced her aunt and uncle. Since there was a great crush of people near the main entrance to the ballroom, Alethea and the Truscotts could not linger. After exchanging a few more words, they moved on.

"Why, Lord Worcester was quite civil," said Elizabeth. "He is rather grand, I admit, but he was not in the least unpleasant. And I believe he was happy to see you, Alethea. He didn't seem at all vexed with you."

"At least he didn't toss us out," said Alethea with a smile. Glancing back toward the marquess, she was a bit taken aback to see that he continued to stare after her. She hurriedly looked away and they proceeded across the ballroom, greeting a number of friends and acquaintances.

Sometime later, Feversham stood surveying the crowd. The orchestra had begun to play and the dancing had begun. Feversham was standing beside Lady Catherine and her mother, Lady Huntingdon. The ladies were watching the dancers with keen interest.

"I must say, I have never seen such ill-cut coats in all my life," said Feversham, taking out his snuffbox and tapping it open. "Look at that person there near the punch bowl. Appalling, don't you think?"

Lady Catherine laughed. "One shouldn't expect to find fashionable people here, Feversham. We have seen enough of Worcester's neighbors before this to be well aware of that."

"But that fellow positively offends me," said Feversham, languidly taking a pinch of snuff. "And that waistcoat. Would you call that shade aquamarine?"

"I should call it hideous," said Lady Catherine. She sighed. "How I hate these country affairs. They're so dull. And there are so few gentlemen one would wish to dance with. I shall die if one of those country louts asks me to stand up with him."

"Why, they wouldn't dare," said Feversham, taking up his quizzing glass and peering through it. "I've seen one or two young bucks casting their eyes upon your fair countenance, my dear Lady Kate, but none would be so bold as to ask for the honor of a dance. But you must stand up with me as soon as some civilized dance is played."

"I shall be delighted, Feversham," said Catherine, smiling at him.

"I fear it is a dead bore," said Lady Huntingdon. "I shall be glad to have supper and gladder still to leave. Thank God the Season will be starting and we will have some decent society in town." She turned to see her husband coming toward them with Worcester in tow. "It seems your father is bringing Worcester to us, Catherine. We have seen very little of him."

Worcester and Lord Huntingdon approached them. The marquess was looking very solemn. He bowed to the ladies. "I hope you are enjoying the ball."

"Yes, of course," said Catherine.

"It is exceedingly interesting," said Feversham. "You have some fascinating neighbors, Worcester." Smiling sardonically, he scanned the room. "Oh, there is Miss Brandon. She's with Lady Prudence."

Catherine followed his gaze. When her eyes alighted on Alethea, she scrutinized her critically. "I will say that dress is an improvement over the frightful thing she was wearing at dinner that evening. Still, I don't think Miss Brandon's looks are above the ordinary."

"My dear Lady Catherine," said Feversham, "she is above the ordinary in this society. Why, I've never seen so many ill-favored females in all my life. Indeed, Miss Brandon is a veritable Helen by comparison."

Worcester frowned. "Miss Brandon would look well in any company. And I find nothing lacking in the appearance of the ladies."

"What a gentleman you are, Worcester," said Lady Catherine, not too pleased to note that her future husband seemed very quick to come to Alethea's defense. "We are very wrong to criticize your guests. They cannot help it if they are in the provinces, obviously far from a decent dressmaker. And I will say that Miss Brandon's gown is passable."

"Why, yes, it is quite passable," said Lady Huntingdon. "And I've seen one or two gowns that were not altogether dreadful. But doesn't your sister look exquisite, Worcester? What a dear, sweet girl she is."

"I should go to her," said the marquess, eager to break away. "Do excuse me." He left rather abruptly, heading toward Alethea and Prudence, who were standing with a group of people including Alethea's aunt and uncle and several others.

When Worcester came up beside them, Elizabeth smiled broadly. "Lord Worcester, it is a lovely ball."

"Yes, indeed," said another lady standing beside her. "We haven't had the like for some time. And we are so enjoying talking with your sister. Lady Prudence is so delightful."

The marquess smiled slightly and nodded to the woman, but it was Alethea who commanded his attention. She was looking at him, a pleasant smile on her face.

"Miss Brandon," he said suddenly, "would you do me the honor of the next dance?"

Surprised, she nodded. He extended his arm, which she took. As they walked toward the dancers, the music ended and there was applause. "I didn't expect you would ask me to dance," said Alethea, glancing over at him.

"And why not?" said Worcester.

"Because you were so exceedingly vexed with me."

"I believe I wronged you, Miss Brandon. Seeing my sister with

Chandler, I quite lose my temper. I apologize. I hope you will for-give me."

"Yes, of course," said Alethea, smiling at him.

Worcester wished he could take her into his arms and kiss her delectable lips. Instead he smiled. "I warn you, I'm not a good dancer."

"I'm rather out of practice myself," said Alethea. "There are so few houses in the vicinity with rooms suitable for dancing. It is a great treat for everyone to be here at Hartwood."

"I'm glad you're here," said Worcester, gazing into her hazel eyes with an intensity that quite discomfited her.

Alethea looked away. "We had best join the others, my lord," she said.

Worcester nodded in reply and then led Alethea to where the other ladies and gentlemen were assembling. The music started. It was a spirited country dance with a good many steps and forma-tions and Worcester was soon at sea. Yet he did the best he could, even once laughing good-naturedly when he took a wrong turn. Alethea couldn't help but smile at him.

When the dance was over, he bowed and she curtsied. "I thank you very much, Miss Brandon."

"You quite astonished me, Lord Worcester."

"Yes, it wasn't that I danced well, but that I danced at all."

She laughed. "And see how everyone is regarding you. They are quite delighted for now you appear far less formidable."

"I appeared formidable?" he said, feigning surprise.

"Of course, you are a very formidable personage."

He smiled. "You never seemed to find me so."

"Well, I'm not easily cowed, my lord."

"I know that well enough," said the marquess, smiling down at her upturned face. Then his expression grew serious. "You are also very beautiful, Miss Brandon."

Alethea feared she was blushing at this unexpected remark. Her heart was pounding and she was feeling a powerful attraction to him.

Worcester immediately regretted his words. He told himself that he'd spoken like a damned idiot, revealing his feelings in such a manner. A man engaged to another lady shouldn't be pay-ing such compliments. the marquess had never said such things before, and he was aware that he'd disconcerted her.

"I must find my aunt," said Alethea, looking down in some confusion.

"Yes, of course," returned Worcester, escorting her back to her aunt and uncle, who were now standing alone. Prudence, who had been asked to dance by Feversham, was being led away by him.

After exchanging a few courteous words with the Truscotts, Worcester took his leave. "How very exciting for you to stand up with the marquess," said Elizabeth. "You and he seem to get on exceedingly well. And to think that you didn't even wish to attend the ball because you thought he was vexed with you.

"Well, I'm glad to see him so amiable. I had thought him so very aloof. He is very different from his brother, who is so very charming, and his sister, who is such a sweet girl. But I don't believe she really wished to dance with Lord Feversham. I can't imagine why. He is the most handsome young man."

"He's a fop," muttered Alethea's uncle, who, as a man of few words, seldom voiced such opinions.

"Mr. Truscott," said Elizabeth, "you mustn't say such things."

Alethea's uncle ventured no further remark, but only frowned in his usually taciturn way.

"I don't like him either, Uncle," said Alethea, watching Prudence walking away with Feversham.

"Lady Prudence is such a nice girl," said Elizabeth. "She isn't the least self-important. Not like that Lady Catherine. I have been watching her. It's clear she considers herself far above this company. I'm told they are engaged. Worcester and Lady Catherine."

"Are they?" said Alethea, trying to sound indifferent. "I was informed that he intended to ask for her hand."

"It seems he has done so and that they are to be married," said Elizabeth. "I just heard it from Sir Roger Metcalf, who happened by while you were dancing. He was speaking with Lady Catherine's father, Lord Huntingdon."

"Oh," said Alethea. So they had become engaged? It shouldn't have surprised her. Yet only a few moments ago, when they were dancing, she had thought he cared for her.

"Well, Lady Catherine is believed to be a very considerable prize," said Elizabeth. "I admit she is a beauty."

"Yes, she is," said Alethea, glancing in her direction to see that Worcester had joined Catherine and her mother. They were standing there surveying the crowd.

"Oh, look!" said Aunt Elizabeth. "It's Robert Chandler."

"Robert?" said Alethea, turning to see the physician coming toward them. He looked handsome in his black coat and knee breeches, although his blond hair seemed a bit wild-looking.

"Good evening to you all," said Chandler, grinning broadly at them.

Alethea eyed him with considerable surprise. "I thought you had gone to London."

"Oh, I was going to leave, but then I started thinking it over, and I decided I couldn't go without paying my respects to his lordship and Lady Pru. Yes, I didn't wish to miss the Hartwood ball. No, indeed, I shouldn't want to do that."

A frown appeared on Alethea's face as she detected the distinct smell of alcohol. He'd been drinking! While this was hardly a surprising state of affairs for a young gentleman, Alethea was somewhat alarmed. She had never known Chandler to drink to excess. "Why don't we sit down, Robert?" she said.

"Sit down? No, indeed. I'm in the mood for dancing. Will you do me the very great honor, Miss Brandon?"

Noting that her aunt and uncle were regarding Chandler with keen interest, she took his arm. "Yes, I'll be happy to dance with you." As Alethea led him away, she whispered, "Robert, have you been drinking?"

"Yes, I have," he replied in a loud stage whisper. "And why shouldn't I? But I'm not drunk, if that's what you think."

"I don't know what to think. You don't seem yourself at all. Do be sensible, Robert. I think you should leave."

"I'll leave when I'm damned ready to leave, Alethea." These words were spoken very loudly, causing several heads to turn and Alethea to redden in embarrassment. "And I want to dance!"

"Then we'll dance," said Alethea in a low voice, "but if you don't behave yourself, I shan't forgive you."

"Don't worry, I'll not cause a scene. I'll be a good lad." Grinning again, he took her by the hand and pulled her toward the group of ladies and gentlemen who were dancing.

"We must wait until they are finished," said Alethea. "The music will end soon." She stood there with him, uncertain what to do. She saw that he had spotted Prudence, who was dancing with Feversham.

His merry grin turned to a frown. "It's Lady Prudence dancing with some damned coxcomb! By God, how I should like to plant him a facer."

"Robert," said Alethea, grasping his arm firmly. "Don't talk like a fool."

"Oh, I wouldn't really plant him a facer," muttered Chandler. He frowned again. "God, Lady Prudence is so beautiful. There is no one like her."

"I'm feeling very thirsty, Robert," said Alethea, hoping to divert his attention. "I should like some punch. Let's go get some."

"In a moment, Alethea," said the doctor, fastening his eyes on Prudence and regarding her with a forlorn expression.

Alethea was sure that everyone was watching them. Chandler was a well-known and popular figure. Those in attendance would be utterly scandalized to know that he had come there in what appeared to be an inebriated state.

When the music ended a short time later, the ladies and gentlemen who were dancing bowed and curtsied. Alethea saw Feversham offer his arm to Prudence, who took it somewhat reluctantly. "She doesn't care a fig for him," said Chandler.

"Of course, she doesn't," said Alethea. "Now, come, let us go get some punch."

At that moment Prudence caught sight of the doctor. Her face first expressed surprise, and then she smiled at him. Chandler smiled in return. Then, pulling away from Alethea's grasp, he hurried toward Prudence.

"Robert!" said Alethea, following after him. He arrived beside Prudence before Alethea could catch up with him.

"Lady Prudence," he said. "How do you do?"

"I am very well, thank you, Dr. Chandler," said Prudence, blushing prettily.

"You look utterly enchanting!" cried Chandler. Feversham regarded the doctor with an annoyed look, but said nothing. Chandler continued. "May I have the next dance, Lady Prudence?"

"I fear, sir," said Feversham, casting a disdainful look upon the physician, "that Lady Prudence has promised me the next dance."

"Perhaps we should ask her to decide who should be her partner," said Chandler in a loud voice.

Alethea tugged at his arm. "Robert, you are to dance with me. Have you forgotten?"

Chandler turned to regard her in some confusion. "Oh, I did ask you, Alethea. I'm so sorry. Lady Prudence, the dance after that, if I may."

"You're not dancing with my sister at any time," said a stern masculine voice that Alethea recognized immediately as Worcester's. She turned to see him staring at Chandler with a grim expression. "I suggest you leave, sir."

"I am commanded to leave, am I?" said Chandler, opening his eyes wide in an expression of incredulity. "Well, my lord, I'll leave when I'm ready. And I wish to dance with Lady Pru and I'm going to do so."

"You're not going to do anything except leave my house," said the marquess. "You're drunk, sir, and making a spectacle of yourself."

"Drunk? I'm not drunk." He smiled at Prudence and then took a step toward her. "I only want to dance with you."

A very disgusted Worcester took hold of his arm. "Come away, Chandler. You're to leave at once or I'll have my servants throw you out."

"Let go of me," said the doctor, pulling his arm out of Worcester's grasp. Then to Alethea's astonishment, Chandler shoved Worcester hard, causing the marquess to fall backward against a large gentleman who was standing behind him. Fortunately, the guest caught his host, preventing the marquess from landing on the floor in an undignified heap.

Feversham recoiled in fear. "The man is mad!" he cried.

Several gentlemen were upon Chandler in a moment, and two of Worcester's manservants soon assisted them in subduing him. The doctor was then led, struggling, from the ballroom.

Horrified, Alethea stood watching him. When she looked over at Worcester, he was staring after Chandler with a furious expression. "I must say, that was rather exciting," said Feversham, who had recovered from his frightening experience. "At least I shall have an interesting anecdote to take back to town. I do hope he didn't upset you, Lady Prudence."

Prudence murmured that she was fine, but she was, in truth, very much upset. And to make matters worse, now everyone was staring at them. Fortunately, Lord Edward told the musicians to begin playing and there was some return to normalcy as music once again filled the room.

Alethea stood there with a worried expression on her face, deciding that the Hartwood ball had turned into a disaster.

Chapter 25

The late-morning sun streamed in through the window of the library at Crow's Nest Cottage. Alethea sat at the desk, staring idly at the manuscript of her book on herbal medicine. She was finding it very hard to concentrate, for she kept thinking about the ball.

Alethea sighed. Last night had been dreadful. After Chandler's ignominious departure, the guests hadn't been able to talk of anything else. It was hard for anyone to believe that Robert Chandler could have acted in such a manner, appearing drunk and causing a scene. There was a good deal of gossip that Chandler had lost his heart to Lady Prudence Beauchamp. That he could have formed such an inappropriate attachment seemed quite extraordinary to the ladies and gentlemen in attendance.

Since it was well known that Alethea was a dear friend of Chandler's, she was barraged with questions. She soon developed a headache and begged her aunt that they might go home.

Resting her head in her hands, Alethea stared at the window. Suddenly there was a loud cawing and Hector the crow flew into the room, landing on the desk.

Nelson, who had been lying on the floor near Alethea's feet, lifted his large head to stare at the bird. "Hector," said Alethea, "this won't do, sir. Out with you!"

The glossy black bird cocked his head and uttered a guttural sound before flying back to the windowsill. Rising from her desk, she went to the window. "Everything is a fearful muddle," said Alethea, sitting down in the window seat and addressing her avian visitor. "First of all, I've lost my heart to the Marquess of Worcester. Can you imagine anything more ridiculous? And Robert is in love with Lady Prudence. And he made a dreadful scene at the ball last night." Hector cocked his head again, as if considering this information.

"Miss," said Molly, entering the library, "Dr. Chandler is here." Molly, who had had a brief account of what had happened at the ball, raised her eyebrows slightly.

"Show him in," said Alethea.

When the physician arrived in the library, he had a very somber expression on his face. "Thank you for seeing me, Alethea," he said. "I wasn't sure whether you'd receive me after last evening. I know I made a cake of myself."

"You did indeed," said Alethea, "but do sit down, Robert."

Nelson had risen to his feet and had approached the doctor, his tail wagging happily. "Hello, Nelson, old boy," said Chandler, reaching down to pat the dog's head. "And there is Hector. Good day to you, sir." The crow only stared at the new arrival. Smiling wearily, Chandler pulled a chair near the window seat and sat down. "I'm so sorry about what happened."

Alethea shook her head. "You poor goose, why did you do it? You've always been the sensible one."

"I don't know. I was feeling very sorry for myself I suppose. I kept thinking about Prudence, and the fact that I'd never see her again. I started drinking, and before long, I wasn't thinking clearly. I decided to go to the ball." He paused a moment before continuing. "How was Prudence? What must she think of me?"

"I don't know, Robert. Prudence was upset by what happened, I'm sure of that. But I didn't have much opportunity to talk with her. But I do know this. You must get over her. There is no other choice."

"I know," said Chandler, "but it won't be easy."

"Thank heaven, you have your work. And you'll be very busy with your new duties in town."

"Yes," he replied, rising from the chair. "I must go, Alethea. I'm starting for London."

"Now? But you've only just arrived."

"I only intended to stay a short while, but I must be on my way. It's late as it is. But I couldn't go without seeing you. You are coming to town with your aunt and uncle, aren't you?"

Alethea nodded. "Yes, in a week or two, I suppose."

"Good, then I'll see you then."

She rose up and accompanied him to the door. "Good-bye, Robert," she said.

"Good-bye, Alethea." After kissing her on the cheek, he took his leave. Alethea sighed as she watched him ride off.

Prudence sat in her bedchamber, gloomily looking out the window. It was a fine, sunny day, but the bright sunlight did little to dispel her somber mood.

There was a knock at her door and Edward poked his head in. "May I come in, Pru?"

"Yes, of course," said Prudence.

As Edward made his way in, he noted that his sister was still attired in her nightdress and dressing gown. "I was told you hadn't come down for breakfast. I was a bit worried."

"There is nothing to worry about, Ned," she replied. "I have a slight headache. That's all."

"I know you were upset about last night."

"It was quite awful. Geoffrey was so angry with Dr. Chandler."

"Well, he was a trifle foxed, and he did shove our dear brother. It was deuced undignified behavior for the doctor, I must say." When Prudence only frowned at this remark, Edward folded his arms across his chest and regarded his sister with a serious look. "You're fond of Chandler, aren't you?"

Prudence nodded. "Oh, Ned, I'm in love with him. I know that you'll understand."

"I do understand, Pru, but are you sure? You don't know Chandler very well."

"But I am sure," said Prudence. "Just as you're sure about Miss Whitfield."

Edward nodded. "It seems we're in the same boat. Did you tell this to Geoffrey?"

"I tried to tell him last night, but he wouldn't listen. He treats me like a child. And I told him I wouldn't marry Feversham if he locked me in chains in the tower at Worcester Castle."

Edward grinned. "I wouldn't give him any ideas if I were you, Pru."

Prudence smiled in spite of herself. "If only he could understand what it's like to fall in love. He doesn't love anyone. He is so cold and unfeeling. How else could he marry Catherine Percy even though he cares nothing for her?"

"Well, he isn't like you and me," said Edward. "We're both romantic fools, it seems."

"And he's a cold fish," said Prudence with a sigh. "I wish he could fall in love. I wish he could fall in love with someone 'un-suitable.' "

"I'd like to see that as well," said Edward, "but I don't think it likely. Well, you mustn't hide away here, Pru. Our guests are leaving in the morning and you have only one more day to be civil to them."

"Thank goodness," said Prudence.

"And I shall leave for town as well tomorrow. Our lord and brother says I might."

"Ned, you wouldn't leave me alone!"

"You'll be coming back to town in a few days. Geoffrey told me so. Now get dressed and come down. It's a fine day. We'll take a nice walk."

Prudence nodded and her brother left her room. When she was alone, she sat down on her bed. If only Geoffrey knew what she was feeling, perhaps he'd be more understanding, she felt. Her eye fell upon the book that had been sitting on her night table for some days, the book on spells that Alethea had left. Prudence kept meaning to return it to her, but it kept slipping her mind.

Opening the old volume, Prudence began paging through it. She had looked at it several times before, although doing so made her rather nervous. After all, it was a book about witchcraft and spells and potions.

A thought suddenly occurred to Prudence. Spells and potions? What about a love potion? Perhaps there was a way to make her brother fall in love. Stopping at one page, she began to read carefully.

The following day, the guests departed from Hartwood. Prudence was very happy to see the back of them. She was decidedly less happy to say farewell to her beloved brother Edward.

Once the guests and Edward had all left, it seemed strangely quiet in the house. Worcester stood in the drawing room, contemplating Alethea's flower painting that hung over the mantel. He found himself remembering how they had danced at the ball and how wonderful she had looked. He envisioned her black curls and bright hazel eyes and the way her full inviting lips had smiled at him. He thought, too, of the enticing display of her charms afforded by the low-cut bodice of her peach-colored dress.

Worcester turned away from the picture in some frustration. He must cease thinking about her, he told himself grimly.

"Geoffrey," said Prudence, entering the room. She carried Poppet in her arms and the kitten's tail hung down, twitching back and forth.

"Prudence," he said.

"Geoffrey, I'm sorry that I have vexed you. I wish to apologize."

The marquess frowned. His sister had been very difficult lately and he wasn't sure that he was in the mood to forgive her. Since the ball, she had steadfastly maintained that she wouldn't marry Feversham or anyone else he threw in her way. He had been quite angry with her. Indeed, his ill temper and frustration over Alethea made him not very kindly disposed toward his sister at that moment. Still, it was good to see her in a more conciliatory frame of mind. "I imagine you're glad now that our guests are gone."

"Yes," she said, "aren't you?"

He frowned again. He was exceedingly glad to be rid of the company, but he didn't like to admit it. After all, Lady Catherine was his fiancée and it would hardly do to say that he was very happy that she was no longer there. "It will be easier on the servants now that the guests are gone."

Prudence almost laughed. Her brother had never been one to consider the servants. "When are we returning to town?"

"I should think Friday. Will that give you enough time to pack?"

"Oh, yes, that is quite sufficient," said Prudence.

"Then you don't mind going back to London?"

"No, indeed not." Prudence paused. "I shall miss Alethea." Worcester made no reply to this remark, and his sister continued. "Could we call on her tomorrow?"

"Call on Miss Brandon?"

"Yes, I really don't see how I could go back to town without saying good-bye to her. Couldn't we call at Crow's Nest Cottage?"

Worcester hesitated. He didn't want to see Alethea again, he thought. Or, in truth, he wanted to see her more than anything in the world, but he knew it wasn't a good idea. No, it would be best to go back to London and try to forget her. "I really don't know that it's necessary to call. Why don't you send her a letter?"

"Oh, I couldn't do that. It would be so very rude. And she has been such a good friend to me. And don't forget how she saved your life."

"She didn't save my life," said Worcester.

"I think she did," said Prudence. "In any case, she worked very hard to help you. We owe her the courtesy of a visit. I know you dislike her because of Dr. Chandler."

"I don't dislike her," said the marquess.

"Then can't we call at Crow's Nest Cottage?"

"Oh, very well," said Worcester.

Prudence smiled. "Thank you, Geoffrey." Sitting down on the sofa, she stroked Poppet's soft fur. She had a most ingenious plan and tomorrow she would put it into action.

Chapter 26

It had taken a good deal of time for Prudence to decipher the instructions for making a love potion from Alethea's book, but she was finally able to copy the recipe down onto a piece of paper. She had heard of most of the ingredients, although a few items rather mystified her.

Prudence had taken the recipe to the kitchen, telling the cook that it was a remedy that Miss Brandon had recommended for headaches. The cook had been only too happy to assist her young mistress, but there had been several items they didn't have. The worthy servant had suggested that Prudence send to the apothecary in the village for the rest of what was needed.

When the servant entrusted with this errand had returned with two bottles and a small packet of dried brown powder, Prudence and the cook had set about mixing the ingredients. The mixture then had been heated slowly and stirred constantly. The result was a greenish brown liquid that they poured into a small bottle.

"If this works well, m'lady," said the cook, "we'll have to make up a large batch for the servants."

"Oh dear," said Prudence, alarmed at the prospect of the household staff partaking of what Alethea's book claimed to be a powerful love potion, "I feel it is better that I test it out first. Miss Brandon wasn't sure if it worked well with people. I believe she had good results with horses."

"Horses, m'lady?" cried the cook. "Do horses have headaches?"

"Oh, yes, I'm sure they do," said Prudence.

"Well, I shouldn't take any of that without asking Miss Brandon first."

Prudence assured her she wouldn't do so. After thinking the

cook for her assistance, Prudence left the kitchen. When she arrived in her room, she sat staring at the bottle. Now she had the potion. The book said that two persons drinking it at the same time would be in love forever.

Her brow furrowed in concentration, Prudence considered the matter. There was only one person she wanted her brother to fall in love with and that was Alethea Brandon. She smiled. Wouldn't it be wonderful if Worcester and Alethea fell in love? He would then understand what she and Edward were going through.

Prudence nodded thoughtfully. Yes, Worcester would be far more sympathetic to them once he knew what it was to lose his heart. And indeed, how could he marry that odious Catherine Percy if he loved someone else? No, he certainly wouldn't do so, decided Prudence. Why, he would marry Alethea instead. Finding the prospect of Alethea as her sister-in-law a very happy one, Prudence resolved to do her best to put her plan into action.

That afternoon Worcester and Prudence set off for Crow's Nest Cottage in his lordship's carriage. The short ride passed without unpleasantness. The marquess was glad to see that his sister's spirits had improved and that she appeared eager to be on good terms with him.

His lordship found himself thinking about Alethea. He had had a particularly restless night. He had lain awake envisioning Alethea beside him, and his imagination had quite run away with him in a decidedly disturbing fashion. Worcester thought that it was a bad idea visiting Alethea, but he had promised Prudence and therefore had no choice. He would have to endure it somehow, he told himself.

Alethea hadn't expected them to call and when Molly came to the library to announce the visitors, she had been rather dismayed. Having concluded that it would be far better to avoid Worcester, she had no wish to see him.

Yet she had little choice but to receive them. Adopting a serene expression, she walked into the drawing room, followed by Nelson. "Prudence," said Alethea, smiling at her young friend. "And, Lord Worcester. How good of you to come."

"Miss Brandon," said The marquess, making a polite bow. "And Nelson. You are looking well."

Nelson acknowledged the remark by wagging his tail.

"It is so good to see you, Alethea," said Prudence, going to her friend and kissing her first on one cheek and then the other.

"Good afternoon, Nelson," she said, smiling at the dog, who continued to wag his tail. Prudence was carrying Alethea's book in her arms. "Here is the book you left at Hartwood, Alethea. I'm sorry that I didn't return it sooner."

"Thank you. It is a curious old book. I hope you didn't learn too many spells, Pru."

Prudence laughed and handed the book to Alethea, who took it and placed it on a table. "We're here to say farewell, Alethea," said Prudence. "We are going back to town tomorrow."

"So soon?" said Alethea.

"Yes," said Prudence. "I shall miss you awfully, Alethea."

"And I shall miss you," said Alethea, directing a warm smile at the other young lady. "But do sit down, won't you? And will you have tea?"

Worcester was about to say that they could only stay a short time, but Prudence jumped in, saying that they would be very happy to have tea. Alethea rang for Molly and asked her to bring them refreshments.

"I imagine you'll be glad to return to town, Lord Worcester," said Alethea, making polite conversation but avoiding eye contact."

"Not really," returned his lordship. "I much prefer the country to town."

"Yes, my brother doesn't enjoy the Season," said Prudence. She made a face. "Nor do I. I wish you would be there with me." She brightened. "Couldn't you come and stay with us, Alethea?" Prudence turned to Worcester. "Wouldn't it be wonderful if Alethea could visit us in town? I wouldn't mind all the parties and things if she could be with me. Do invite Alethea to stay with us, Geoffrey."

The marquess stared at Alethea. She was dressed in a simple blue frock fashioned from striped muslin with long sleeves and a high collar. Her dark hair was in a state of charming dishabille. He thought she looked ravishing. "Of course, you are welcome to stay with us in town, Miss Brandon." As he said the words, the picture of Alethea residing at Worcester House came to mind. How could he bear to have her there sleeping in a bedroom near his?

"That is kind of you, Lord Worcester, but I couldn't possibly inconvenience you."

"But you must come," said Prudence. "It isn't in the least inconvenient."

"But Lord Worcester will be very busy, I'm sure, with his wedding plans." Alethea looked at the marquess, fastening her hazel eyes on his gray ones in a way that made him decidedly uncomfortable. "I must wish you joy on your upcoming marriage, my lord."

"Thank you, Miss Brandon," said the marquess. This exchange seemed to cast a pall on them.

Prudence spoke next. "You could still come stay with us, Alethea."

"Well, I do intend to be in town for a time and I shall be sure to call on you. I promised my aunt and uncle that I will visit them for a fortnight or more. They are taking a house in London for the Season and I shall stay with them."

"At least I'll see you in town," said Prudence. "That is good news. I do hope Poppet likes London." Mention of her cat made Prudence talk for a time about her pet and then Molly entered with tea.

Prudence watched Alethea pour the tea and hand the delicate blue-and-white cups and saucers to her guest. She had formulated a plan, although she wasn't sure whether she could carry it off. She had placed the small bottle of brownish green liquid into her reticule. Now she only had to get it into the cups of Worcester and Alethea.

But how to get the liquid into the teacups without anyone's knowledge? It wasn't going to be easy. Prudence sipped her tea and waited.

"Have you finished your work on your book, Miss Brandon?" said Worcester.

"Yes, I am done with it. I shall be taking it to the publisher when I accompany my aunt and uncle to town."

"How thrilling it will be to see your book in print. I shall certainly buy a copy," said Prudence.

"Thank you, Pru," said Alethea. "I must say I'm happy to be finished with it." She put down her teacup.

Prudence noted that both Alethea's and her brother's cups were now on the table. Her chance had come. "Oh dear!" she cried. "There's a man at that window! A hideous, awful man!"

Prudence spoke in such a shocked voice that Alethea and the marquess turned to the window in some alarm. Nelson started to bark furiously. "Oh, do go to the window, Geoffrey!" cried Prudence.

The marquess jumped to his feet and Alethea rose as well. He went quickly to the window and looked out, with Alethea following behind. Nelson continued to bark ferociously. Prudence hurriedly took the bottle out of her reticule and poured some of the potion into each of the two cups.

"What is the matter with you, Prudence?" said Worcester, turning away from the window. "There is no one out there."

"Are you all right, Pru?" said Alethea.

"Oh, I thought I saw someone," said Prudence, "but now I see that it was only the branch of the tree. I'm sorry to have startled you so. Do come and drink your tea."

Alethea and Worcester sat back down and picked up their teacups. They were both regarding Prudence with curious looks. "You gave us such a start," said the marquess, frowning at her. "A face in the window, indeed."

"I am sorry, Geoffrey," said Prudence. "It was silly of me." She watched them intently while they drank their tea. She was glad that neither seemed to notice that anything was different about it. Prudence made a few remarks about the weather while she watched their faces. She wondered how long the potion would take to work. "Have you seen Hector lately, Alethea?" asked Prudence.

"Yes, he came by yesterday."

"I do wish we could see him. Do you think he might come while we are here?"

"One never knows," said Alethea. As she finished her tea, she decided it had a strange flavor. She would have to ask Molly if she had bought some new tea. "Sometimes he comes to the garden."

Prudence looked at her brother, who was staring solemnly at Alethea. It seemed that he was regarding her with unusual intensity. Prudence watched as Alethea glanced over at Worcester. She saw that their eyes met for a rather long time. Looking from one to the other, Prudence couldn't help but smile. The potion was working!

"Wouldn't it be wonderful to see Hector, Geoffrey?" said Prudence.

Worcester seemed barely aware of his sister. He was staring at

Alethea with a gloomy look. "What?" he said. "Oh yes, I would like to see Hector."

"Would you like to go outside?" suggested Alethea.

"Yes, why don't we do so?" said Prudence.

They rose from their chairs and proceeded from the room and out of the house to the garden. Alethea looked up into the trees. "I don't see him, but he may come if we wait for a while."

Noting the way her brother was looking at Alethea, Prudence was now very confident that the potion had worked. "Oh, I should have brought a teacake for Hector in case he does come. I shall go fetch one." Prudence turned and hurried back to the house.

Worcester watched his sister in some frustration. He didn't want to be left alone with Alethea. She was looking too beautiful and he could smell the subtle fragrance of the perfume she was wearing. Prudence was acting in a peculiar fashion, he thought, first imagining a hideous man at the window and now rushing off to get a teacake for a crow who was nowhere to be seen.

Nelson, who had followed them outside, made his way around the garden. It was another fine day with bright sunshine and warm breezes rustling the leaves of the trees.

They stood in awkward silence for a few moments, and then Worcester spoke. "Miss Brandon, I believe I should thank you for all your assistance while we've been at Hartwood. I shall not soon forget how you nursed me back to health. And you've been a good friend to Prudence."

"I'm very fond of her," said Alethea, smiling at him. Her smile made him feel strangely week. Why had Prudence left them alone like that? Where the devil was she?

"Do you think you will come back to Hartwood, my lord?" said Alethea. "That is, when you and Lady Catherine are married?"

Worcester frowned. Why must she remind him about her? "I don't know," he said. "I imagine I shall spend most of my time in the country at Worcester Castle once the repairs are completed there." A rueful smile crossed his lips. "Well, perhaps the Beauchamp family weren't meant to stay at Hartwood."

"Perhaps not," she said, gazing up at him. Alethea was finding Worcester's closeness sorely trying. Why did she have this maddening attraction to such a man, she asked herself.

The marquess looked into her lovely hazel eyes. Her lips were raised toward him in the most inviting way. Suddenly Worcester reached out to her. Grabbing her by the arms, he pulled her to him and kissed her.

Alethea was so thoroughly astonished that at first she had no reaction. His lips were on hers, kissing her with a passionate longing that caused a tremor of excitement to pass through her body. Then, lost to all reason, Alethea returned his kiss with the fervor of suppressed ardor.

It was Worcester who first came to his senses. What in God's name was he doing! He pulled away from her. "Miss Brandon, I am sorry! I don't know what came over me! I beg you to forgive me."

Alethea looked down in confusion. She didn't know what to say or how to respond to what had happened.

"I am so sorry," repeated the marquess. "I completely lost my head." He looked toward the house, where Prudence was just now coming out of the door. Why had his sister gone off and left him like that, he thought bitterly. He had acted like a debauched rakehell and now Alethea must think him some sort of unprincipled beast.

"Did you see Hector?" said Prudence, hurrying toward them with a tea cake in her hand.

"No, we did not," said Worcester curtly. "I believe it is time we took our leave, Prudence. We have taken advantage of Miss Brandon's hospitality long enough."

Surprisingly, Prudence made no protest. "Do promise you will call at Worcester House as soon as you arrive in London," she said.

"Yes, of course," said Alethea.

"Good-bye, then, my dear Alethea," said Prudence, hugging her friend.

"Good-bye, Pru," said Alethea. When she had extricated herself from Prudence's embrace, she looked over at Worcester. "Good day, my lord."

"Miss Brandon," he said stiffly. Alethea ushered them back through the house and out the front door. As she stood watching the carriage drive off, she thanked Providence that Prudence hadn't witnessed the lamentable scene in the garden.

Prudence leaned back on the carriage seat and stared thoughtfully at her brother. He was deep in thought and in a terrible mood.

A worried look came to Prudence's fair countenance. Although Alethea had thought her friend hadn't seen the shocking kiss, Prudence had been watching them through the window. After retreating into the house and obtaining a tea cake for Hector, she had gone to the library, where she knew there was a window facing the garden. There she had stood, triumphantly spying on her brother and Alethea.

Yet when Worcester had pulled Alethea to him and kissed her in that passionate way, Prudence had been horrified. It seemed the potion was far more powerful than she had thought. Prudence had then rushed out from the library to the garden, where she had found her brother and Alethea, both looking stunned by what had happened.

Prudence stared reflectively out the carriage window. It seemed she had caused a great deal of mischief. She frowned and felt on the verge of tears. Why hadn't she thought more about Alethea? It was all very well for Worcester to get his comeuppance, but what about her friend? Now Alethea would be hopelessly in love with Worcester. And what if her brother still felt compelled to marry Catherine Perry?

Prudence looked over at the marquess, who was staring grimly out the window, and wished that she had never thought to concoct a love potion.

Chapter 27

Alethea arrived in London two weeks after Worcester and Prudence left Hartwood. The trip hadn't been too arduous, for the Truscotts possessed a fine carriage suitable for long journeys. Since Mr. Truscott abhorred rushing about the countryside, they had proceeded at a decorous pace, stopping frequently to rest and take in the sights along the way.

Elizabeth was very excited about finally going to town. She loved spending the Season in London amidst the excitement and hustle and bustle of the great metropolis. She adored the theater and parties and evenings at Vauxhall Gardens.

Alethea's aunt was looking forward to this Season even more than usual, because she felt that she now had an entrée into the more elite circles of society. She was now acquainted with the Marquess of Worcester. Of course, Elizabeth was well aware that she scarcely knew the marquess. Yet because her niece was on terms of considerable intimacy with that nobleman's sister, she was certain they would receive invitations from Lady Prudence. Who knew whom they might meet when dining at Worcester House?

The only troublesome thing in her aunt's view was that Alethea continued to insist that she only wished to stay a fortnight in town. Since it was inconceivable to Elizabeth that anyone would travel such a distance to stay such a short time, she continued to insist that Alethea remain with them for a month at the very least.

Alethea, to her aunt's frustration, had no wish to linger in town. Having left Nelson at Crow's Nest Cottage, she missed him very much. The first day that she was in town, she found herself sitting in the nicely furnished room where she was to stay, wishing she were back at her home near the sea.

The noise and dirt of London depressed her and she never got used to seeing such crowds of people everywhere. And there was always the knowledge that Worcester was there nearby.

Alethea didn't want to see him again. He was probably soon to be married, and it would be far easier if their paths never crossed.

It was soon clear, however, that Elizabeth had different ideas. Ever since leaving Towmouth, she had talked about calling on Lady Prudence. It was hard for Alethea to think of any reason for not doing so. After all, she and Prudence had become good friends and she did want to see her.

The morning after they arrived in London, Alethea sat at breakfast with her aunt and uncle. Mr. Truscott occupied himself with eating kippers while his wife chattered happily. "I do think this is a very fine house," said Elizabeth. "And Henley Square is a very respectable address. Oh, I know it isn't the most fashionable place in town, but one need not be ashamed of it."

"It's a lovely house," said Alethea. "And so conveniently located."

"Yes, isn't it?" said Elizabeth. "There are wonderful shops everywhere. I daresay you'll want to do a good deal of shopping while you're here."

"In truth, Aunt, I don't really need anything."

"Don't need anything?" exclaimed her aunt. "My dear, if you don't mind my saying so, you have need of a number of improvements to your wardrobe. One cannot attend parties in town wearing gowns several seasons old."

"But I don't wish to attend parties, Aunt, and I won't be here very long."

"Alethea Brandon, I caution you not to vex me. I've wanted you to come with me to town for years and now that you're here, you will humor me. There are a good many charming gentlemen who will be very eager to meet a young lady of your accomplishments."

"Well, perhaps I shall meet one at the British Museum," said Alethea.

"At the British Museum?" said Elizabeth.

"Yes," replied Alethea with a mischievous smile. "I intend to spend a good deal of time there."

"Whatever for?"

"There are a good many specimens I wish to see."

"Specimens!" cried her aunt. "Mr. Truscott, do tell your niece that she mustn't fritter her time away at such a place."

"I'll not venture to tell Alethea anything," said her uncle, continuing to eat his breakfast.

"You are no help whatsoever," said Alethea's aunt. "Well, I thought we might visit some shops today. And then we could call on Lady Prudence."

"But I must take my book to the publisher. I promised Mr. Ward that I'd bring it to him as soon as I arrived. I shall write to Prudence and we can call on her tomorrow."

"Oh, very well," said Aunt Elizabeth, rather disappointed.

After luncheon, Alethea set off for her publisher while her aunt went shopping. Mr. Ward, a distinguished elderly gentleman who was a good friend of her father, was very pleased to see Alethea. After a very pleasant and fruitful discussion, Alethea returned to Henley Square. She had scarcely removed her bonnet and pelisse when a maid knocked on her door. "Excuse me, miss, but you have a visitor. Dr. Chandler is here. I've shown him to the drawing room.

Pleased at the idea of seeing him, Alethea hurried to the drawing room. "Robert!"

"Alethea!" He held out his hands to her and she clasped them happily.

"Oh, how good it is to see you, Robert. It appears London agrees with you."

Chandler smiled. He looked a very dapper and prosperous young gentleman. "My uncle has been very kind and the work is deuced interesting. And I've been enjoying life in the great city. I've already seen its greatest attractions, the Elgin marbles and Kean."

"I should love to see both," said Alethea with a smile.

"I shall take you," he said. "Anytime you like. Or at least when my duties allow." Pulling his watch from his pocket, he glanced down at it. "I fear I haven't much time. But it is good to see you, Alethea."

"And it's good to see you looking so well and happy."

He smiled. "If you're worried that I'm pining away for Lady Prudence, you may rest easy. Oh, I feel very strongly about her, of course. I feel that I shall always love her, but I've become reconciled to the idea that I'll never see her again. I was such a fool. For a time I was thinking that we could be married. I believe I was reading too many radical pamphlets about the equality of man.

"But a physician doesn't marry a marquess's daughter. That's true enough."

Alethea nodded and said to herself, *And a botanist's daughter doesn't marry a marquess.* Aloud, she said, "Poor Robert. It must be very difficult. And poor Prudence."

A rueful smile came to Chandler's face. "Poor, dear Prudence," he said, "but she'll find someone else and forget all about me. Indeed, I hope she does. I wish her only happiness." He paused. "You'll be seeing her now that you're in town?"

"Yes," said Alethea. "My aunt and I will call on her tomorrow."

"Well, I hope you find her well." Chandler rose to his feet. "And now I must be going. I have many appointments and must return to my office. I'll call again when I have more time."

After he took his leave, Alethea sat down to write a brief note to Prudence.

Worcester stared solemnly at his future bride as Lady Catherine poured tea. He was seated across from Catherine and her mother in the Huntingdons' lavishly appointed drawing room. The ladies had been talking for some time about the upcoming wedding, a subject that depressed his lordship.

Lady Huntingdon and her daughter had determined a date for the ceremony that was scarcely six weeks away. While Worcester would have liked to delay the event for some months, he could think of no excuse for doing so.

"There are so many arrangements to be made," said the countess. "One's head just spins thinking of all the details. It will be a splendid occasion to be sure. The prince himself has assured me he will attend."

"He didn't attend Caroline Fitzwilliam's wedding," said Catherine. "She'll be green with envy."

"Well, who is Caroline Fitzwilliam compared to you, my dear?" said the countess. "No, there won't be another such wedding this Season."

The conversation turned to prospective bridesmaids. Since his lordship had no interest whatsoever in this topic, he found his mind wandering. As usual the object of his thoughts was Alethea and he wondered what she was doing at that moment.

Worcester scarcely listened as the ladies chattered on. They were finally interrupted by the entrance of the Huntingdons' butler, who announced that Lord Feversham had arrived.

"Oh, we must see Feversham," said the countess. "His opinions would be very useful. Do show him in."

In a few moments, Feversham sauntered into the drawing room. Dressed in his trademark sartorial splendor, the viscount wore a dove gray coat over a yellow-and-black stripped waistcoat and pale buff-colored pantaloons. He bowed to the ladies and nodded to Worcester.

"How good of you to call, Feversham," said Lady Huntingdon. "We were just discussing Catherine's wedding plans."

"Indeed?" said Feversham, taking a seat.

"Mama was saying that I must have my cousin Penelope Cavendish as a bridesmaid. While she is a good sort of girl, she is so frightfully plain."

"Well, I shouldn't worry about that," said Feversham, taking his snuffbox out of his pocket. "I daresay all eyes will be upon the beautiful bride."

Catherine was quite delighted by the compliment. She knew that Feversham was a critical judge of appearance and not the sort of man to offer flummery to a lady. Fixing a dazzling smile upon the viscount, Catherine continued to discuss her bridesmaids with him.

The marquess was growing increasingly irritated as his fiancée and future mother-in-law eagerly sought Feversham's advice on a number of matters concerning the wedding plans. The two ladies listened raptly to the viscount as if he were some great oracle. Feversham talked on and on, delighting the countess and her daughter with his cutting witticisms.

Worcester sat stonily silent, regarding the viscount with a disapproving expression. He wondered how he could have ever considered such a coxcomb as a husband for his sister. It was fortunate that Prudence had been so adamant in her refusal to marry the fellow. The match would have been a terrible mistake.

Turning his gaze from Feversham to Catherine, Worcester's face grew exceedingly grim. At least his sister Pru had been spared from a disastrous marriage, he thought to himself. Certainly he wouldn't be so lucky.

With his wedding fast approaching, Worcester felt himself trapped. As a man of honor, he could not renege on his pledge to marry Catherine, but the thought of taking the lady to wife and to his bed was becoming more and more intolerable to him.

The marquess continued to stare glumly at his intended bride. Catherine, who was laughing at one of Feversham's remarks, seemed to be totally oblivious to Worcester's presence. He reflected that there was no doubt that the lady was a remarkable beauty. However, of late, that seemed little consolation. Worcester was increasingly aware of Catherine's defects of character. He found her shallow, spiteful, and conceited, with no interests outside of fashion or society.

Looking away from Catherine, Worcester's thoughts wandered once again to Alethea. He remembered their last meeting and how he had taken her into his arms. Lingering on the vivid memory of their kiss, the marquess was unaware that Lady Huntingdon had asked him a question.

"Worcester," said Catherine in a loud voice, abruptly interrupting his pleasant reverie. He glanced over to find her regarding him with an exasperated expression. "Mama was asking you a question."

"I beg your pardon, Lady Huntingdon."

"Worcester," said Lady Huntingdon, "I was just wondering what your preference would be?"

"My preference?" he asked, raising his eyebrows slightly.

"Why, for the wedding feast, of course. We're discussing the menu."

The marquess wanted to say, "Hang the wedding feast," but he merely shrugged. "That's a subject best left to you ladies. I'm certain that anything you decide will be quite adequate, ma'am."

Lady Huntingdon was not overly pleased with the word "adequate," but she nodded. "Very well." There was a momentary lull in the conversation as both of the ladies regarded the marquess with slightly disapproving looks.

"Well, Lady Catherine," said Feversham, deciding to change the subject, "aren't you glad to be back in town after your sojourn in the country?"

Catherine nodded. "I am, indeed. I know that some prefer the country, but I always find it so frightfully dull."

"Precisely," said the viscount. "There are always such frightfully dull persons about the bucolic landscape." He paused. "Of course, I must admit, that the countryside around your Hartwood boasted at least one rather interesting personage, Worcester." The marquess did not deign to reply to this.

"Hartwood?" repeated Catherine, her lovely face looking perplexed. "Surely you didn't find any of the provincials there interesting?"

"Oh, yes. I did find one lady there rather intriguing—Miss Brandon." On hearing Alethea's name, Worcester frowned.

"Miss Brandon?" said Catherine. "Why, you surprise me, Feversham. I didn't think the lady at all above the ordinary."

"Indeed," added her mother, "the young lady was tolerable-enough-looking, I suppose, but she was rather singular, don't you think? Writing a book about, oh, what was it about?"

Catherine rolled her eyes heavenward in amusement. "Herbs, Mama."

"Herbs," said Lady Huntingdon with an expression that implied she had proven her point.

"Yes, it's not surprising that she is well versed upon the subject," said Feversham. "Apparently the lady uses them in her sorcery."

"Sorcery?" asked Catherine. "Whatever can you mean?"

Feversham nodded. "I do wish I had found out about it earlier, but after we returned from Hartwood my valet informed me that many of the local peasants believe Miss Brandon practices the powers of witchcraft."

"That is utter nonsense," said Worcester testily.

"Yes, you are being ridiculous," said Catherine with a smile.

"Well, perhaps, but it is rather curious. Apparently this Miss Brandon has a pet crow and spends her time concocting various potions over a cauldron. And she did have raven tresses as I recall."

"Good heavens, Feversham," said Lady Huntingdon, "next you will tell us that she flies about the countryside on a broom."

Feversham laughed. "I have not heard any such report, ma'am. But it is said that she has amazing healing powers which she uses on the local hogs and such."

"Hogs?" said Catherine and she and her mother burst into laughter. "Yes, I do remember her running off from Worcester's dinner party to see to some farmer's cow. Can you imagine that?"

Feversham looked slyly over at the marquess. "Didn't she use her witchcraft on you, Worcester? To cure your illness, I mean to say."

The marquess bristled. "Miss Brandon is knowledgeable in plant cures, that's all. Only a complete bottle head would believe such rubbish."

Feversham did not appear at all insulted by this remark. "I daresay you're right, Worcester. But it does make a good tale, does it not?"

Catherine and Lady Huntingdon laughed again, but it was obvious that the marquess was not amused. He was relieved when Feversham changed the topic of the conversation to the Prince Regent. After sitting for what seemed an interminable time, but was in reality only a few minutes, Worcester stood up rather abruptly.

"Excuse me, Catherine, Lady Huntingdon," he said, "but I have some business and must go."

His fiancée, who was not at all unhappy to see the sullen marquess depart, merely nodded. Making a slight bow, Worcester took his leave.

After the marquess's departure, the mother and daughter remained talking to the viscount for some time. A servant entered the room, announcing that there was a problem in the kitchen that needed Lady Huntingdon's immediate attention. Lady Huntingdon reluctantly followed the servant from the room.

Left alone with Catherine, Feversham smiled over at her. "It appeared that Worcester didn't appreciate my talking about Miss Brandon."

"I fear he doesn't have a sense of humor, Feversham."

"I suppose Worcester is grateful to the girl for tending to him when he was ill," said Feversham. The viscount leaned toward her. "I do hope Worcester realizes what a fortunate man he is, Catherine."

Meeting his gaze, Catherine was surprised by the look of admiration in it. She had never considered Feversham as a possible suitor, for it had always been common knowledge that the Duke of Cranworth had intended to marry Lady Prudence Beauchamp. Now, of course, the gossip was that Prudence had rejected him. As Catherine smiled over at the handsome viscount, she decided that if that was true, then Worcester's sister was a very foolish girl indeed.

Chapter 28

Prudence sat on the floor of the drawing room watching Poppet's antics. The gray-striped kitten batted a ball of yarn about with her small paws, chasing after it as it got away from her.

When the door opened, Prudence looked up to see the butler enter the room. "Look at Poppet play with the yarn, Talbot. Isn't she a darling creature?"

The servant nodded. "Indeed, she is, my lady." Although Talbot had little use for cats and would scarcely refer to them as "darling," he was glad to see that the animal was cheering up his young mistress. He was well aware that she and his master had seemed particularly unhappy since their return to town. Indeed, a gloom had settled over the entire household.

Walking over to Prudence, Talbot bent down to extend a silver salver to her. "There is a letter for you, my lady."

The smile on Prudence's face quickly faded. "Oh dear," she said, certain that it would be another invitation to some society function. Since returning to town, Prudence had already attended several parties and a ball and she was not eager for another engagement. Sighing, she took the letter from the tray and broke the seal. "Why, it is from Alethea!" said Prudence, her face brightening. "Miss Brandon, that is to say. Oh, thank you, Talbot."

The butler nodded and quietly left the room as Prudence read Alethea's communication. Poppet, who was distracted from her yarn, came over to her mistress to stare up at her with a quizzical expression.

After finishing the short note, Prudence smiled down at the cat. "Oh, Poppet, it's very good news. Alethea is in town and she'll be calling on us tomorrow." The cat meowed as if in reply and Prudence laughed.

While Prudence had been reading Alethea's note, her brother had returned from his unpleasant visit to Lady Catherine and her mother. Frowning, he handed his hat to the butler. "Where is Lady Prudence, Talbot?"

"In the drawing room, my lord," said the servant, who could not fail to note that his master appeared to be in a particularly ill humor. Worcester nodded and then made his way down the hallway toward the room.

Opening the door, the marquess found his sister sitting on the floor intent upon a piece of paper before her. Poppet had returned to her ball of yarn and was chasing it about the floor, a long strand of blue yarn trailing after her. "Really, Pru," said Worcester in some irritation, "must you sit upon the floor? It is scarcely ladylike. And that cat has yarn all about the place."

Prudence looked up at her brother. "Don't be cross, Geoffrey. We're only having a little fun." Rising from the floor, she gave him a welcoming kiss on the cheek.

A slight smile appeared on Worcester's face, softening his stern expression. "Oh, very well, I shan't lecture you or the creature." Taking a seat on the sofa, he noticed the note in his sister's hand. "What's that? Another invitation?"

Sitting down beside him, Prudence shook her head. "No, it's far better than that. It's a note from Alethea! She's in town and will call on us tomorrow!"

As Worcester stared at the letter, a slight flush appeared on his face. "Miss Brandon is in town?" he managed to say in what he hoped was a tone of polite indifference.

However, Prudence could plainly see that the news had very much affected him. It was clear that the potion had worked with a vengeance and her brother was still madly in love with Alethea.

"Yes, you remember that she was going to be staying in London with her aunt and uncle?" said Prudence, handing him the letter. "Here, you must read her note."

Taking the paper, the marquess gazed down upon it. "I know you'll be glad to see Miss Brandon again." He paused. "I fear I shan't have that pleasure, for I'll be away all afternoon." Worcester handed the note back to her. "But I daresay Miss Brandon will scarcely notice my absence. It's you she wishes to see."

"Yes, of course," said Prudence, casting a sympathetic look at her brother. She could well understand why he didn't wish to be there for Alethea's visit. Certainly, seeing her would be very painful for him. After all, he was to marry Catherine Percy in a few weeks' time. And poor Alethea! Prudence devoutly wished that she had never seen the recipe for the love potion.

Worcester stood up. "Now if you'll excuse me, Pru, I have some business that I must attend to." Prudence merely nodded and watched dolefully as her brother exited the room.

Taking up the letter again, she stared gloomily at it. "Poor Geoffrey," murmured Prudence. She was well aware of what it was like to love someone that you could never have. Prudence thought of Dr. Chandler constantly. Knowing that he was in London made it even worse, for despite his proximity, she doubted that she would ever see him again.

Sighing, Prudence appeared thoughtful. She had concocted the potion so that her brother would know how it felt to be in love. It was obvious that she had succeeded beyond all of her expectations. As she folded up Alethea's note, Prudence could not help but feel guilty.

Prudence glanced down at the kitten curled up next to her. "Oh, Poppet," she cried, "I think I have made a terrible muddle of everything!" The small cat looked up at her and twitched her long tail.

The following afternoon, a carriage pulled up in front of Worcester's townhouse. Staring out the vehicle's window at the redbrick building, Alethea experienced considerable trepidation at the thought of seeing Worcester again. Her Aunt Elizabeth, who sat next to her, felt no such qualms. She was quite eager to pay a call upon the august marquess.

As a footman assisted her down from the carriage, Elizabeth glanced about with considerable satisfaction. As a woman who craved a place in the higher echelons of society, she was well aware that she and her niece were visiting in the most fashionable neighborhood in town.

As the two ladies arrived at the front door of the elegant residence, Elizabeth fixed a final critical gaze upon her niece. She had wished that there had been time for Alethea to have had some new clothes made, but she had to admit that her niece appeared quite presentable. In fact, attired in an olive green dress and matching pelisse, her dark curls peeking out from beneath a lace-trimmed bonnet, Alethea looked quite charming.

The door opened and they were met by the butler. "Good day, Talbot," said Alethea, smiling at him.

"Miss Brandon," he said with a deferential nod. "Lady Prudence is expecting you. Please follow me." He led the two ladies to the drawing room, where they found Prudence sitting upon an elegant French sofa with Poppet.

"Miss Brandon and Mrs. Truscott, my lady," said Talbot.

Jumping up from the sofa, Prudence rushed over to them. "Alethea!" she cried, giving her friend a hug. "I'm so happy to see you."

"And I am glad to see you, Pru," said Alethea. "You remember my aunt, Mrs. Truscott?"

"Oh yes," said Prudence, smiling affably at that lady, "I am pleased you could come, ma'am."

Elizabeth beamed and curtsied. "Thank you, Lady Prudence."

Prudence steered them into the room, where Mrs. Truscott happily took a place in a Queen Anne chair. Alethea joined her friend on the sofa. Reaching over to pet the kitten, Alethea glanced up at Prudence. "It appears Poppet is in fine fettle."

"Oh, yes, she's grown quite a bit, don't you think?"

"She has, indeed," said Alethea.

"And how is Nelson?" asked Prudence. "Did you bring him to town?"

Alethea shook her head. "I fear Nelson doesn't like being away from home. He is at Crow's Nest Cottage, where I'm sure Molly and Sarah are spoiling him outrageously."

"Oh," said Prudence, slightly disappointed that she wouldn't get to see her friend's huge canine. "I suppose it's best Nelson stayed at home. I don't think he would like town overmuch."

Although Elizabeth was fond of animals, she was growing a little impatient with the talk of the young ladies' pets. "And how is Lord Worcester, Lady Prudence?" she asked, changing the conversation to human subjects. "I do hope he is well."

"My brother is very well, thank you," said Prudence. Glancing over at Alethea, she continued a trifle sheepishly, "I'm afraid he won't be joining us. He had a previous engagement."

The news that she wouldn't see the marquess after all struck Alethea with surprising force. While she had been dreading meeting him again, she was now experiencing a sense of profound disappointment.

"Oh, that is too bad," said Elizabeth, who was also disappointed to hear that the marquess would not be in attendance. "Well, I don't doubt that his lordship is very busy. After all, he's soon to be married."

Prudence glanced sideways at her friend, knowing that Alethea wouldn't want to discuss the topic of Worcester's upcoming marriage. She hastily continued. "My brother Ned is staying with friends in Brighton, but he's expected back in a day or so. I know he'd very much like to see you, Alethea."

"I'd like to see Lord Edward," said Alethea. "I hope he's well."

"Oh, yes," said Prudence. "And have you brought your book to town, Alethea?"

"Yes, and I have already delivered it to the publisher."

"I shall be very eager to purchase a copy of it," said Prudence. "And I shall, of course, want my copy signed by the author."

"I think that can be arranged," said Alethea with a smile.

The three ladies continued to talk for a time and then Prudence called Talbot to bring in tea. A short time later the butler returned, followed by two other servants carrying silver trays laden with china and a tempting selection of cakes and biscuits.

After dismissing the servants, Prudence reached for the teapot. She was just about to pour out a cup when the drawing-room door opened again. Alethea glanced over and was startled to see Worcester standing in the doorway.

"Geoffrey!" cried Prudence, regarding him in surprise. "I didn't expect you."

Worcester walked into the room and stood before them. "My appointment was mercifully short," he said. Looking at Alethea, he made a slight bow. "Miss Brandon," he said. Then turning to Alethea's aunt, he bowed again. "Mrs. Truscott."

Alethea merely nodded, hoping she was not blushing. However, Elizabeth quickly spoke up. "Lord Worcester," she said, "it's very good to see you. We have been so enjoying our visit with your delightful sister."

"I am glad to hear it, ma'am," he said.

"Well, do sit down, Geoffrey," said Prudence. "We were just about to have tea."

The marquess obliged by taking a seat across from Alethea. He then proceeded to stare intently at her.

Prudence, who was finding the situation somewhat awkward, began pouring out the tea. Fortunately, Elizabeth was quite eager to talk and she chatted on about Worcester's lovely home and what a wonderful visit they were having. She then began to discourse on the coming delights of the Season in town.

The marquess managed to nod politely every now and then, but in truth, he was scarcely listening. He found it almost impossible to turn his attention away from Alethea. She was as lovely as he remembered her, and he had an almost overpowering urge to take her into his arms again and fasten his lips upon hers.

Of course, such a shocking action was impossible, so he contented himself with gazing at her. He knew that his appearance there was imprudent. He had had every intention of staying away from the house while Alethea was there, but his resolution had failed him. Knowing that he desperately wanted to see her again, he had hurried home, hoping that she'd still be there.

Alethea felt uncomfortable under Worcester's intense scrutiny. Reminding herself that he was soon to be married, she tried to maintain a calm pose. She was glad that her aunt chattered away, sparing her the necessity of making many comments.

After what seemed to Alethea a very long time, Elizabeth finally announced that they should be going. "I fear we really must take our leave," said Elizabeth in a tone of regret.

"Yes," said Alethea, quickly getting up from the sofa. Worcester immediately rose to his feet.

"I've enjoyed myself very much," said Elizabeth. "And I must get the recipe for that poppyseed cake."

"Of course," said Prudence. "I shall have Cook write it up for you." She turned to Alethea. "I do hope you'll call again. Or perhaps I might visit you."

"Oh, please do," said Alethea, warmly pressing her friend's hand.

Elizabeth hesitated a moment before turning to the marquess. "I was wondering, Lord Worcester, if you and Lady Prudence might join a small dinner party I'm having on Tuesday next."

Alethea, who hadn't expected her aunt to issue an invitation to dinner, regarded Elizabeth with alarm. "We would be very pleased to do so, Mrs. Truscott," said the marquess, surprising both Alethea and Prudence with his ready acceptance. "You are very kind."

Elizabeth was thrilled. "How wonderful!" she exclaimed.

"And, of course, I shall send an invitation to Lady Catherine and her parents."

Worcester's face clouded. He realized that he had made a dreadful blunder. "That would be good of you," he murmured glumly.

After a brief leave taking, the ladies were soon on their way back to the Truscotts' residence. Elizabeth, who was quite thrilled by the outcome of their visit, talked excitedly.

Alethea tried to hide her dismay. Not only would she have to see Worcester again, but she now had to face the prospect of a dinner party that included his future bride. As the carriage continued on, Alethea could only wish that she were back at Crow's Nest Cottage.

Chapter 29

Alethea sat at a desk in the Truscotts' small library, a thick book propped open before her. The volume was a biography on Sir Francis Drake that she had purchased that morning on a shopping expedition with her aunt.

Although the recounting of the naval hero's life was quite exciting, Alethea found that she was having trouble concentrating. No matter how hard she tried to put the marquess out of her mind, her thoughts continued to dwell on him.

It had been two days since she had called on Prudence, yet the memory of the visit was still quite vivid. Frowning, Alethea rose from the desk. It was ridiculous to keep thinking of Worcester. She was acting like a silly moonstruck schoolgirl.

Walking over to the window, Alethea glanced outside at the busy city street. Although it had rained all morning, the weather appeared to be clearing, with the sun attempting to break through the clouds. Deciding that she would go out for a walk, Alethea went to her room, where she hastily put on a pelisse and donned a broad-brimmed bonnet. Then, after informing her aunt that she would be back directly, she left the house and made her way down the sidewalk.

The moment she was outside, Alethea's spirits were considerably brightened. The cool temperature was invigorating, and she could not help but appreciate the profusion of colorful flowers that lined the street.

There was a small, picturesque park that was a mere four blocks from the Truscotts' house. It had become a favorite destination for Alethea during her stay with her aunt and uncle.

When she was halfway to the park, Alethea noted a gentleman walking toward her. She realized in some surprise that it was

Lord Edward Beauchamp. That gentleman broke into a broad grin and hurried to meet her.

"Miss Brandon," said Lord Edward, tipping his tall beaver hat, "what good fortune to meet you."

"Lord Edward," said Alethea, smiling at him, "I am surprised to see you walking here."

"Well, after all that rain this morning, I was deuced glad to be able to go out and get some exercise."

Alethea nodded. "Then we both had the same idea."

After learning that Alethea was on her way to the park, Edward asked if he might accompany her there. When she assented, he gallantly offered her his arm and they began to stroll down the street together.

"I'm glad that I happened upon you, Miss Brandon," said Edward with a charming smile. "Actually, I was on my way to pay you a call. My sister told me you were in town. I just got back myself last night."

"Yes, Prudence said you were expected back soon."

"Pru wanted to come with me this afternoon, but, unfortunately, she had already agreed to accompany Lady Catherine to the dressmaker. They were to see about Pru's gown for the wedding."

Alethea made no reply and they continued walking. "Yes, it will be a very grand wedding," said Edward. "Poor old Geoffrey."

"Poor old Geoffrey?" asked Alethea, regarding him with a questioning glance.

Edward laughed. "Well, I know it is rather bad of me to say so, but I don't envy his marrying Lady Catherine. I fear he's making a dreadful mistake."

"Is he?"

Edward nodded. "I believe he is. You see, Miss Brandon, my brother looks at marriage in a cold, practical way. He thinks of it as a business transaction, a merger of two families of rank and fortune." He smiled at Alethea. "I suppose I'm a romantic fool, but I cannot imagine how Geoffrey could be happy with a woman for whom he has not one ounce of affection or regard."

"Perhaps you are mistaken about Lord Worcester's feelings for Lady Catherine," said Alethea.

Edward shook his head. "I don't believe so, and I don't think the lady cares one whit for him, either. No, I'll wager that Geoffrey and his bride will soon make each other miserable. I only wish that he would not be so eager to inflict the same fate upon Pru and myself."

"Your brother cannot want you to be unhappy," said Alethea, having a strange desire to defend Worcester.

"Oh? You saw how he was ready to foist Feversham upon Pru, even though she thoroughly disliked the fellow. Thank God my sister stood her ground and refused him." Edward stopped and faced Alethea. "I don't mean to paint my brother as a monster, Miss Brandon. I'm really dashed fond of him, but he can just be so devilish difficult at times!"

Alethea smiled. "Yes, I know him well enough to be aware of that, Lord Edward."

Edward nodded. He appeared to hesitate for a moment, before continuing. "I feel I can confess a certain matter to you, Miss Brandon. You see, I'm in something of a predicament myself."

"Oh dear," said Alethea.

Edward took her arm again and they continued walking along the street. "It's actually a rather wonderful predicament. You see, a few months ago I met a girl and I fell head over heels in love with her. Her name is Thomasina Whitfield and she is absolutely adorable."

Alethea smiled. "But what is the problem with that?"

"My brother is the problem," replied Edward.

"I gather Lord Worcester doesn't approve?"

"You've hit the nail upon the head, Miss Brandon," said Edward. "Or at least I'm certain that he wouldn't approve. You see, I haven't told him about Miss Whitfield. Her father is very wealthy, but his fortune has been made in trade. When Geoffrey finds out that I'm engaged . . ."

"You're engaged?" asked Alethea in surprise.

Edward nodded. "It's a secret, of course. I know Geoffrey will be furious when he finds out. I daresay he'll disown me and never wish to see me again.

"While I have no desire to sever all ties with my brother, Miss Brandon, it seems that I'll have no choice. I intend to marry Thomasina no matter what Geoffrey says."

Alethea considered this for a moment in silence. "I do think it would be best if you spoke to Lord Worcester as soon as possible about the matter," she said finally. "If you're determined to marry Miss Whitfield, you'll have to talk to him sooner or later"

"Yes, I know you're right," said Edward. "I've been trying to work my courage up to the sticking point, as it were."

Alethea pressed his arm sympathetically. "Perhaps Lord Worcester will be more understanding than you think."

"I do hope you are right," said Edward. As they continued along on their walk, Alethea very much hoped so, too.

Prudence called at the Truscotts' the following day. Although Alethea was happy to see her friend, she was far from pleased when Prudence informed her that Lady Catherine was planning to attend her aunt's dinner party the following week. Of course, Elizabeth, who was quite ecstatic at the news, could scarcely wait for the day of the great event to roll around.

Unlike her aunt, Alethea spent the next several days dreading the dinner. She had hoped that Catherine and her parents would refuse her aunt's invitation and that the marquess would beg off as well. But, unfortunately, all the guests were expected to attend.

When the day of the dinner party arrived, Alethea was almost relieved. She decided that at least she would finally get the ordeal over with.

As she got dressed, Alethea reflected on the unpleasant evening ahead of her. She glumly watched as her maid began to work on her hair.

When the servant was finished, Alethea stared at her reflection critically in the mirror. Attired in a rose-colored silk gown, her dark hair was festooned with silk roses. Alethea decided that she looked good enough, although she didn't doubt that Catherine would surely find some fault with her. Reluctantly, she got up from the table and went downstairs.

As soon as Worcester and his guests arrived, Alethea realized that the evening was going to be even worse than she had imagined. Catherine and her parents had adopted a condescending attitude that bordered on rudeness. Instead of being insulted by this, Alethea's aunt fawned over her top-lofty guests, much to her niece's disgust.

Although she tried to avoid Worcester, Alethea found it rather difficult in such a small party. It didn't help matters that her aunt had placed him directly across from her at the dinner table. Sitting between Lord Huntingdon and her uncle's old friend, Colonel Webster, Alethea attempted to focus her attention on them. However, since those two gentlemen were intent upon the meal and seemed little inclined toward conversation, she didn't have much success. Whenever she glanced over at the marquess, she was disturbed to find his gaze upon her.

Alethea was much relieved when the final course was over and the ladies left the gentlemen to their port. Adjourning to the drawing room with the other women, Alethea quickly took a seat in the drawing room next to Prudence. However, to Alethea's disappointment, Catherine placed herself in a chair beside her.

After informing Alethea that she would be glad to refer her to her own dressmaker, Catherine proceeded to disparage the dinner, the other guests, and Alethea's aunt's interior decoration. Alethea, who was having some difficulty controlling her temper, decided that Catherine was one of the most odious persons she had ever met.

When the gentlemen joined them, Elizabeth suggested that some of her guests might enjoy a game of cards. Hoping to escape Catherine, Alethea rose to take a place at the card table. Unfortunately, her aunt suggested that the marquess and Catherine join her.

Alethea found the card game quite excruciating. Catherine, who only a few moments ago had been loquacious, lapsed into silence. She sat staring at her cards, a decided pout on her lovely face. Worcester also scarcely spoke a word, and since Alethea's own partner at the table was her taciturn uncle, it was a very dull group, indeed.

Since Alethea was nearly as skilled at whist as she was at chess, Alethea and her uncle were winning handily. Catherine, who seemed quite befuddled by the game, played miserably, causing Worcester considerable frustration.

Perhaps the only person at the gathering having an even worse time than Alethea was Worcester, who was feeling more wretched than he had ever felt in his entire life. It was horrible for him, sitting so close to Alethea all evening. He was dismayed to find that she was treating him with cool politeness, as if he were some distant and not-much-liked relation. Of course, he could scarcely blame her. Worcester knew he had behaved quite abominably at his last visit to Crow's Nest Cottage. The memory of that passionate encounter returned to him again and he colored slightly.

Worcester frowned grimly. Surely Alethea had every reason to despise him. He attempted to focus his attention on the card game, but it was very difficult. As the game continued, the marquess desperately wished to be anywhere but there at the Truscotts'.

Unlike her niece and the marquess, Elizabeth was heartily enjoying the party. Well aware of her triumph in having such august personages in attendance, she was in high spirits all evening. In fact, her only disappointment occurred when Worcester and the others announced much too early that they had to depart.

When the guests had gone, Elizabeth smiled at her niece. "Wasn't it a lovely dinner party, my dear?"

"It was very nice," said Alethea.

While a bit disappointed at her niece's lack of enthusiasm, Elizabeth still basked in the glow of her success. "I had the most interesting discussion with Lady Huntingdon. I'm sure that we'll receive a good many invitations now. Isn't it wonderful?"

Elizabeth continued to talk excitedly about the party and it was some time before Alethea was finally able to retreat to her room. Feeling quite exhausted, she was very glad to go to bed.

Unfortunately, as soon as Alethea climbed into the large canopied bed, she found it impossible to go to sleep. She kept dwelling on Worcester and Catherine and their upcoming wedding. It was a long time before Alethea fell into a fitful slumber.

The next morning, Alethea found herself thinking again about Worcester. Try as she would, she couldn't get him out of her thoughts. Frustrated by this, Alethea suddenly made a decision. She would not stay in London any longer. She would go home, away from the marquess and Lady Catherine.

After she dressed, Alethea made her way downstairs. She was surprised to find that her aunt was already having breakfast. "Good morning, Aunt," she said, managing to smile at Elizabeth. That lady regarded her with a cheerful expression.

"Alethea, I'm so glad you're up. Wasn't it a wonderful evening?"

Fortunately, Alethea was spared the necessity of a reply by the appearance of her aunt's butler. "I beg your pardon, ma'am," he said to his mistress, "but a message has been delivered for Miss Brandon." He walked over to Alethea and extended a salver toward her. Alethea picked up the envelope and glanced down at it.

"Don't keep me in suspense, my dear," said Elizabeth. "Who is it from?"

Breaking open the seal, Alethea glanced down at the missive. "It's from Robert Chandler. He asks if I might meet him this afternoon for tea. He says there is a tea shop right near his office."

"Well, you must refuse, Alethea," said Elizabeth, lathering her slice of toast with marmalade. "I wish you to accompany me today on my calls. My dear, I can't wait to tell everyone of last evening!"

Alethea shook her head. "I'm sorry, Aunt Elizabeth, but I would prefer to see Robert." She paused. "And it will be my last opportunity to do so for some time."

Elizabeth looked up from her toast in surprise. "Whatever do you mean, your last opportunity?"

"I've decided to return home tomorrow."

"What?" cried her aunt. "What foolishness is this, my girl? You've scarcely been here more than a week."

"I know, Aunt, and I do appreciate you and Uncle's kindness in having me here. But I really must return to Crow's Nest Cottage."

Elizabeth was silent for a moment as she fixed a rather incredulous look on her niece. "You can't be serious, Alethea. Why, after last night, I'm certain that we'll receive a great number of invitations from Lady Catherine and her friends. My dear, you'll be able to attend the most elite functions this Season. You can't think to leave now!"

"I'm sorry, Aunt, but there's no purpose in arguing with me," said Alethea firmly. "I've decided to return home tomorrow and I won't change my mind."

Seeing the resolute expression on her niece's face, Elizabeth sighed. It appeared that Alethea was determined to leave and she knew her niece well enough to know that there was no way to persuade the stubborn girl otherwise.

Chapter 30

That afternoon, Worcester walked down a busy street in the center of London. After having paid a lengthy visit to his tailor's, his lordship was on his way to see his solicitor. Since that gentleman's office was merely a few blocks away, the marquess made his way there on foot.

The sidewalk was crowded with hawkers selling their wares and people hurrying about. However, Worcester took little note of the bustle around him. As he strode past the shops and offices, his mind was still focused on the previous evening at the Truscotts'.

After having suffered through the dreadful dinner party, the marquess had returned home, feeling utterly depressed. His future had never before seemed so bleak to him as it did now.

That morning, after having spent a sleepless night, Worcester had attempted to pull himself together. He had decided it was no use bemoaning his fate. What was done was done and he must go ahead and do his duty. It was an unpleasant duty, to be sure, but as a man of honor what choice did he have? No, he would marry Catherine and somehow forget about Alethea.

Yet as Worcester made his way toward his solicitor's office, he found his stoic resolve beginning to crumble. It was not so easy, after all, to dismiss all thoughts of Alethea and what he viewed as his only chance for happiness.

As he walked down the street, he couldn't help but think of how beautiful Alethea had looked as she sat there at the card table. Worcester began to imagine taking her up into his arms and pressing his lips upon her delectable mouth. In his fantasy, Alethea smiled up invitingly at him and he proceeded to loosen her gown from her lovely shoulders. . . .

Worcester was abruptly shaken from his pleasurable daydream

when a boy, hurrying along the street with a large package, ran into him. "Beggin' your pardon, sir," said the youth, a rather grimy-faced urchin who was wearing a cap that was much too big for him. When his lordship eyed him with disfavor, the lad quickly scurried away.

Brought back to reality, Worcester frowned. He mustn't think about Alethea, he told himself, and especially not in *that* way. Feeling frustrated and quite blue-deviled, he continued along the street.

The marquess hadn't gone very far when his eyes alighted on a sign hanging out from one of the offices he was passing. It said "Henry Chandler, Physician." Staring at it, he wondered if there was some connection between this Chandler and the irritating fellow who had tried to ingratiate himself with Prudence.

Worcester grew thoughtful. The whole episode with Chandler had been most unpleasant. He remembered how his sister had claimed to be in love with the man. Of course, thought Worcester, he had managed to put an end to that nonsense. Since their return from Hartwood, Prudence hadn't mentioned Chandler once. Still, he suspected that she hadn't forgotten about him. After all, Prudence had seemed very gloomy since returning to town.

Frowning, the marquess continued on his way. He had gone but a few steps farther when he glanced across the street and suddenly stopped dead in his tracks. Walking along the opposite sidewalk toward him was Alethea.

Worcester stood there, staring at her, unsure what to do. Then, stepping off the sidewalk, he started into the street. He did want to see her!

However, after taking a few steps, he stopped. What was he doing, he asked himself. Hadn't he decided that very morning that he had to forget her? He couldn't just go up to her. Indeed, he wasn't sure if he could trust himself not to snatch her up into his arms right there in public view.

He continued to hesitate, standing in the street. Alethea, who was glancing in the shop windows as she walked along, hadn't seen Worcester. He watched her, a faint smile on his face. How could he bear not to speak with her, he asked himself. No, it wasn't to be endured. Oblivious to the traffic on the busy street, he started across, walking directly into the path of a fast-moving carriage.

There was a shout as a passerby saw Worcester's danger.

Robert Chandler, who had come out of his office a few moments ago, heard the cry of alarm. Seeing that a man was in the street, about to be run over, Chandler jumped into action, dashing across and shoving Worcester out of the way as the vehicle bore down upon them. The two men went falling forward as the vehicle rushed by, missing them by a hair's breadth.

Alethea, who had looked into the street at the sound of the shout, had witnessed Chandler's rescue of the marquess. Although she had at first been very much shaken, she had quickly recovered. Hurrying to them, she knelt down beside Worcester, who was still on the ground near the sidewalk. "Lord Worcester!" cried Alethea. "Are you all right? Oh, Robert!"

Chandler, who hadn't been aware of the identity of the man he had saved now recognized the marquess with considerable astonishment. "Worcester!" he said. "Alethea!"

But Alethea was more concerned with Worcester. "Are you hurt?" she said, casting a worried look at him.

Embarrassed, he shook his head. "I'm fine, Miss Brandon," he said. Chandler, who had got to his feet, helped the marquess up.

"I don't hear you inquiring about my condition, Alethea," said Chandler with a smile.

She took his hand. "Oh, Robert, are you all right?"

He nodded. "It would appear so."

"You were wonderful, Robert. You saved Lord Worcester's life."

A group of curious onlookers had gathered around them by this time, and several people in the crowd now stepped forward to congratulate Chandler on his heroic feat. The marquess, feeling like an utter fool, brushed himself off and tried to regain his dignity.

Then stooping over to pick up his hat from the street, Worcester winced slightly. "You are injured!" said Alethea, noticing that his left hand was scraped rather badly and bleeding.

"I assure you, Miss Brandon, it's nothing."

Not content with this reply, Alethea took his wrist and examined his hand. "You must have it seen to at once. Robert, do look at Lord Worcester's hand."

"That is a nasty scrape," said Chandler in a businesslike tone. "Come, my office is right across from here. I'll see to it."

The marquess frowned, finally pulling his hand away. "That is unnecessary, sir," he said irritably. "It is a trifling thing."

"Lord Worcester," said Alethea, speaking to him as if he were a recalcitrant child, "you will do as Dr. Chandler says." She glanced over at the physician and cast her eyes heavenward. "It appears, Robert, that his lordship is still a difficult patient."

The doctor smiled slightly. "I fear, Lord Worcester, you have no choice. You know how headstrong Miss Brandon is, and she insists upon you receiving treatment. I, for one, should not like to go up against her."

The marquess looked from Chandler to Alethea. That lady was eyeing him with a mischievous gleam in her hazel eyes.

"Oh, very well," he said, "but there is no need for making such a fuss."

The three of them made their way back across the street to Chandler's office. When they entered, they found a well-furnished waiting room. The physician led Worcester and Alethea to another room, where there were a table and two chairs and a large glass cabinet filled with bottles and other medical paraphernalia. "Do be seated, Lord Worcester," said Chandler, motioning to one of the chairs. "And, Alethea, you may sit in that chair."

After waiting until Alethea had taken her place, Worcester sat down. Chandler then went over to the table, where he poured water from a pitcher into a ceramic bowl. After washing Worcester's hand and drying it off with a linen cloth, the doctor then began to wrap a bandage around it.

The marquess was finding the experience rather awkward, especially with Alethea sitting there. As he watched Chandler expertly tie the bandage around his hand, Worcester could not help but think of the ill will between them. Of course, he could scarcely be blamed for his dislike of the man. After all, Chandler had had the effrontery to insinuate himself into Prudence's affections.

"Well, I don't think you'll be much the worse for your mishap," said Chandler, "but I'll advise your lordship to take more care crossing the street in future."

"Yes," said Alethea, "there are so many reckless persons driving about. One must be careful. Thank heaven that Robert was there to push you out of harm's way."

Worcester frowned. He didn't like to be reminded that he very likely owed his life to Chandler. Watching the doctor as he placed a bottle back in the cabinet, the marquess grew thoughtful. What if Chandler wasn't the fortune hunter he had taken him for? What if the man was genuinely attached to Prudence? In his present situation, Worcester could be somewhat sympathetic to the physician's predicament.

"Thank you, Chandler," he said. "I feel I owe a great debt to you."

"It's only a bandage, Lord Worcester," said Chandler.

"I mean for saving my life, man. If you hadn't pushed me away from the carriage, I might have been killed."

"I assure you that you have no need to feel any obligation," said Chandler.

Worcester met the doctor's gaze. He could see that Chandler had little friendly feeling for him. No doubt, the fellow was now regretting his action in saving his life.

Rising from the chair, Worcester took up his hat. "I must be going."

"Are you sure you shouldn't rest for a time, my lord?" said Alethea, who had gotten to her feet. "It must have been a rather unsettling experience for you."

Worcester looked at her. If only she knew that the most unsettling experience for him that afternoon was seeing her again. "I'm quite recovered, Miss Brandon."

She paused. "Dr. Chandler and I were about to have tea. There is a little tea shop just down the street from here. Won't you accompany us?"

"Thank you, Miss Brandon," said Worcester, "but I really must take my leave of you."

Alethea nodded and the three of them made their way out of the room and back to the reception area of the office. A lady was now sitting in one of the chairs in the waiting room. A thin woman of about thirty, she immediately jumped up as soon as she spied Chandler.

"Oh, Dr. Chandler!" she cried, rushing toward him, "I wanted to come in and thank you. My Tom is so much better."

Chandler smiled at the lady. "I'm glad to hear it, Mrs. Mac-Neil."

"If it wasn't for you, Dr. Chandler, I don't know what I would've done." She turned to Alethea. "My boy was so very ill I began to fear that he would leave us." A tear trickled down the woman's cheeks, and she hastily pulled out a handkerchief. "Dr. Chandler saved him. He is an excellent doctor and such a good man."

"Indeed, he is," said Alethea. "I'm very glad that your son is better."

As the woman continued to talk, singing Chandler's praises, Worcester stood there eyeing the doctor with a thoughtful expression. The doctor was an admirable man, he decided.

The marquess frowned. Why should he feel so superior to the physician, he asked himself. At least Chandler was doing something worthwhile in the world. And what had he done himself but merely live the idle life of a rich lord?

When they were finally outside, Worcester turned once again to the physician. "Thank you again, Chandler. I'm very grateful to you." He extended his hand to the doctor, who shook it.

The marquess then turned to Alethea. "I'll say good-bye to you then, Miss Brandon."

Alethea's hazel eyes met his gray ones for a moment. "Goodbye, Lord Worcester," she said, extending her hand to him.

Worcester was forced to use all his self-control not to betray his emotions. Taking her hand, he politely bowed over it. "Goodbye, Miss Brandon," he said. Then, somewhat abruptly, he turned and walked away.

Chapter 31

Two days after Worcester's near accident, a stylish phaeton pulled up in front of his lordship's town house. Handing the reins to his groom, Lord Edward Beauchamp nimbly jumped down from the vehicle and proceeded to make his way to the house.

Standing at the front door, Edward nervously straightened his cravat. After putting off seeing his brother for several days, the young gentleman was finally there to talk to him about his engagement to Thomasina Whitfield. Since Edward knew that Worcester wouldn't take the news well, he very much dreaded their meeting.

The door opened and Talbot appeared before him. "Good day, Lord Edward," said the butler, nodding.

Smiling, Edward handed his hat to the servant. "Hello, Talbot. I'm here to see Lord Worcester."

The butler looked apologetic. "I'm sorry, my lord, but his lordship isn't at home."

Edward felt a combined sense of relief and disappointment. Although he wasn't eager to talk to Worcester, he had very much wanted to get the unpleasant business over with. "What deuced bad luck," he said.

"Would you care to wait, my lord?" asked Talbot. "I don't expect that his lordship will be gone long. And Lady Prudence is in the drawing room."

"Thank you, Talbot. I'll go and see her." Edward walked down the hallway and entered the drawing room, finding his sister ensconced on the sofa reading. Poppet was curled up in the corner, sleeping.

Prudence looked up as he came into the room. "Ned!" she

cried, smiling at him. "I thought you were purposely staying away from us. I'm so glad you decided to visit."

Edward walked to the sofa and leaned over to give his sister a peck on the cheek. "Actually, I was staying away, Pru. But I have finally worked up my nerve to talk to Geoffrey and so here I am."

Prudence eyed him with a concerned look. "You mean you are going to tell him about Miss Whitfield?"

Her brother plopped down on the sofa next to her and reached over to pet Poppet. "Yes, I'm going to tell him how I wish to marry Miss Whitfield. No, that I *am* going to marry her." He paused and looked at his sister. "You see, Pru, the truth of the matter is, Thomasina and I are already engaged."

"Oh, Ned!" cried his sister, giving him a hug. "I do wish you the greatest happiness!" She then pulled back, a worried expression on her face. "Oh, I do hope Geoffrey will be reasonable."

Edward sighed. "Yes, I fear that most unlikely. I'm quite certain he'll be furious. But, there's no helping it. I'm in love with Thomasina and I'll marry her no matter what our brother says."

"Perhaps Geoffrey will understand now and give you his blessing after all."

Edward regarded her with a perplexed look. "What do you mean, Pru?"

Prudence stroked Poppet and then turned her gaze back on her brother. "Remember when we were at Hartwood and I said Geoffrey could never be sympathetic to us because he'd never been in love?"

"I seem to recall such a conversation." Edward met his sister's gaze and regarded her in astonishment. "What? You can't mean that Geoffrey has fallen in love?"

Prudence suddenly appeared sheepish. "Yes. He's in love with Alethea."

"In love with Alethea?" cried Edward, regarding her in amazement. "Miss Brandon?"

Prudence nodded. "And it's all my fault!"

Edward continued to eye her with an incredulous expression. "You can't be serious. Geoffrey and Alethea Brandon? Good God!" He stopped. "But, whatever do you mean, it's all your fault, Pru?"

Prudence proceeded to tell her brother the story of how she had concocted a love potion and given it to Worcester and Alethea.

Edward listened to the tale and then burst out laughing. "My dear sister, you are a silly goose! A love potion, indeed!"

Prudence shook her head. "You may laugh, Ned, but I tell you, it worked! As soon as I gave it to him, Geoffrey fell madly in love with Alethea! And she with him!"

"Don't be ridiculous!"

"But it's true, Ned. After I gave them the potion, I saw how they looked at each other. And then I managed to get them alone together in Alethea's garden. You see, I went back to the house and then spied on them from the window. And then . . ." Prudence stopped in some embarrassment.

"And then what?" asked Edward impatiently.

"Why, Geoffrey grabbed Alethea and kissed her!"

"What?" cried Edward. "Geoffrey kissed Miss Brandon?"

Prudence nodded. "He did. And it was a very long kiss, Ned. Oh, dear, I have made a terrible mess of things! Now Geoffrey is hopelessly in love with Alethea and he's to marry horrible Catherine. Of course, he's quite wretched. And poor Alethea! She is doubtlessly pining away for Geoffrey. Oh, Ned, I wish I'd never given them the love potion!"

"Really, Pru," began her brother, "you can't really think that your so-called love potion . . ." Before he could finish, the door to the drawing room opened and Worcester walked in. Both Edward and Prudence exchanged guilty looks.

Fortunately, the marquess didn't seem to note anything unusual in their expressions. He regarded his younger brother with a slight air of disapproval. "So you have finally seen fit to pay us a visit, Ned."

Edward smiled. "I've been devilishly busy, Geoffrey." Then noting the bandage on the marquess's hand, he added, "Are you hurt?"

"It was nothing," said Worcester, taking a seat in an elegant armchair across from the sofa. "It's only a minor scrape."

Edward wasn't encouraged by Worcester's gloomy tone. It appeared the marquess was in an exceedingly ill humor. He began to think that perhaps he should put off his interview with his brother for a time. However, Prudence intervened. Getting up from the sofa, she turned to the marquess. "I know Ned wants to talk with you, Geoffrey, so I shall leave you two alone." After giving an encouraging smile to Edward, she left the room with Poppet in her arms.

Worcester eyed his younger brother expectantly. "So you wish to speak with me, Ned?"

Edward met his brother's gaze and nodded nervously. "Yes, I do, Geoffrey." He hesitated, fearing his brother's reaction.

"Is something the matter, Ned?" asked the marquess.

"Yes, well, no. That is to say . . ." Edward stopped and took a deep breath. He then continued in a rush of words. "To come directly to the point, I have met a girl whom I wish to marry. I know you think I'm too young, but I assure you, I'm not."

Worcester regarded him with some surprise. "When did this all happen and who is the girl?"

"I met her a few months ago," said Edward, knowing the worst was approaching. "I don't doubt you will think it too short a time, but it isn't at all. I think I fell in love with her the moment I saw her. Her name is Thomasina Whitfield and she is an absolute angel."

The marquess looked thoughtful for a moment. "Whitfield? I don't think I can place the name."

"Her father is Josiah Whitfield," said Edward. "He is a very fine man and he is quite wealthy." He paused and regarded his brother with a defiant look. "You've heard of Whitfield Breweries." Not giving his brother a chance to respond, Edward raced ahead. "I know you'll disapprove, Geoffrey, but I will marry Thomasina no matter what you say! I don't care a fig that her father is in trade. We love each other." To Edward's surprise, his brother's only response was to continue to regard him with a thoughtful expression.

"Are you certain that you are in love with this lady?" asked Worcester finally.

"I've never been so certain of anything in my life," said Edward in a fervent tone.

"And she shares your feelings?"

"Indeed, yes, Geoffrey," said Edward, very much surprised at his brother's words.

The marquess leaned back in his chair and nodded. "Well, if that's the case, Ned, I must congratulate you and wish you happiness with this Thomasina of yours."

Edward regarded Worcester in considerable astonishment. "You mean, you're actually giving your consent to the match?"

A slight smile appeared on his brother's face. "Surely you aren't disappointed, Ned?"

Edward smiled. "Indeed, I'm not. But I was quite sure you'd be furious when I told you about Thomasina's father."

Worcester shook his head. "I used to think that all that counted was a person's rank in life, and that love was of no consequence in marriage. I realize now that I've been very much mistaken. I've been a great fool, Ned, and now I must pay for my ridiculous pride. I find myself soon to be shackled to a woman for whom I have not the least regard. No, I shouldn't wish the same fate upon you."

Edward continued to regard his brother with an expression of amazement. "Good God, Geoffrey! Then Pru was right! You *are* in love with Alethea Brandon!"

Worcester reddened. "Prudence? What the deuce has she been saying?"

"She told me that you are desperately in love with Miss Brandon." Edward suddenly broke into a grin. "In fact, Geoffrey, our dear sister thinks she is to blame for your feelings toward that lady. You see, Pru slipped both you and Miss Brandon some powerful love potion."

The marquess raised his eyebrows and regarded him with a ludicrous expression. "What?"

Edward proceeded to tell his brother the story of Prudence's romantic scheming with a supernatural elixir as Worcester listened with a look of incredulity upon his face. Finally the marquess shook his head. "How could Pru be such a great gudgeon to believe such nonsense?"

"Well, perhaps it isn't nonsense," said Edward, still grinning. "After all, brother, you are in love with Miss Brandon, aren't you?"

Worcester met his gaze. He abruptly got up from his chair and walked to the window. Then he turned around and faced his brother. "Yes, I'm in love with her, but it wasn't the result of Pru's silly potion. I was in love with Alethea Brandon long before that."

Edward appeared quite pleased at this confession. He leaned back in his chair. "And what are you going to do about it?"

The marquess eyed him with some irritation. "What the deuce do you mean? I can't do anything about it. Have you forgotten I'm to marry Catherine? It's all settled."

His younger brother shook his head. "If you marry Catherine, Geoffrey, then you're a blockhead! Good God, how could you even think of doing such a thing when you're in love with Alethea Brandon?"

"But I have given my pledge . . ." began Worcester.

"Then you must break it!" cried Edward. "There is no other way out of the business." He got up from the sofa and walked over to his brother. "You can't marry her, Geoffrey. Both you and Catherine would be unhappy for the rest of your lives."

Worcester considered this for a moment. "Yes, I don't doubt that we'd be miserable."

"Of course, you would be," said Edward. He continued matter-of-factly. "This is what you must do. First you must break off your engagement with Catherine, and then you must marry Miss Brandon."

The marquess frowned. "What makes you think she would have me?"

"Well, Pru is of the opinion that the lady is pining away for you."

"What nonsense," muttered Worcester.

Edward smiled. "Don't you think you had better find out for yourself? You do wish to marry Miss Brandon, don't you?"

"Of course I want to marry her," he growled.

"Well, then, you must ask her," said Edward. "Really, brother, I think it's time you took my advice for a change."

Worcester hesitated and then a slight smile appeared on his face. "Very well, Ned, I shall do as you say."

"Good!" said Edward. "Now you mustn't waste any time. You must go and see Catherine immediately." The marquess nodded, and then he rang for a servant to have his carriage brought around.

Chapter 32

A short time later, Worcester's carriage pulled up at the Earl of Huntingdon's impressive residence. The marquess looked somber as he walked up to the door. While he didn't relish telling Catherine that he was breaking off their engagement, he was eager to correct the dreadful mistake he had made in proposing marriage to her. He knew that Lord Huntingdon would be furious, but he really didn't care.

The Huntingdon's butler admitted him. "Lord and Lady Huntingdon aren't at home, Lord Worcester," said the servant.

"Is Lady Catherine here? I should like to see her."

"Of course, my lord," said the butler, disappearing a moment before returning to escort the marquess to the drawing room. There he found Catherine sitting in a chair, reading a fashion magazine.

"Good day, Catherine," he said.

"Good day, Worcester," replied Catherine, placing her magazine on the table. He noted that she didn't appear happy to see him. "I'm glad you've come. You've spared me the need for writing. Perhaps you should sit down. I have something I wish to say to you."

The marquess regarded her curiously as he took a chair. "Yes?"

"I shan't beat about the bush, Worcester," she said. "I don't wish to marry you."

His lordship regarded her in surprise. "What!"

"I'm sorry, but I've come to realize that I made a mistake. We don't suit very well, you know. And, in truth, I've found someone else. I'm going to marry Feversham."

"Feversham!"

"Yes," said Catherine.

Worcester stared at her, scarcely believing his good fortune. *She* was breaking off the engagement!

"My mind is quite made up," said Catherine resolutely, "so there is no point in trying to convince me otherwise. And I assure you, my father has agreed with my decision. He's fond of Feversham. Of course, he was irked with him when he bought that horse he wanted, but that is all forgotten now. I do hope you won't make a fuss."

"A fuss?" said the marquess, feeling an unaccustomed urge to break into song.

"I know you were expecting the Derbyshire estate."

"What?" said Worcester.

"It was to be part of my dowry."

The marquess rose to his feet. "No, I won't make a fuss, Catherine," he said. "And Feversham may have the Derbyshire estate with my blessing. You'll be far happier with him."

"You are taking it very well, Worcester," said Catherine. "I'm very glad."

"I shall take my leave of you then," said his lordship, bowing before making his exit. Leaving the house, he returned to his carriage. As he commanded his driver to take him to the Truscott residence, the servant reflected that he had never before seen such a broad grin on the marquess's face.

A short time later, Worcester was at the Truscotts' front door. A maid led him into the drawing room, where he found Elizabeth perched in a chair, some embroidery in her lap. "Oh, Lord Worcester," she said, smiling up at him, "what a delightful surprise!"

The marquess took her proffered hand and bowed over it. "Good day, ma'am. I was hoping to speak to your niece. Is she at home?"

"Oh dear, I'm sorry, my lord, but Alethea isn't here. She insisted on returning home to Crow's Nest Cottage yesterday and I couldn't change her mind."

The news came as a great disappointment to his lordship. "Then I must take my leave of you, ma'am."

Elizabeth shook her head in some bewilderment. "But you have just arrived, my lord."

"Do forgive me, ma'am," he said, and bowing again, he quickly left the room. Elizabeth could only watch him go, wondering at his strange behavior and why he was so anxious to see Alethea. A sudden suspicion came over her about Worcester and her niece. Perhaps that was why Alethea was so eager to leave London, she speculated. Mulling over this surprising and disturbing conjecture, Elizabeth watched the marquess's carriage drive away.

Alethea sat at the desk in the library of Crow's Nest Cottage, her gaze intent upon a wildflower in a vase before her. She then looked down at a sheet of paper, attempting to sketch the delicate flower.

After considerable effort, Alethea cast a critical gaze on the drawing. She was far from pleased with the results of her labor. The plant's tubular petals did not seem quite right to her. Sighing, she put down her pencil.

Alethea had just arrived home at Crow's Nest Cottage the previous afternoon. While it had been good to be back, she could not shake the depression that had settled over her. It seemed all she could think about was Worcester and the fact that he would soon be married to Lady Catherine Percy.

Pushing aside her paper, Alethea frowned. She wished that Worcester had never come to Hartwood. Indeed, she was sorry that she had ever met him. Alethea sighed again and wondered how long it would take for her to get over her unfortunate feelings for the marquess.

Nelson, who had scarcely been away from his mistress's side since her arrival the prior day, seemed to sense her dismay. He put his massive head on her lap and gazed up dolefully at her. Alethea smiled and fondly gave him a pat. "Dear old Nelson," she said. "I shan't have you in the doldrums as well. Why don't we go on a walk?"

The mastiff's mournful expression suddenly became joyful at hearing the word "walk" and he gave a happy bark. He followed his mistress eagerly as she made her way toward her room to fetch her straw bonnet.

A short time later, Alethea and her canine companion stepped outside the cottage. There was a familiar cawing noise overhead and Alethea looked up to see the crow Hector in the large oak tree behind the house. She smiled up at the bird. "Good day to you, sir." Hector cawed again and then, seeing no evidence of any biscuits, he flew away.

Alethea and Nelson continued walking along until they reached the scenic path that led from Crow's Nest Cottage down to the sea. The wind had become strong and some dark, threatening clouds appeared menacingly over the turbulent-looking water below them. However, Alethea seemed invigorated by the approaching storm and showed no inclination to cut short their expedition.

Stopping at one of her favorite overlooks, Alethea gazed out at the sea. She remained there for some time, watching the waves as they crashed upon the shore. Nelson remained happily by her side, staring up at her with an adoring expression on his jowly face.

As she stood there, Alethea's thoughts once again were on Worcester. She remembered how she had first met him when he had been so desperately ill. A host of other memories came to mind and she smiled as she thought of the ceremony in which she had removed the curse from Hartwood.

Alethea's smile faded since the episode made her think of Prudence. She felt very bad that she had to sever her relationship with Worcester's sister. Alethea had just written a letter to Prudence that morning, informing her that she was back in Devonshire. She hoped that her young friend would not be too upset about her abrupt departure from town.

Still gazing out at the sea, Alethea grew thoughtful. Perhaps when Worcester was safely married, she could invite Prudence to come and visit her. However, this thought was hardly likely to cheer her up since it again made her dwell upon the marquess's upcoming nuptials.

Nelson, who had been sitting quietly at Alethea's feet, suddenly got up and gave a deep, excited bark. "What is it, Nelson?" she asked. The mastiff continued barking at something behind them. Turning around, Alethea was startled to see Worcester standing on the path. "Worcester!" she cried.

The marquess didn't speak. In a few long strides he was standing next to her. He looked down into her hazel eyes for a brief moment, and then he swept her into his arms, pressing his lips fiercely upon hers. Alethea responded fervently, kissing him back passionately.

When their lips finally parted, Worcester smiled down at her. "Alethea, my darling," he murmured. Then, pulling her close, his mouth once again sought hers. Overwhelmed with his desire for her, the marquess kissed her long and passionately.

Alethea, realizing her danger, suddenly came to her senses. "No!" she cried. And with a forceful shove, she pushed Worcester away from her.

Worcester regarded her with some surprise. "What is the matter, my darling?"

Alethea fixed an indignant expression on him. "Don't call me that. Have you forgotten, my lord, that you are soon to be a married man?"

He looked down at her and smiled. "No, I haven't forgotten, and you'll be my wife."

"What!"

"Say you'll marry me, Alethea. I love you so desperately."

"But you're engaged to Lady Catherine."

"No, I'm not, my dearest, Alethea. She called it off. It was quite fortuitous, actually, since I was just going to break the engagement myself." He gazed down at her, an intent look in his gray eyes. "I was a fool for some time, thinking I must go ahead with the marriage, even though I knew I'd be miserable with Catherine. Luckily my brother Ned talked some sense into my thick skull. I knew I couldn't marry her, not feeling about you as I do. If you care for me at all, you will agree to be my bride."

Alethea's hazel eyes met his. "Oh, I do love you, Worcester, but are you sure? I don't know anything about being a marchioness."

The marquess replied to this by kissing her firmly.

Sometime later, Molly was very much surprised to see her mistress coming toward Crow's Nest Cottage, her hand in Worcester's. Both Alethea and the marquess looked radiantly happy and Nelson bounded ahead of them.

When they entered the drawing room, Worcester took the opportunity to embrace Alethea again. "I cannot imagine why Providence has been so good to me when I have been one of the greatest blockheads imaginable.

"But I shall be a better man and a better brother. Ned has told me he wishes to marry. He is in love with a Miss Whitfield. Whitfield Breweries."

"And what did you say to him?"

"I told him that I shan't object if they are truly in love. And I'll say the same thing to Prudence. If your friend Chandler wishes to pay court to her, I shan't object."

Smiling delightedly, Alethea hugged him tightly. "You astonish me, Lord Worcester."

He smiled in return. "I rather astonish myself," he said.

Then looking up at him, a mischievous look came to her face. "I believe I understand, my lord. Now that you are going to marry me, you can hardly object to whatever connections Prudence and Edward wish to form."

He laughed. "What can you mean, madam? You are Miss Brandon, after all. And it appears that the Brandons will once again take their rightful place at Hartwood."

"My rightful place is beside you, my dear Worcester," said Alethea, reaching up to kiss him once again.